Behind The Magnolia Tree

To order additional copies, please contact us.
BookSurge, LLC
www.booksurge.com
1-866-308-6235
orders@booksurge.com

DENNIS R. MAYNARD

BEHIND THE MAGNOLIA TREE

BOOKSURGE PUBLISHERS
2005

Behind The Magnolia Tree

*S*teel Austin is young. He is idealistic. He is an Episcopal priest on fire with enthusiasm for the ideals of the Gospel.

He is called to be Rector of one of the most prestigious congregations in the old South. Historic First Church in Falls City, Georgia, however, has its own understanding of the Gospel.

Falls City, itself, is a town that thrives not on Gospel ideals, but secrets. For nearly two hundred years things have always been done in a certain way. Secrets are best guarded by familiar traditions.

The Gospel of the Reverend Steele Austin was bound to clash with that traditional way of life. Those with the deepest secrets of sex, greed, and power are most threatened. They will stop at nothing to insure that their way of life is preserved and that their secrets are never revealed. They will do whatever it takes. Even if it means the young priest must be...

Dedicated To My Brothers And Sisters

Who Wear The Collar.

FORWARD

Anovel is the ultimate yarn. It is first spun in the author's imagination. When imagination becomes reality for the author, a novel is born.

The themes of any good tale are universal…good versus evil, love and betrayal, death and resurrection.

I am grateful to the thousands of people who have listened to me "spin a yarn" from the pulpit and lecture hall over the past four decades. With rabbinical license I have expanded on reality and created fiction in order to instill a message of hope.

I am grateful to the people in my life who have continually encouraged me to devote my energies to this particular novel, especially those who have allowed me to be teacher, pastor, and friend in the congregations I have served from South Carolina to California.

I am particularly grateful to my sweet wife, Nancy and my children Dennis, Andrew, Kristen, and my daughter-in-law Kristin Zanavich. Their encouragement and enthusiasm for my writing has inspired me to try and try again. I only wish I had the confidence in myself that they seem to have.

The various personalities and events in Falls City, Georgia are the product of my own creativity. Any attempt on the reader's part to find a parallel with my personal journey will be frustrating. Since I am a priest who has served multiple congregations—it needs to be stated clearly—the story that unfolds in this quaint little southern community is **completely fictional and does not depict any actual person or event.**

While I know that the characters that perform on this novel's stage are not real, nonetheless, I have become deeply devoted to each of them and the story line they weave together. My hunch is that not every reader will share this same admiration. It will be difficult to immerse oneself in the lives of the people on the following pages without seeing the characteristics of someone you know, or your own. It is my hope, dear reader, that you will be reminded that God uses imperfect people to accomplish the Divine purpose simply because there are no others available.

Since the Church is the center of the lives of the people on the following pages, the uninformed observer may at first be surprised by the actions of those inside. My devotion to the Church in general and the Episcopal Church in particular, is not based on some notion of perfection. To the contrary, I love this Church precisely because the clergy and the people inside it are imperfect and confess that imperfection each Sunday.

If we don't like one of the good citizens that expose their inner selves to us in this wonderful old southern community, perhaps we should ask ourselves, why? The answer will be found internally. It just might provide us with an opportunity to grow and mature.

It has been said we do not keep secrets. Our secrets keep us. Rare to non-existent is the person who is not being kept by one or more secrets. How we respond to the folks in Falls City, albeit, how we respond to this yarn is, in the final analysis—information about us.

So, fellow traveler, I ask you to look with compassion on the various people that interact with The Reverend Steele Austin. I appeal to you to understand that their words and deeds are but an expression of the fear and pain common to us all. It is only when we look at each other through the eyes of compassion that relationships begin to change. When we look at one another with charity, each of our communities and our very world becomes a better place for all of us. The people on the following pages can teach us if we are willing to learn. They can teach us to be better people. As we become better people, those around us change in response.

The overwhelming majority of my years have been lived out in what many of us affectionately call "the old South." There is a gentleness about the South and about Southern people that is not easily forgotten. That gentleness can often mask resistance to new ideas and new ways of doing things. Although I currently wake up each morning in the arms of the San Jacinto Mountains in one of the most beautiful valleys on the West Coast, there is a very special place in my heart for the Confederacy. It is now and always will be—home.

The bells in the old First Church Steeple are ringing. The congregation is gathering. Welcome to Falls City, Georgia and historic old First Church. We are so glad that you are here.

Happy reading.

Dennis Maynard
Rancho Mirage, California

CHAPTER 1

Mrs. Chadsworth Purcell Alexander the Third turned the water hose on the big magnolia tree sitting on the front lawn of historic First Church. Most folks had learned to address her by her first name with the mandatory, but respectful, Miss, in front of it. She was known to most everyone who mattered in Falls City, Georgia simply as Miss Almeda. Today, she felt especially pleased with herself and with her lot in life.

In spite of her seventy years, Miss Almeda knew that she was still a beautiful woman. Or, at least that is how she appraised the reflection in her dressing room mirror. Of course, there was no reason to doubt what she saw. With the help of her Atlanta surgeon, she would routinely have a nip here and a tuck there. An occasional lift and a few injections, oh well, a woman has to do what a woman has to do.

On this particular South Georgia morning there was a hint of autumn in the air. The breeze was a bit on the cool side, but it was gracefully balanced by the warm morning sun. In the distance, there was just a whiff of smoke from a wood burning fireplace. Life was good for Miss Almeda.

She had taken great care in the selection of her morning attire. She chose the dark blue garden dress that she just recently purchased at Rich's Department Store. The large brimmed hat complimented the dress and gave a particular brilliance to her solid black hair. Tastefully appointed shoes and pure white garden gloves put a finishing touch on her presentation.

Miss Almeda particularly liked standing in front of old First Church. It was right on Main Street at a critical intersection. The corner stop light insured that anyone who was anyone would have to stop in front of the church as they traveled from their exclusive homes on River Street to the Women's Club, the Magnolia Club, or the Country Club. Miss Almeda took pride in knowing that Falls City's finest knew that she was a dedicated churchwoman who took her church work seriously.

There was a time when life was not so good for Miss Almeda. Even now she shuddered when she thought of the stench in the trailer house. Melon Town, Alabama seemed so far away. Still, she remembered the fights, the beatings, the poverty, and the tears. It was a secret she had lived with her entire life. Had it not been for her natural beauty, her youthful cunning, and a healthy dose of Jim Beam, Chadsworth Purcell Alexander the Third, who was a full ten years her junior, would never have stood before the Justice of the Peace with her that night. God only knows where she would be now.

Chadsworth had been a good husband. His family money had certainly been a plus, but he was not content to sit back on his family fortune as had so many. No, Chadsworth continued to improve himself and to be a good provider. They had been cursed with two sons. Both had been hell raisers their entire lives. One was married but living like he was single. The other single and living like he had never seen the inside of a church. Again, she shuddered.

Chadsworth was not a very affectionate husband. He really didn't make any demands on her body. Even when they were very young his affections were few. As for her own satisfaction, this she had been left to find in the passion of the novels she kept locked away in her attic trunk. On occasion, in her younger days, there were the arms of a stranger on one of her New York City theatre trips with the ladies in her bridge club. Still, her heart belonged to Chadsworth even if she seemed completely unable to stir him with her womanly charm.

Miss Almeda was awakened from her musing by the horn of a passing auto. She returned the greeting with a big smile and a genteel wave. Her thoughts returned to the beautiful magnolia and historic old First Church. Anyone who was anyone was a member of First Church. It was the most prestigious congregation in the entire state. Even the Governor would drive all the way from Atlanta to be seen at First Church on Christmas and Easter.

The church historian recorded that General Robert E. Lee himself had once worshiped at First Church. It was definitely the church of the elite. It was the church in which to be married, and if one were to have aspirations for public office, one needed to be a member of First Church. A cursory glance at the listing for the board of directors of the country club, the Magnolia Club, the Women's Club, the cotillion, and the Original

Debutante Society revealed that the very same names were also proudly listed on the membership roles of First Church.

While new people of distinction were welcome at First Church and certainly marriage into a First Church family was an acceptable path of transfer; no passionate effort was directed toward new member recruitment. This sort of thing was best left to the Baptists and the Presbyterians. The granite sign in front of the church proudly stated the church name. Large capital letters spelled out—**HISTORIC FIRST CHURCH**. Smaller letters underneath surrounded by parentheses spelled out (Episcopal). And then in italics was written: *Established in 1813*. No service times were listed. And there was no provision made for the listing of the Rector's name. Almeda was grateful that the Episcopal Church was a church of good taste.

"Willie! Willie!" she cried. Where is that lazy good for nothing darkie? Every one of them is the same. She had sent him for an additional hose attachment twenty minutes ago.

"Willie! Where have you been?" She knew the answer to her own question. He had been the sexton here at First Church for well over fifty years. He had his hiding places well disguised. He had also learned how to cover up the smell of the bottle of "medicine" he kept hidden in his overalls.

"There you are. Willie, who has been cutting branches off this magnolia tree?"

"Miss Almeda, Mistuh Howard Dexter told me to cut those branches so he could make an arch of magnolia for the Titus wedding."

The Titus wedding, she snarled. Just who do they think they are? They are just a bunch of upstarts without proper breeding or class. They make such a show of their wealth. The word on the street was that the entire thing was tasteless and downright tacky. Of course, she and Chadsworth were not invited, but it was her understanding that any of the proper people who were invited simply sent their regrets.

"Willie, is it true that the bride's mother stood out in the parking lot waiting on the limousine to pick her up so that she could be driven around the corner and dropped off in front of the church?"

"Yes'em Miss Almeda, I saw her for myself. That's exactly what happened. That Mrs. Titus, she stood out there by the family car for fifteen minutes waiting on that big sleek limousine to pick her up. When it finally got there the dead could hear her cussin' that driver out for being late. Then he put her in the back seat and drove her 'round the corner so she could make a grand entrance."

With that the two of them let the laughter roll.

"Willie, from now on you tell Howard Dexter or anyone else that they are not to touch this magnolia tree without talking to me first!"

"Yes'em Miss Almeda, but the Junior Warden say it was okay."

"Willie, I don't care what the Junior Warden says. I don't even care if the Bishop says it is okay. No one is to touch this magnolia tree until they talk to me first. Now if I see any sign that anyone has touched so much as one leaf on this tree without talking to me first, you, Willie, are going to get the full force of my wrath. Do you understand?"

"Yes'em Miss Almeda, I'sa tells 'em."

Just then she heard someone calling her name.

"Miss Almeda! Miss Almeda! We need your help. You've got to help us."

It was Virginia Mudd and her two pale faced little daughters. Almeda really didn't like the Mudds even though they were from an old and prestigious Georgia family. She particularly did not like those pasty faced little girls who were always dressed just like they had stepped right out of a Laura Ashley Store.

"Where have you been, Virginia? You look absolutely ravishing. And just look at these beautiful girls. Virginia, they get prettier every day. My, oh my, where do you find these darling dresses? You girls must have the biggest closets in Falls City; I don't believe I have ever seen you wear the same thing twice. Now just what is this nonsense about needing help? What can I do for you?"

"Miss Almeda, have you not heard? We just came from the Rectory. We went over to call on the new Rector and his wife." Virginia Mudd shuddered.

"Oh, no," Miss Almeda grabbed at her breast. "You don't mean it?"

"It's worse. It's so much worse," Virginia Mudd shook her head.

A grim faced Almeda asked, "Then it is as bad as I heard?" Almeda felt her face grimace. The look on Virginia Mudd's face confirmed that the rumored tragedy at the Church Rectory had not been exaggerated.

"Miss Almeda, they put foil wallpaper in the dining room! Can you believe that, Miss Almeda? Foil paper, they have put gold and silver foil paper in our Rectory dining room. Poor old Doctor Stuart must be turning in his grave with shame and embarrassment."

"I know—I know, Doctor and Mrs. Stuart brought such grace to our Rectory. They never did anything to it without consulting the Ladies Guild first. Why, they didn't even buy a new piece of furniture or a piece of glassware without first consulting us. Now foil wallpaper, for shame Virginia, do they think we're a bunch of Baptists? I have a hunch that he is not even an Episcopalian by birth. Someone told me he was raised a Methodist -- or worse."

"Miss Almeda, I hear that it was worse."

"Worse than a Methodist?"

"Worse," Virginia shook her head.

Almeda wanted to visibly demonstrate her own displeasure of the new Rector for Virginia Mudd's benefit so she pretended a shudder had just run the length of her body.

"Well, Virginia, we will just have to do something about that wallpaper. What goes up can also come down. We just have to do it quickly before the word gets out."

"Oh, Miss Almeda, the wallpaper is the very least of our problems."

"You don't say. You mean there's more?"

Virginia Mudd pointed to her own mesh of sandy hair. "Miss Almeda, I met the wife. She's bleached blonde!"

"Are you sure it's a bleach job?"

"Right out of a bottle of Clorox."

"Obvious?"

"Obvious."

This time Almeda did not have to pretend to shudder. She felt an involuntary chill rush over her body. She then held her hand to her heart as though she were having difficult time breathing. "Is there more?"

"False eyelashes."

"Now stop it! You're just making that up, Virginia Mudd! That's not even funny. Now don't you run around Falls City exaggerating your story. Bad enough is bad enough without making things worse."

"Miss Almeda, that's not an exaggeration. She has great big old black false eyelashes underneath that bleached blonde hair. My God, Miss Almeda, she looks like Bambi! First Church is going to be the laughing stock of Falls City. What are we going to do?"

Miss Almeda pulled herself straight up. This is a time for composure and action, she said to herself. Almeda began picking up the dead leaves under the tree as she muttered to herself. "Awful, this is just awful. Just wait until I get home. I'm going to give that idiot of husband of mine a real piece of my mind. I can't believe he agreed to bring that hillbilly to First Church."

She turned to face Virginia Mudd and started shaking her head in disgust. Then she pointed her finger at the Mudds in order to emphasize her point. "I'll tell you what we are going to do. We're going to call an emergency meeting of the Altar Guild. We're going to make sure everyone knows just what a tragedy this is and just what a threat it is to our church. Then we'll hand out the list of telephone numbers for the Search Committee, the Vestry, and the Bishop. One by one, we'll have the ladies of the Altar Guild call each of these men and give them a piece of their mind. We'll tell them that we want this joke of a Rector they hired for us out of here by Christmas. Honestly, I don't know what those men were thinking. And I'm going to begin with that man I live with. Chadsworth should've known better."

"Do you think that will work, Miss Almeda?"

"Virginia Mudd, how long have you known me? When I make up my mind that I'm going to do something there is no stopping me. And I'll be hanged if I'm going to let those hillbillies stay in our Rectory any longer than it takes to call up a moving van and get them out!"

As Almeda stood watching Virginia and her two pudgy little girls waddle back down the sidewalk toward the parking lot, her distaste for them became even stronger. In fact, she didn't like a lot of the people she had to associate with at First Church. She particularly disliked those who were continually putting on airs. She knew so many that had inflated opinions of their own importance. She was a woman of distinction and she was personally offended by those who pretended to be equal to her stature.

Almeda turned again to face the magnolia tree. It had almost been ruined when Willie cut some of the branches off for the Titus wedding. She walked closer to the tree so she could stand in its shadow. The sun was warm and she did not want to get sunburned. Over the past few years she had often thought of presenting the idea to the Vestry that First Church needed a membership committee. She would volunteer to be that committee. A committee of one was exactly what was needed. She would then be in the position of deciding just who could be a member of First Church and who should *politely and with Christian charity* be referred to one of the other congregations in the city that would be more suitable.

She smiled to herself as she considered the possibility yet one more time. Now, that Titus bunch is a perfect example. Sure they had some money or at least it appears that they have some wealth. But wealth and good taste are not always wed. That Mrs. Titus dresses like her outfits were purchased at Victoria's Secret or worse. After all, they did move here from New Jersey or New York or one of those other god-forsaken "new states" up north. No, they did not fit at First Church and she for one would be happy to assume her role as a committee of one, authorized by the Vestry of course, to inform them of the fact. Yes, she nodded, that is exactly what is needed.

Almeda was developing a full head of steam. It was time to make some changes at First Church. Things were beginning to go downhill. The calling of this hick for a Rector and his blow-up doll wife was the final straw. First Church has a long history of being a place of distinction in the state of Georgia. It is rightly to be envied by the other congregations and sought after by those who had improved themselves just as she had. But that needed to be the measure of their acceptability. If the candidates for membership at First Church could demonstrate to her that they were cultured ladies and gentlemen with a deep affection for the finer things in life then she would admit them.

She refined her idea even further. Membership in the Country Club would not be enough to qualify them. No, the standards for admission to First Church needed to be more stringent. Clearly, she was the only person that could distinguish between the qualified and those that were not.

Almeda was now ready for action. She would present her membership committee idea in the near future, but first she needed to rally the faithful to save their beloved Church before this new priest had a chance to completely destroy everything she had worked for all these years. She started charging toward her car in the parking lot. Almeda felt God had chosen her to save First Church and she knew exactly where she needed to begin. She would start with her husband Chadsworth. He had been on the Search Committee and the Vestry that brought that Okie to Georgia. What on earth was he thinking?

CHAPTER 2

The Reverend Steele Austin pulled his mini-van up the circular driveway in front of the First Church Rectory. It was an old white colonial framed by large columns in desperate need of paint.

Steele stepped out of the van, tugging at his Levi's and stretching his feet into the Dan Post boots he was wearing. He leaned back on the van and stared at the great white house that was to be his home for the next few years. You've come along way from the hills of Eastern Oklahoma, Steele told himself. His mind flashed back over the little two-bedroom house he had grown up in. The fact that his father and mother struggled most of their lives just to make ends meet only made him wish that he could have done more for them.

He thought about how proud his mother would be to know that he had become a priest. She would be proud to see his beautiful new church and this grand house. But she was gone now, and that wasn't possible. His beautiful little grandmother flashed before his eyes. Of all the people he had known in his life, she had been his greatest spiritual influence.

As a boy, he would accompany her to church. She had always insisted that she was a Presbyterian, but she liked to go to the Pentecostal Church. Steele recalled how the lively music had moved him. He liked the fervor and enthusiasm of the congregation. The preacher was a great storyteller and was able to hold the attention of both children and adults.

Many of Steele's boyhood friends attended that church. There were great parties, hayrides, camp outs, and mission work trips. The church became as much a part of his life as was his school and his family. Early on, Steele entertained the notion of becoming a minister. He often played the lead in the Christmas pageant and was elected president of the youth group.

Steele remembered, however, that for a period in his life, his interest in the church was greatly diminished. That period began when his interest in girls took precedence over his interest in religion. He would go wherever the girls were. He attended most every church in the community; he would go to church with whomever he was dating at the time, or in search of someone he wanted to date.

Steele Austin was no angel during his high school and college years. There were the nights that they would form a drinking party. One of them would go over to the all night gas and grocery. It was common knowledge in his crowd that you only needed to show the night clerk your older brother's driver's license and they would sell you some beer. He and his friends would then take the beer to the local drive-in. Steele would put all his buddies in the trunk of his car before getting to the entrance. Once inside he would open the trunk and they would all pile into the car. They would drink, hoot, flirt, and smoke cigarettes until the beer was all gone or the movie over—whichever came first.

Then there were the dates he arranged with only one goal in mind. Steele was always prepared. He would take a quarter down to the local gasoline station. The machine was in the bathroom. He kept the contents in his wallet well hidden from his parents, but available for use in an instant just in case he got lucky.

The girls he knew were always more than willing to neck. Most had no problem with him going to second base. The line usually got drawn when he would reach for the snap. Then they would cool it and get argumentative.

There were those girls that would let you go all the way, but they were always so desperate. They had marriage on their mind. Marriage was the very last thing on Steele's mind.

At the University of Texas he was introduced to the wonders of pot smoking. The girls at the university were free spirits. Just get them to inhale a few times or get them to drink some wine or beer and they were all over you. There was no talk of marriage or babies or anything else.

Vietnam heated up and Steele knew he was going to have to keep his grades up in order to maintain his student deferment. The first time he was called back home to be a pallbearer for one of his high school chums was a living nightmare. They couldn't even open the casket. The director of the funeral home said that the body was in pieces. His childhood friend was only twenty years old. Steele sat staring at the flag-draped casket. He recalled the nights at the drive-in and the football games and the school dances. Then it hit Steele between the eyes. Vietnam is a place young boys go to die.

It was his junior year at the university when he spotted her. She had long black hair and the most incredible blue eyes you could ever hope to see. If there were such a thing as love at first sight, Steele found it with Dawn.

Her long black hair framed her face. She had big blue eyes that sparkled when she saw him coming toward her. They would study together in the library for hours and never speak, but the bond between them was still not broken. Their song was "Blue Velvet". She wore a blue velvet dress the night he gave her a ring. Steele could not imagine a life without her.

They would talk for hours on the telephone. He rose early each morning before her first class. He would meet her at the door to the classroom. They would just stand in the hallway. He would hold her hand. They would gaze into each other's eyes. He thought of himself as the luckiest guy in the world.

Sometimes after school they would go to the park. He would read to her. He preferred to simply lie on the grass with his head in her lap as she read to him. Their parents approved of their relationship. On school breaks, Steele would go with her to her parent's home. Her mother would hug Steele's neck. Her father showed his approval as well. When Dawn went with Steele to his home, Steele's mother fussed over her. His dad was shameless with his flirtations.

Dawn was an Episcopalian. Steele found it a strange church at first. The clergy wore vestments like the Roman Catholic priests. There were kneeling benches in the pews. The first few times he went to the Episcopal Church with Dawn he was nervous. He was not sure what would be expected of him. He did not want to embarrass himself, but Dawn was helpful. After a few Sundays, he relaxed; he became more familiar with the ritual. He would hold Dawn's hand during the sermon. They would hold hands when they knelt to pray before and after communion. There were some changes taking place inside Steele Austin. Not only had he fallen in love with Dawn, but he had fallen in love with her church.

She went with him to membership classes. She giggled at his clumsy attempts to learn how to genuflect and to cross himself. She gave him a Prayer Book for his service of confirmation. Sharing in her faith increased his own convictions. Sharing their faith together brought them even closer.

They began to talk about getting married after graduation. Steele surprised Dawn one evening as they were talking about their future. He told her that he could see himself becoming a priest. Dawn's eyes grew moist. She reached up and hugged his neck. Then she drew back and looked deep into his eyes. "Steele Austin, I love you."

It was the beginning of their senior year at the university. It started simply as an infection in the big toe on her right foot. The antibiotics did not work. They had to amputate. Deep down they knew that once the surgeons starting whittling on her it was but the beginning. Next they removed her foot and then her leg below the knee. Then the other leg had to be removed as well.

Even now, Steele's eyes filled as he thought about that last night. He held her hand and watched the disease that she had lived with since childhood take the last bit of life from her. He watched her struggle for air and he so wanted to be able to breathe for her. He watched her crystal blue eyes roll back into her head. He listened desperately for the next breath. None came. There was only silence. And then off in some distant place he heard a heartbreaking scream. As he collapsed to the floor he realized that the scream was his.

He awoke in a strange room. The tear-stained faces of his mother and father were staring down at him.

"The doctor has given you something to help you sleep, son," his father said. "Sleep now. There's nothing else you can do for Dawn."

The next few months he remembered just walking around in a daze. Every muscle and bone in his body hurt. He was so empty, so hopeless, and so lonely. He regressed to some of his less than admirable behavior. He drank too much. He smoked every marijuana cigarette he could buy. The family doctor gave him a prescription to help him sleep. Sometimes if he could combine all three things he could sleep—for days. Steele thought of enlisting to go to Vietnam. He would volunteer for the most dangerous assignment. He would die for his country, but more than that, he would die so that he could go be with Dawn.

With the passing of time Steele's grief lessened. He knew he would always miss Dawn. He would always grieve for the life they had dreamed of having together. There was one part of their dream that he could still fulfill. He knew that it was what she would have wanted him to do. Even more, he knew it was what he needed to do. It was the right thing to do. It was his destiny.

He entered the seminary in New York City. There were plenty of single women available for him to date in that metropolis, but he just was not interested. He dated some, but he simply went through the motions. Steele could not forget Dawn.

Steele recalled his ordination at St. Paul's Cathedral in Oklahoma City. There were seven of them being ordained that day. They stood before the Bishop at the high altar. Together they responded to the Prayer Book vows. Then together they prostrated on the Cathedral floor before the Bishop as he and the choir chanted the *Veni Creator*. The words of the ancient prayer invoking the Holy Spirit burned into Steele's soul. He prayed that the Holy Spirit would be his constant companion in ministry and guide his every word and deed.

The Bishop stared deep into his eyes before laying his hands on his head. It was at that moment that all doubt was shaken from Steele Austin's soul. He knew beyond a shadow of a doubt that he was answering God's call. He was fulfilling his destiny. He was put on this earth to be a priest. After being ordained he stood to look up at the cross above the altar. Dawn's face flashed before him.

His first Rector did not want a Curate. The man made it clear that had he wanted a Curate it sure would not have been Steele Austin. The Bishop assigned Steele to him anyway.

The Rector took great delight in pointing out Steele's mistakes in front of the entire congregation. He would try to disguise his criticism by asking the congregation to overlook his "youthful enthusiasm." But each time the Rector publicly critiqued him, Steele could feel the blood rush to his face. He was humiliated to hear the congregation have a great laugh at his expense. Steele resolved then and there that it would be the shortest curacy on record.

He tried his best to get a new assignment, but not before his life was changed forever. He was distributing communion on Easter Sunday when their eyes met. Her beautiful face was framed with a full-brimmed hat. Her eyes were the blackest he had ever seen. She smiled at him, and he smiled back.

After the service he casually inquired after the name of the beautiful young woman in the white lace dress and the full-brimmed hat. It didn't take long to discover her name, Randi, and that she was single.

He telephoned her that afternoon. She responded to his greeting with her most deferential voice. "Yes, Father, it is so nice of you to telephone me. What can I do for you? Do you need help with one of the programs at the church?"

He had not counted on her treating him as a priest. He was a man who had been smitten by her beauty.

"Are you seeing anyone?" he inquired.

There was silence. Then she answered uncomfortably. "You mean like a psychiatrist or a counselor?"

Steele chuckled. "No, I wasn't calling about your personal life uhh... well; I am, but not that way."

"Well, then Father Austin just what aspects of my personal life are you calling about?"

Steele became frustrated and it was difficult for him to find the words he needed to undo his opening question. He feared he was off to the wrong foot with Randi. Turning the tide of the conversation took some doing, but he finally succeeded. Clearly Randi had not considered him as a potential date. "Please call me Steele. Would you consider going to dinner with me and then, perhaps a movie?"

"Father uhh ur Steele, are you asking me to go on a date with you?"

"Yes, I would really like to get to know you."

"As a parishioner?"

"No." There was a very long, very uncomfortable silence before she agreed. He picked her up the following Friday. The chemistry between the two of them was explosive. They shut down the restaurant and then continued talking in his car until sunrise. They saw each other every day after.

Just six months later he once again stood in front of the Bishop waiting for her to come down the aisle on the arm of her father. He took her hand and looked into her eyes. For the second time in less than a year he knew beyond a shadow of a doubt that he was doing what God had put him on this earth to do.

CHAPTER 3

Mistuh Austin, I'm Howard Dexter."
The voice came from a runt of man wearing an English driving cap. Steele remembered that he was on the Vestry. He had met him in the search process.

"And I'm Chadsworth Purcell Alexander."

The second voice came from one of the most incredibly good-looking men Steele had ever seen in his life. He had a full head of beautiful gray hair. And while he had to be in his late fifties or early sixties, it was apparent he was no stranger to the gym, the tanning booth, or the plastic surgeon. Steele remembered that he too was on the Vestry.

"We are the co-chairs of the Rectory Committee. We just wanted to come over and make sure that everything is acceptable."

"Gentlemen," Steele began, "I am glad that you came by. I do have some questions for you. I believe that my Letter of Agreement states that you would do some things to the Rectory prior to our arrival. It doesn't appear to us that much has been done."

Howard Dexter gave a nervous chuckle. "Well, Mistuh Austin, as you know it costs a lot of money to maintain a house of this size and the church just isn't in a position to do much more than we've already done."

Steele felt the blood surging into his face. "Mister Dexter...."

"Oh, call me Howard."

"Yes, and call me Chadsworth," the man who looked like an aging male model repeated.

"And please call me Steele," he responded. "Gentlemen, my wife is very disappointed that the work that we agreed to has not been done. The Vestry agreed to replace the dishwasher. You simply painted the door. It looks terrible. You also promised to paint the house inside and out and replace all the carpet. You also agreed to hang drapes and curtains."

"Now, now, Mistuh...uh...ur...-- Steele." Howard Dexter started waving his hand in an effort to calm down Steele Austin. "You young clergy just don't seem to understand how much it costs to maintain a big house like this. We did touch up the paint and we did steam clean the carpets. The Vestry is in a quandary. It just can't see itself clear to do more."

Steele had a flashback to the first dinner that they had with the Search Committee. He remembered the other committee members teasing Howard Dexter. They had taken Steele and his wife to the Country Club for their initial interview. The other committee members teased Howard about wanting to take everyone for Happy Meals at a McDonald's. More than one committee member had remarked just how much Howard Dexter hated to spend money. They insinuated that Howard was so stingy that he squeaked when he walked. He had appointed himself the keeper of the treasury at First Church. Not only did he hate to spend his own money, but he didn't want to spend any of the church's money either. One person suggested that Howard so needed to make sure that the church didn't spend any money he didn't want them to spend that he had made arrangements for all the church accounts to be placed in his bank. He didn't charge the parish any bank fees, thus insuring that he could keep the accounts in his bank. Control over the money meant more to him than even collecting fees for his services.

On recalling this information about Howard Dexter, Steele decided to try another tactic. "Howard, Chadsworth, please come inside, I want to show you something."

The two followed Steele into the house. Steele reached into his brief case on the kitchen counter and pulled out the Letter of Agreement. He started reading them the section entitled "Rectory Improvements."

Howard Dexter interrupted. This time it was apparent that his face was flushed and his voice shook as he tried to restrain himself. "Mistuh Austin, we know what the agreement states. The church simply does not have the funds to do the work. You young priests should learn from men like Doctor Stuart. He and Mrs. Stuart lived in this house eighteen years and they never asked us to do one thing to it. They felt honored and proud to live in this grand old house. That was enough for them. I would like to suggest that you and your wife try to emulate their behavior."

The disbelief in Steele Austin's voice could not be disguised. "You didn't do anything to this house in the eighteen years that the Stuarts lived here? That is incredible."

Again, Howard Dexter rebutted, "Mistuh Austin, please, there is no reason to get upset. The Vestry at First Church has to be careful with the way it expends money. We don't want the congregation or the people in the community to think that we are putting on airs. We don't want to spend their offerings recklessly. We are a conservative people. Frugality is a virtue."

"But Howard," Steele continued, "please try to understand things from our perspective. This house has sat over here empty for almost two years while you tried to find a new Rector. A fresh coat of paint and some new carpets hardly seem like an extravagance after twenty years of deferred maintenance."

Just then Steele heard his wife scream from the other room. "Steele, come quick! It's a rat on the baby's head!"

Steele ran for the den just in time to see a rat the size of a small cat running past his two-year-old son's head. The child was sleeping on a blanket on the floor in the den.

"You mean you guys didn't even have this house exterminated?" Steele could not help but raise his voice.

"Now, Mistuh Austin, we are reasonable people. If you will try to see things from our point of view, I think you will understand. We feel it is our responsibility to provide you with a house. It is your responsibility to maintain it."

"That is not what we agreed to. It is right here in writing. It is signed by the Chair of the Search Committee, the Wardens, and the Bishop. There is nothing in it about us maintaining the house. Quite the contrary, you guys agreed not only to maintain it, but to make the list of improvements on it." Steele was trying to keep himself polite and under control, but he felt he needed to hold his ground.

Howard Dexter shook his head. He too was firm, but in his most soothing voice he appealed to Steele. "Mistuh Austin, the church does not have the money…."

Steele cut him off mid-sentence, "Howard, I understand that the parish may be hesitant to spend any money on the Rectory, but I thought we made a deal. It is all here in writing and signed by all the appropriate officials. I resigned from one perfectly good job, sold a house that we owned, and put my family through the trauma of a move across country because I thought we had a deal."

"Now, now, Steele, don't be overly dramatic," Howard Dexter tried once again to calm Steele down. "I was a part of the team that came out to see your quaint church in Oklahoma. We saw that cute little house you had, but they are all pale in comparison to First Church and this grand house. Steele, you and your little family should consider yourself fortunate that First Church has chosen you to be our Rector. What a privilege it is for you to be here. Your wife and child will now move among the finest circles in Falls City."

Steele was beginning to feel manipulated and frustrated. "Howard, Chadsworth, I really need you to honor the deal that we made. I need you to honor the terms of our Letter of Agreement."

"Sir," Howard Dexter pleaded, "please don't call our honor into question. In the great state of Georgia it is a dangerous thing to question a man's honor."

Steele took a deep breath. He wanted to be polite. He did not want the men to lose face, but he wanted them to honor their contract. "Will the two of you see if there is not some way that the Vestry can make the agreed repairs and improvements on the Rectory?" Steele looked over at Chadsworth, who had not spoken a word up to this point.

Chadsworth nodded. "Howard, the young man might have a point. Let's go down to the club. Have some lunch and see if we can't get some of the boys to chip in. We may not be able to raise all the money and it may take us a while to get all the work done, but we'll see what we can do. After all, we do want our new Rector and his family to be happy."

Steele began to relax. "Then our deal is still good?"

Chadsworth again nodded and extended his right hand, "We'll see what we can do."

Howard Dexter turned to leave. It was apparent that he was not a happy man. It appeared that the teasing Steele had witnessed about Howard not wanting to spend money was well earned. Steele did not want Howard to be an enemy, but he knew that if First Church was going to live into the vision he had for the congregation they were going to have to spend some money. He had a hunch that this was not going to be the last time that Howard Dexter and he would square off on the use of church funds.

Steele stood watching after the two of them as they went down the drive. His wife joined him. He put his arm around her as they watched them drive away. As Steele thought about the exchange he had just had with Howard Dexter, he began to feel nauseous. Steele had the sinking feeling that he had just made one of the biggest mistakes of his life.

CHAPTER 4

The Magnolia Club forms the third side to Falls City's equivalent of the Bermuda Triangle. The other two are the Falls City Country Club and old First Church. For generations, the finer people of Falls City have lived out their entire lives inside this Triangle. Most have done so without a thought of escape. On occasion, one of the Falls City young people would turn their back on the University of Georgia, Georgia Tech, or Auburn and escape to some far off school like the University of North Carolina or Duke. Some of the more adventurous would go all the way to the University of Virginia in Charlottesville. Still, unlike Brigadoon where some are allowed to escape every one hundred years, the young people of Falls City seem unable to escape. Upon graduation they are drawn back into the Triangle where they live out their lives following in their parent's footsteps.

As a club for gentlemen of distinction, the Magnolia Club boasts a waiting list at least two decades long. Women cannot be members of the Club. Wives, daughters, and their female guests may eat in the Parlor. They are not allowed down the hall into the larger ballroom that is reserved for the gentlemen members and their male guests. Likewise, the ladies are not allowed downstairs in the bar and the gentlemen's café, nor are they allowed upstairs in the private meeting rooms.

To be sure, this large old antebellum house that was converted into the Magnolia Club during the early 1950's is always a place of dignity and decorum. Jackets and ties are required of all males in attendance, and ladies are required to wear dresses -- hats and gloves remain optional. There are rumors in the community that at the annual Christmas Party, decorum is put aside. There are hushed whispers of female entertainers being brought in from Atlanta just for the occasion. Speculation is that the young women provide more than just a dance to some of the less reverent members. Nothing, of course, has ever been confirmed. The wives all choose to look the other direction and the male members remain tight-lipped about the party.

From its beginning the membership of the Magnolia Club has remained all white, protestant, and male. A few years ago, the waiting list to the club membership did face a deficit of qualified male candidates. This caused quite a stir for the Membership Committee. A popular monsignor at the local Roman Catholic parish had applied for membership. That he would have been the first Catholic admitted to membership was, in itself, reason for great concern. The Membership Committee became even more exercised when they read on his application that his mother's maiden name was Lieberstein.

The Membership Committee was concerned that a dangerous precedent was about to be set. If they made this one exception they feared that it would be more difficult to maintain their current membership standards in the future. After a lot of drinking and pulling in the cleverest of the clever for counsel, it was decided to implement the "male heir" option. Regardless of their age, the sons and grandsons of all current members were placed at the top of the waiting list. This pretty much insured that the club membership would remain white, Protestant and male for the foreseeable future.

The large ballroom and the downstairs bar is opened to the guests of members for wedding receptions, dinners, The Cotillion, and of course, the Original Falls City Debutante Society. It must be noted, however, that there is an unwritten rule that members do not invite people of color or members of the Jewish religion to these events. Should that happen, be sure that the offending person will be called before the Membership Committee and his privileges temporarily revoked.

Howard Dexter was still fuming when he entered the bar in the club. He and Chadsworth took a table near the fireplace in the corner of the room.

"Bring us each doubles, Henry," Howard shouted.

Chadsworth touched him on the arm. "Calm down, Howard. We'll figure it all out."

Just then a couple other members of the First Church Vestry entered the bar.

Howard motioned, "Hey, you boys come on over here and have a seat. We need to talk."

"Dexter, what on earth is wrong with you? You're sweating like a darkie at a Klan Rally," one of them asked.

"Guys," Howard began, "we've got trouble. That damn Rector we hired is going to be a problem. He had the nerve to question my honor. He thinks that just because we didn't do everything to the Rectory, we can't be trusted. It looks like he's going to make a stink. Chadsworth thinks we ought to take up a collection and do the work."

Chadsworth shrugged, "I don't want us to forget just how much trouble we had even getting a Rector. Don't forget we had to cross several state lines to find a mullet because any one who knew anything about this parish wouldn't even talk to us."

"Some damn mullet!" Howard Dexter pounded the table. "I am telling you boys this guy is going to be trouble and we're all going to live to regret the day we ever heard the name Steele Austin."

"Now, now, Howard," Chadsworth interrupted. "We've had clergy who were too big for their britches before. We know what to do. We know how to deal with them. He'll either conform or he'll leave."

"I just don't want the honor of the church to be impugned. If he starts running around town or the Diocese saying that we didn't keep our word -- what will people think?"

Chadsworth took a deep swallow of his Johnny Walker Black. "Should we call the Bishop? Maybe the Bishop can come down on him and get him to fall into line. Or, we can always unleash the Altar Guild on him. If there was ever a group of women that knows how to make a priest miserable, it's that flock. Every one of us who are married to one of them knows that for a fact. Can you imagine having to deal with all forty of them at one time?"

With that all the men enjoyed a good laugh.

One of the men punched Howard on the shoulder, "Are you sure that the Church doesn't have the money to fix up the Rectory? I'll bet if you open up your safe, of course, all the moths will fly out and block the sun..."

Again, the group broke out in laughter.

Again, Howard interrupted the laughter, "Now you guys all know I only have the best interests of the church at heart. My granddaddy was finance chair for this Church. Then, he was Senior Warden six times. My daddy followed in his steps. He served on the Vestry over forty years. My family has always held a high regard for First Church and we have always made the long term financial security of the parish a priority. But hell, all you boys know that. Most of you men knew my granddaddy and all of you knew my daddy. If memory serves me right, my daddy taught a lot of you boys how to shoot. You all know me. I just don't want us to spend our member's hard earned money on things that we simply don't need." Howard took another sip of his drink and then his face brightened. "Let me tell you what I think we ought to do. We'll tell him that we're going to do the work, but we'll have to wait until all the money has been collected. That ought to satisfy him for now. It will also give us time to make a plan. If he gives us too much trouble we can always turn the Klan loose on him. He'll head back to Oklahoma like a bat coming out of hell."

Again, they laughed.

CHAPTER 5

Steele Austin awoke early for his first Sunday at First Church. Unlike Oklahoma, they had been able to sleep with the windows open. The attic fan in the Rectory had pulled the cool, damp South Georgia breeze into the bedroom. Since the Rectory was located close to the city zoo, the roar of the resident lion pulled him out of his slumber long before his alarm was set to go off. He was excited to celebrate his first Sunday with the congregation.

Steele put on a new black clerical shirt, new black pants, and a brand new sports coat he had purchased in Oklahoma just for this Sunday. He slid his feet into his black western boots and then studied himself in the full length mirror. He heard Randi stir behind him. She came up and wrapped her arms around his waist and smiled at him in the mirror. "Go get'em cowboy. You can do it." They both giggled like school children.

As he pulled into the staff parking lot he was struck by the fact that the other members of the staff had their names painted on their parking spaces. His parking space, however, simply read "Rector". He remembered that when touring the buildings in the search process there was no listing of the past Rectors. He was Rector number twenty-one but nowhere in any of the buildings was there any notice of previous Rectors. There was no listing of Rectors, no engraved plaques of gratitude for their ministries, no gallery of Rector's pictures. He found that curious since it was such a common practice.

Standing at the gate of the church was a young man leaning up against the pillar. He had his face buried in his hands, and he was holding a handkerchief. He was obviously distraught.

"May I help you?" Steele asked.

The young man did not look around. He just shook his head.

Steele placed his hand on the young man's shoulder. "I'm the new Rector, Steele Austin. If you're upset, I really would like to help."

The young man turned so that he could make eye contact with Steele. His eyes were moist with tears.

"I'm Ronnie. My name is Ronnie Williams. I've been coming to this church for the past few Sundays. Everyone has been so excited for you to come. I'm from Oklahoma too. Durant, Oklahoma."

"Pleased to meet you, Ronnie Williams. Now tell me, what has you so upset on this beautiful fall morning?"

"I talked to the head usher a few weeks ago and asked if I could be an usher. I particularly wanted to usher on your first Sunday. He told me to be sure to wear a tie and a jacket. I bought this new pink shirt yesterday and this sports coat to go with it. When I reported a few minutes ago, however, the head usher told me that I couldn't usher at First Church dressed like this. He said I had to wear a white shirt and a dark suit. I don't have the money to buy another shirt and suit. I sure don't have enough money to wear a different shirt and suit every week."

"Who told you that?" Steele had the familiar feeling of blood rushing to his face. "What's the head usher's name?"

"Oh, I don't want to get anyone into trouble. I'll just find another church where I'll be more comfortable."

"No," Steele replied. "If I have anything to say about it, you'll be welcomed in this church and you'll be an usher, but first I have to speak to the head usher. Now what was the name of the man who said this to you?"

"I believe his name is Mitchell. Yes, that's it. Colonel Mitchell." The young man appeared thoughtful for just a moment. "Reverend Austin, do you know what you have gotten into here?"

"What do you mean?" Steele queried.

"Reverend Austin, all my friends over at the plant told me not to come to this church. People like me really aren't welcome here. Some of my friends told me that not even God had been able to get into this place. Everyone in town says this is just a country club with a cross on the top of it."

Steele felt himself shudder. "Oh, surely it isn't that bad. Come on in and worship with us. I'll see what I can do to get you an ushering job."

Ronnie stared at him for a long time. "Reverend Austin, I'm going down to Saint Joseph's Catholic Church. I had been going there. I should've stayed. I'll pray for you. And Reverend, if what I have seen from the pew is even a sample, you are really going to need it in the pulpit."

With that, Ronnie turned and walked toward the parking lot.

Steele began to wonder just what he had gotten himself into. He felt his stomach do a flip.

As he rounded the corner going into the church, he encountered a very elderly man struggling to come up the stairs from the basement.

"Can I help you, Sir?" Steele extended his hand. "I'm Steele Austin, your new Rector. What were you doing in the basement?"

The man stopped and took a breath. "Young man, when nature calls you have to answer. At my age, nature calls more and more often."

"But why didn't you use the bathroom upstairs? It is small, but it would keep you from having to go up and down these stairs."

The man grimaced, "Young man, look at me. I'm a large man. That bathroom was once a broom closet. The door is small and the room is even smaller. Besides you would have to go through the Altar Guild Sacristy to get to it. No one goes into the Altar Guild Sacristy but the Altar Guild and the clergy."

"Then we should find a place to put a suitable bathroom on the same level as the church. There must be other elderly members who can't negotiate these stairs. What about disabled people? What do they do for bathroom facilities?"

The elderly man shook his head, "Sir, I don't think that there is any way that you will be able to put a bathroom in the church. This is a historic building. We are on the historic register. No, I'll keep climbing these stairs as long as I'm able. If the day comes I can't negotiate the stairs, then I reckon it'll be time for me to stay home."

Steele muttered to himself, "Well, that doesn't seem right."

The man walked past Steele muttering to himself as well, "You young people. You just can't leave well enough alone."

The Reverend Steele Austin stood in the back of his new church. It smelled of mildew and brass polish. There was no shortage of brass, stained glass, crushed red velvet carpeting, or needlepoint. Every pew was padded. What was it he had been told about churches with padded pews?

He slid into the back pew, pulled down the kneeler and knelt to recite his morning prayers. The members of the congregation were beginning to arrive. He sat back in silence for a few minutes to watch the people entering their pews and to mentally rehearse his sermon one more time.

Just then, Steele Austin saw something so shocking that at first he did not believe his eyes. An elderly woman wearing a gardenia blossom walked past him. She was superbly dressed in hat and gloves. While her black house servant was holding one of her arms, she was leaning very heavily on a walking cane with a silver handle. The woman and her servant walked slowly down the aisle to the front of the church. They did not glance either direction and took no notice of the other worshippers. Then, the duo stopped just short of the front of the church. The woman turned to look at a young family that was sitting on the end of the third pew in front of the pulpit. Steele noticed that she just stood there and stared at them. The husband looked back at her and then stood in his place to allow her pass into the pew. The woman continued to stand there. The wife looked at her husband, confused. The man shrugged and sat back down. Then the elderly woman, without saying a word, took the end of her cane, tapped the husband and the wife on the shoulder with it and motioned for them to move. The couple looked at each other, gathered up their children, and went up the side aisle and left the church through the side door. The woman and her house servant sat down. Steele thought that there had to be more to this than what he just witnessed.

Steele went into the Sacristy to put on his vestments. A woman with a strange looking napkin on her head wearing a matching apron imprinted with "First Church Altar Guild" greeted him.

"Mistuh Austin, I am Mrs. Gordon Smythe, the Altar Guild Directress."

Steele could not help but notice the condescending look the woman had on her face. She was literally looking down her nose at him.

"Yes, Mrs. Smythe I have been looking forward to meeting you. I hope we can get together in the next few days so that we can get to know one another better."

"Yes, I will put you in my diary." She continued to look over the top of her glasses at him.

"Mrs. Smythe, it's Mary Alice isn't it? May I call you Mary Alice?"

"No, you may not. I prefer to honor my husband just as I promised him and God on our wedding day forty-seven years ago. I honor him by using his name. In formal relationships, and ours will be a formal relationship, I prefer to be addressed as my husband's devoted wife. I hope that is acceptable, Mistuh Austin?"

"I will certainly honor your wishes with regards to your name, but I am just not used to being addressed as Mister. Please, would you mind just calling me Steele?"

"No sir, I will not do that," she stated haughtily. "I'll not call you Father either. You are young enough to be my son. The Bible says to call no man Father, so don't ask me to call you Father. And I'll not call you Reverend either. I am not a Baptist. Sir, I will give you the title of respect you deserve. I will call you 'Mistuh'."

"Well, now that we have that settled," Steele smiled to himself; "maybe you can answer a couple of questions for me? I understand that we have a pretty strict dress code for ushers here. Can you tell me about that?"

"Listen, Mistuh Austin." She sneered, "I know all about that incident with that boy this morning. Colonel Mitchell was correct in upholding the traditions of First Church. Now, if I could ask you a question?"

"Yes."

"Can you tell me about your costume? I have not seen it for myself, but I understand that you have been seen on the streets of Falls City wearing a clerical collar with blue jeans. I don't believe I have ever seen that combination. Nor have I ever seen a sports coat with such a square cut. What kind of cut do you call that?"

The woman was on the verge of giggling. Steele felt himself blush.

She continued, "I do believe we are going to have to do something about your attire."

Before Steele could respond she confronted him further, "I heard your conversation with old Jack on the stairs a few minutes ago. The bathroom over there was not designed for congregational use. We put it in because Dr. Stuart got so feeble; we felt we needed to provide a place for him. Otherwise, services might start late while we were waiting for him to go down the stairs. The Altar Guild has to use this space to prepare for services. We don't need the members of the congregation coming in here to use these facilities."

Steele figured this woman was a fountain of information so he decided to see what else he could learn from her. "Could you tell me who the elderly woman with the black nurse is on the third pew?"

"Mistuh Austin --- Mistuh Austin --- Mistuh Austin." She was clearly exasperated. "That black woman, as you refer to her, is not a nurse. She is her servant, but I think you already knew that. Mistuh Austin, I am here to help you. Let me begin by counseling you to leave well enough alone. First Church has had twenty Rectors. You are twenty-one and there will be a twenty-two. Mistuh Austin, I have outlived four of those Rectors myself and I will outlive you!"

Steele tried to interrupt.

She turned her back on him and started to walk away. In the process she continued, "If you want to have a happy time here, and I do want you to have a pleasant ministry, you will leave well enough alone. First Church is just like a woman. Treat her gently and treat her with affection, but you rile her up and you will have more trouble than you or any man can handle."

Steele heard the organist begin the opening hymn. He studied his reflection in the full-length mirror. "Welcome to First Church," he said to himself. "We are so glad that you are here. We hope you will have a long and happy ministry with us."

As he continued to stare at himself, he felt what was becoming a familiar sick feeling return to his stomach.

Steele met the crucifer and two torch bearers at the Sacristy door. He nodded to them and they began moving up the side aisle to the back of the nave. There the choir stood leading the congregation in the opening hymn. Steele stopped at the Baptismal Font. The crucifer and torches made the turn down the center aisle and the choir fell in behind them. Steele brought up the end of the procession. When he arrived at the altar he bowed to acknowledge the altar and turned to face the congregation. There were lots of empty spaces in the pews. Steele intensely disliked preaching to empty pews.

The choir only had about a dozen voices in it, but that didn't matter. His gaze fell on a woman who he could best describe as a warbling soprano. She was enjoying her rendition of the hymn enough for all present. Clearly, she was the voice of the choir and the other eleven voices simply could not compete. Steele sought the eye of the organist. He met Steele's gaze and then quickly glanced away. There would have to be some changes in the choir. This Steele knew for certain.

When it came time for the sermon Steele decided not to use the pulpit, but to stand at the crossing in front of the altar. He thought that perhaps on his first Sunday with his new congregation he would simply have a conversation with them.

He began, "My family and I want to thank you for calling me to be your Rector. I am humbled by the trust that the Bishop, Search Committee and Vestry have placed in me. I am well aware that First Church is a great Church in the American Episcopal Family and that you are a distinguished congregation with years of faithful service to our Lord. I come here to serve you. It is my heartfelt desire to live among you as your pastor, teacher, and friend. More than anything else I want to be obedient to the plans that God will reveal to us for First Church."

Steele paused. He could see that there were a few smiles now being returned to him and a few heads were nodding appreciatively. "While I don't know all of your names right now, it is my hope that over the next few months I will be able to put all your names and faces together, but I will need your help with that. If I forget your name it is not because you are not important to me or I don't remember you. It is simply that there are several hundred of you. Nevertheless, I pledge to give it my best effort." The smiles in the congregation continued to grow.

"As I was thinking about our first Sunday together the thought that kept coming to my mind was that today I would see so many faces for the first time, but I would also see your hands for the first time as well." He paused for effect, "I don't know if you have ever thought about it, but a priest soon knows his congregation by their hands as well as their faces. In fact, in my last congregation I could recognize a person by simply looking at their hands. Week by week worshippers come forward and stretch out their hands to receive the Blessed Sacrament. It is not unusual for me to see your hands before I make eye contact with you."

Steele held up his own hands as though studying them for the first time. "Our hands tell so much about us. Hands are used by parents to express love and affection to their children. Hands teach, hands comfort, and hands heal. The homemaker's hands feed. The surgeon's hands repair. The teacher's hands encourage. The poet's hands inspire. The musician's hands lift us up. The factory worker's hands build things that make life better for all of us." With those words Steele's attention was drawn to a couple sitting on the first pew. The man whispered to his wife in a voice loud enough for Steele and those around him to hear, "He's not going to find any factory workers in this congregation. Just who is this guy?" His wife and the couple seated behind them snickered.

Steele lost his thoughts and just stood uncomfortably for a minute.

There was some restlessness in the congregation. A couple of people cleared their throats. He regained his composure and decided to bring his homily to a conclusion. "Consider the role that hands play in the sacramental life of a Christian. The mother and father carry their child in their arms to be baptized. The priest pours water over the candidate with his hands. The Bishop lays hands on us to confirm us. The priest makes the sign of the cross over us when we make our confession to remind us that we are forgiven through the power of the cross of Christ. A couple joins hands as an outward sign of their uniting together in marriage. We are anointed with oil when we are ill and the minister lays his hands on us to pray for us. And finally, every deacon, priest, and bishop since the time of the apostles has been ordained with the laying on of hands."

Steele found that the disturbance in the front pew was still bothering him and had thrown him off his cadence. He fumbled for words, "I come to you today as your new Rector. I bring all the gifts that God has given me. As an outward sign of our ministry together, I pledge to you that I will use these hands as Christ's hands. I promise to be among you to do as Christ would have me do." With that Steele asked all to stand and join him in affirming their faith by reciting the Nicene Creed.

The greetings at the door were courteous, but not particularly enthusiastic. Steele felt welcomed, but the uneasiness in the pit of his stomach that he had first experienced in the Sacristy before the service was still with him. The last couple to come through his line was dressed immaculately. Clearly, they were people of means. The man simply shook Steele's hand. He gave him a sheepish smile, but did not say a word. The woman however, gave Steele a visual examination. "My name is Bernice Southerland. Let me repeat that for you...Bernice Southerland. Now, I don't want to ever have to tell you my name again. I expect you to remember it. Do you understand?"

Steele was caught off guard. "I'll certainly try."

She walked away shaking her head, "Did you hear that? He'll try. Pitiful I tell you. Absolutely pitiful."

Steele walked back into the church. It was now empty except for a couple leaving the side door with the altar flowers that had been placed in large soup cans. They were taking them to the hospital with attached cards reading, "From the Altar of First Church."

The uneasiness in his stomach had now grown to a full case of indigestion. He literally felt like he was about to lose his breakfast. He sat down in the back pew. Cold sweat broke out on his forehead. The joy that he thought he would feel after his first Sunday at his new Church was not there. He was overwhelmed with the feeling that he had made a terrible mistake. He had misread God's will for him.

Steele knelt in the pew, "Oh God, have I made a mistake? Did I not hear you correctly? Did I come to this congregation for the wrong reasons? Were my motives not pure?" There was no answer. He was so confused. He continued kneeling in silence. Tears welled up in his eyes. He thought of his beautiful Randi and their precious child. His mind went back to the green hills of Oklahoma. "Maybe I heard you wrong Father, but I am here now. I am your priest. Use me as you need. My hands are your hands." The tears rolled down his cheeks. He contemplated telephoning Bishop Powers to see if he could simply return to his old parish. He thought that perhaps he needed to meet with the Search Committee and the Vestry to gain some clarification about his call. Perhaps he had been misunderstood. Perhaps he did not hear them correctly. He thought about having a parish forum in which all the members could ask him questions and he could try to help them get to know him better. Time slipped away as he knelt there. After some time his mind went blank and he just knelt in silence.

He jerked in surprise when he felt a hand on his shoulder, "Ya' alright Father Austin?" It was Willie the church sexton. He had turned out the lights and was about to lock up the church. Steele shook his head and wiped his face on his white surplice. "Me 'n my wife gonna pray for you Father. We're glad you're here. Da' Lord brought you here. Everthin' gonna be just fine. You just wait and see."

CHAPTER 6

Sitting on his desk was a large cardboard box. Steele lifted the flaps on the box to discover that it was filled with men's suits. He was overwhelmed by the smell of mothballs combined with the stench of stale cigar smoke. Sitting prominently on the top of the suits was a handwritten note in an embossed envelope. Steele opened the envelope.

Dear Mister Austin:

Several of us have taken notice that you may be in need of additional clothing for your ministry at First Church. This is understandable since I am sure that the salary of a parson does not afford you many of the finer things in life. I have taken it upon myself to offer you some assistance.

These suits belonged to my late husband, Sanders Hampton. He died two years ago, but I have kept them in this box in our attic. I know that he would simply rejoice to know that our new Rector is wearing them. I look forward to seeing you in one of his suits this coming Sunday.

Best Regards,

Mrs. Sanders Hampton

Steele lifted the first suit out of the box. He had to shake the mouse droppings off it. The material looked like it was from a roaring twenties movie set. He couldn't remember seeing an uglier pattern anywhere. The seersucker suit immediately below it was stained in several places.

The pants were far too long and the waist far too wide. If he even had a mind to have them altered for wear the two back pockets would meet in the vicinity of his tailbone. Steele sat down in his chair for a moment so that he could take it all in.

He then turned to his telephone and asked his secretary for the number for Mrs. Sanders Hampton. Her housekeeper answered the phone and then transferred the call to her mistress.

"Mrs. Hampton, this is Steele Austin."

"Oh, yes, Mistuh Austin. I guess you found my little gift. There is no need to thank me. Just knowing that you will be wearing my Sanders' suits is all the thanks that I need. I just know that in the right attire you will pass for a fine southern gentleman. You are planning to wear one of them this Sunday, aren't you?"

"Mrs. Hampton, that is why I am calling, I don't want you to misunderstand. I really do appreciate the gesture. But the suits are just too large for me."

"My dear Mistuh Austin, all you have to do is take them down to the tailor shop and have them altered. After all, they are the finest suits that Henry's Menswear has to offer. My Sanders never wore anything but the finest."

"I am sure that is true, Mrs. Hampton, but I don't believe they can be altered so that they will..."

"We all so want you to be a success here at First Church. I know that you don't get paid very much as a minister, but since I have provided you with some perfectly wonderful suits you need only have them altered."

"But...."

"Good day, Mister Austin. I will see you in one of those suits this coming Sunday."

With that the telephone went dead. Steele Austin sat staring at the box. He then called his secretary and asked her to have them taken down to the incinerator.

He was just about to make another phone call when his secretary returned to his office. She whispered to him across the desk, "Father Austin, the ladies of the Altar Guild are waiting for you down in the Parlor."

"I didn't know there was an Altar Guild meeting today. I didn't see one on the calendar."

She continued to whisper, "Father Austin, I believe it was a called meeting. I think the Parlor is jammed full. Mrs. Gordon Smythe said for me to tell you to come to meet with them right now. No excuses."

Steele couldn't believe his ears. "You mean I am being summoned to meet with the Altar Guild?"

"Father Austin," she whispered, "you don't want to cross these ladies. They take their ministry very seriously. Their altar work is very important to them. They see themselves as the guardians of tradition here at First Church. Many of them are third and fourth generation members of First Church. If they like you they can open a lot of doors for you in Falls City, but if they get down on you—well, Father Austin, you just don't want that to happen."

Steele Austin walked down the hallway to the Women's Parlor. He remembered it to be a finely appointed room with oriental carpets, white silk covered furniture, and a large crystal chandelier hanging from the ceiling. He had been told that the only people who could use the room were the Altar Guild. It was not to be used for any other purpose. Not even the Vestry could meet in the Women's Parlor.

When Steele entered the Parlor he estimated that there were thirty to thirty-five women in the room. The average age had to be well beyond sixty-five. It was clear that they were not a happy group. Steele knew that membership in the Altar Guild was by invitation only. The Altar Guild Directress had final say on membership. Young women who had first completed their training at the Junior League could apply for Altar Guild membership. If accepted, they were assigned the task of polishing the brass candle followers in the chapel. If they were faithful to this duty for several years, they were then elevated to the task of polishing the entire candlestick. Their internship in the chapel would usually take a couple of decades. They would not be granted permission to start polishing brass in the big church until they were well into their fifties. Only the most experienced and elderly of the ladies could earn the distinction of being able to "set up services." This is the way their grandmothers had set up the Altar Guild and so it had been for close to a hundred years.

Mrs. Gordon Smythe greeted the Reverend Steele Austin with a forced smile. No one else in the room returned his smile. "Mistuh Austin, you can sit over here by me." Mrs. Smythe pointed to a straight back chair next to her at the far end of the room.

Steele glanced around the room trying to make brief eye contact with every lady present. "Ladies I really appreciate this opportunity to meet with you and let you know just how much I appreciate the ministry of the Altar Guild. I am a great admirer of your devotion to duty. You work behind the scenes doing an essential work that allows us to offer fitting worship to the Almighty. Without you, those of us who stand out front would not be able to do our jobs. I know that you don't always get the credit that you deserve, but I want you to know that this Rector appreciates you and your ministry. I want to do whatever I can do to help you."

"Mistuh Austin, those are very encouraging words and I am so pleased that you feel that way about the Altar Guild and our work. In fact, we have just been discussing how we can best help you acclimate to First Church. We have chosen to give you the benefit of the doubt on several matters. We believe that you have good intentions, but you just need a better understanding of the way we do things here."

"For example?" Steele asked.

"Well, Mistuh Austin, let's begin with the kneelers in the chapel. You need to understand that the ladies of the Altar Guild worked very hard on those kneelers. We paid for them with Altar Guild money and they were designed and stitched by the Altar Guild. Therefore, Mistuh Austin, those kneelers belong to the Altar Guild. We do not want them used when children are present. They must be removed for Sunday School Services, Vacation Bible School, and for the day school services."

Steele interrupted, "I have seen those kneelers and they are quite beautiful. You have every reason to be proud of them, but ladies, why would you not want the children to use them? It appears to me that anything that is given to the glory of God should be shared with all of God's people, including his children."

"MISTUH AUSTIN!" Mrs. Gordon Smythe reared up in her chair. Then she forced another smile and lowered her voice. She spoke again with obvious restraint. "We are here to share our very best counsel with you. We did not invite you in here for a discussion. We are telling you just what is what." She took a deep breath and then continued, "Further, we want you to understand that members of this congregation are not to be encouraged to use the facilities in the Altar Guild Sacristy. Those are for the Altar Guild and the clergy. Members of the congregation are to use the facilities in the basement."

With that, Steele could feel his own temperature rising. "Ladies, I really want you to re-think that one. The restroom in the Altar Guild Sacristy is the only facility on the same level as the church. Last Sunday I met an elderly gentleman struggling back up the church stairs after going down into the basement. Please, let's think about what we can do for the older people in our congregation. Ultimately, I would like to see us construct a bathroom facility on the same level as the church nave and sanctuary for our people to use."

The entire room broke out in laughter. "Surely you aren't suggesting that we deface our historic worship facility with a bathroom?" Mrs. Smythe countered. "I can guarantee you that will never happen. We are on the historic register. We'll not have our worship services interrupted by embarrassing sounds coming from the facilities. Mistuh Austin, I am sure you are well meaning, but then that's why we are here to help you."

A pudgy little woman with protruding teeth and too much makeup caught his eye. She was wearing a dress far too short for a lady her age. The expression, "Mutton all dressed up to look like lamb," flashed through his mind. "Mistuh Austin, I am Mrs. Howard Dexter."

"Oh yes, Mrs. Dexter, I have met your husband."

"Yes, he told me about your exchange. You have not disappointed me. So far you appear to be everything that my husband told me to expect and then some."

Steele felt a shudder run up his spine.

"Mistuh Austin, there is a very simple solution to the facility question."

Steele shot back, "I am pleased to hear that you agree with me."

"Oh, quite to the contrary, Mistuh Austin, I don't think we shall ever agree on much. What I would like to suggest is that you simply put a notice in the church bulletin that the bathroom in the Altar Guild Sacristy is restricted to the Altar Guild and the ordained clergy. Then, suggest that elderly people who have a difficult time with the stairs to the facilities in the basement should consider wearing diapers to church."

Steele Austin sat in stunned silence. This was one of the few times in his life when he was absolutely speechless. When he thought he had just about heard it all, other members of the Altar Guild began to chime in, "That's a marvelous idea -- yes, that is the perfect solution for all concerned..."

And then he heard one woman say, "Ladies, I am way ahead of all you. I have already told my husband that he has to wear a diaper when we come to church."

Steele thought he was in some kind of comic charade. Any minute now, someone would come out of the closet and announce, "Smile, you're on Candid Camera." Then Steele was given one last jolt.

Mrs. Gordon Smythe gave a self-pleasing smile, "Ladies, I believe we are all in agreement. That's just wonderful. Now there is only one more thing to make clear. Mistuh Austin, it has been reported that you want to bring the altar out from the wall. Suh, that is just not going to happen!"

Again, Steele tried to explain, "But ladies, every altar in most every church in the land has been pulled out from the wall. That was the original position. The clergy are supposed to stand behind the altar in order to better lead the people in worship. Perhaps if I did a series of classes...."

This time Mrs. Gordon Smythe stood up, "MISTUH AUSTIN!" She bent down to put her face directly in front of Steele's face. She then pointed her arthritic finger at him. "Mistuh Austin, the only way you will ever pull that altar out from the wall is with me sitting on top of it!"

And with that, there was a round of enthusiastic applause in the room.

When the applause died down, Mrs. Smythe announced: "This meeting is over. We will see you on Sunday, Mistuh Austin. We trust that you will be properly attired in one of those suits that Mrs. Hampton has so generously provided for you. And one final thing, Mistuh Austin, lose the boots!" That statement was met with yet another round of applause. As the ladies filed out of the room, Steele could hear them congratulating each other on such a frank and open airing of their differences with the new Rector.

Steele Austin sat glued to his chair in stunned silence. He was desperately trying to make his mind accept that which his heart could not understand. Then he chuckled as the image of Howard Dexter wearing diapers and his English driving hat came into view.

CHAPTER 7

"Chadsworth, you're not taking another trip are you?"

Almeda rounded the corner and walked into her husband's bedroom. Chadsworth was carefully packing his suitcase. Throughout their marriage, Chadsworth had made frequent trips to Atlanta. Some of his trips lasted a week or two, but since he was a good provider she hated to complain.

"Oh Chadsworth, I just don't understand why you have to do all your business in Atlanta. Why can't your clients come see you here in Falls City?"

Almeda puckered her lips in a little pout, but she knew that it wouldn't do any good. She knew that her husband had to keep his business going.

"Chadsworth, I just came from the most deplorable meeting of the Altar Guild. We did our best to help that young Mistuh Austin understand how things are done here at First Church, but I just don't think he will ever understand. I tell you Chadsworth; you men on the Vestry made a terrible mistake in calling him here. He just won't do. Chadsworth, you have to help us get rid of him. We need to have him back in Oklahoma by Christmas!"

Chadsworth stopped his packing and drew in a deep breath. Looking sternly at his wife, "Almeda, is your memory really that short? It has taken us almost two years to find anyone who would take this job. Thanks to you fine ladies on the Altar Guild practically every priest in the Fourth Province knows firsthand the hell you put poor old Doctor Stuart and his wife through. You each are getting credit for putting the poor man in his grave and his wife in a bottomless bottle of gin."

"Now Chadsworth, that's simply not fair," she protested.

"Almeda, we had a difficult time getting any priest in a single one of the original Confederate States to even return our phone calls. We had to cross six state lines and go to a part of the country that had never heard of Falls City to find a Rector. Even then any priest with an ounce of sense hung the phone up on us. The only reason we were able to get Steele Austin is because he is young, naïve, and idealistic. But I'm sure that you and the rest of the ladies in this joke of a church will squeeze every bit of idealism out of the boy in short order."

"Now Chadsworth," she whined, "we're just trying to help the boy. We do know what is best for him. But Chadsworth, the church just can't put up with him. If he stays here very long he'll completely destroy our beloved church. You and the Vestry have simply got to get rid of him."

"Almeda, at our age we can't get exercised about a month from now, let alone a year from now. Woman, we are at the age that we shouldn't even buy green bananas. Why don't you ladies just give the boy a chance?"

"No, we won't, Chadsworth. If you and the others on the Vestry aren't men enough to get rid of this upstart then we women will do it ourselves. It won't be the first time that we women have had to clean up a mess you men have made."

Chadsworth slammed down the lid on his luggage and then, red-faced, shouted back at her, "Almeda, you and that whole group you call an Altar Guild are better men than any man I have ever met in my life—so—go to it. Just leave me out of it."

With that he walked out of the house and began his trip to Atlanta.

+

Just off Peachtree Street near downtown Atlanta, Chadsworth walked into his favorite club. He gave a familiar nod and wave to the uniformed officer at the door of Hernando's Hideaway. Once inside, he stopped to take in the room.

Even though the club was pretty dark and lit primarily by strobe lights, Chadsworth could feel the eyes of many of those standing around the bar, and at the tiny tables, on him. Chadsworth knew that he looked good. At his age he was particularly flattered by the attention that the younger patrons of the bar paid him. He figured they looked to an older man for the maturity and security that younger men just do not possess.

Chadsworth ordered a Corona with a twist of lime. He pushed the lime down into the bottle and started walking through the club. While there were several of the patrons who tried to make eye contact with him, he avoided their stares. Chadsworth was taken. He had already made arrangements to meet his long- time lover. He knew that he had gotten the time right, but just where...? And then, off in a distance, he spotted the object of his affection. Their eyes met and a big smile spread across both of their faces.

"Chadsworth, Chadsworth, God I've missed you. You look absolutely fantastic. Just look at your tan. You have been in the tanning booth again. How many times do I have to tell you those things are dangerous? Now promise me you will stay out of those things. I will love you just as much without an all over tan. Now let me feel those arms and that flat stomach of yours. My God Chadsworth, for a man of sixty you have the body of an Adonis. Umm, you do feel good!"

"And you've lost even more weight. Just what is going on with you? Are you bulimic?"

Chadsworth studied the object of his affection. "Have you been sick again? I'm worried about you. You've got to eat. You have to take care of yourself."

"Yes, Daddy, I promise."

They spent the rest of the evening in the club. Earl was a great dancer and Chadsworth loved holding him in his arms. They moved gracefully together. They both knew that there would be plenty of time later in the evening to be alone. For now they were content to hold each other, laugh, and talk with their friends in Hernado's Hideaway.

Later that night at Earl's apartment they let their passion go. Earl was an incredible lover and he brought desire out in Chadsworth comparable to his youth.

Earl had always been beautifully built. The fact that he had lost even more weight only brought out the definition in his muscles. Now, he did not have an ounce of fat on his body. Earl was a consummate swimmer, gymnast, and weight lifter. He earned his living as a personal trainer. He had no hair on his perfectly chiseled chest and stomach, which was just the way Chadsworth liked it. He did have a shocking head full of black curly hair. Chadsworth took delight to run his fingers through those curls. Still, Chadsworth studied Earl's body that night. His arms and legs seemed thinner. His face appeared gaunt. Yet, he was still beautiful. Chadsworth was in love.

They went to sleep in each other's arms. Chadsworth awoke in the middle of the night; Earl was cuddled up next to him with his head on his chest. Chadsworth began stroking Earl's hair. He thought back over his life.

He had known all his life that he was different. Even as a small boy he was attracted to other boys. He remembered that when he went to the country club swimming pool he was more interested in staring at the lifeguards than the girls. He recalled that while his friends liked looking at the nudes in the girlie magazines, he preferred looking at the male models in the ads.

Perhaps it was because of shame or the fear of being discovered, but he refrained from acting on his desires well into his first year of college. His looks afforded him the opportunity to bed more than one co-ed, but he found each of the experiences less than satisfying.

Chadsworth knew that he was gay. He had known that he was gay since he was a very small boy. He didn't know to call himself gay. He had heard people make jokes about queers. In his teens any boy at school that appeared to be a "sissy" was given no mercy. He learned early on to pretend to be something that he was not. He learned to do all the guy stuff. He learned how to hunt, fish, and flirt with women. He knew he had to do it for his own survival.

For the past forty years, Chadsworth had lived a double life. He was the respected, married, heterosexual husband, father, and businessman in Falls City. Here in Atlanta, he was able to be himself. Here he could be Chadsworth—the queer.

He never tried to count the number of men he had known through the years. He had done it all. He had haunted the parks, the department store bathrooms, the bars, and the bathhouses. Earl was his first and only black man. They met at Hernando's Hideaway over ten years ago. In just a few weeks he knew that he was in love and the love was returned a hundred fold. On more than one occasion, he had tried to get Earl to move to Falls City. He would set him up in his own apartment. They could see each other every day instead of every other week, but Earl would have nothing to do with it.

"I'll not be the other woman for a married white man. You dump your wife and we'll make a commitment. Until you do, I'll give you my love when you can get to Atlanta, but the rest of the time, Chadsworth, this boy is going to do whoever this boy wants to do."

The thought of Earl being with another man made Chadsworth want to throw up, but he also knew that for now it was in his best interest to continue the charade.

As they lay there naked together, Chadsworth brought Earl closer to him. Earl looked up at him, "What's the matter white boy? Can't you sleep?"

"No, I don't want to waste my time with you sleeping. I was just lying here thinking about how genuinely happy I am when I'm with you."

Earl began coughing. His coughing caused him to sit upright in the bed. Chadsworth went to the kitchen and brought him back a glass of water. "Are you all right? Listen Earl, have you seen a doctor?"

Earl nodded, "Yes, I've seen a doctor. Yes, I'm fine. I've just had a bad case of bronchitis that won't go away. I'm going to be fine. Now lie back down. Let's get some sleep." With that, Earl rolled over. His breathing was raspy. Chadsworth rolled onto his side as well and put his arm around Earl's waist. He pulled him close. He cuddled up close to him, shut his eyes and prayed, "Oh God, I am so happy with Earl. I don't want this to ever end."

CHAPTER 8

The Reverend Steele Austin was making his morning rounds at Falls City Methodist Hospital. For the most part, it could have been any hospital in any city. Some of the finer citizens of Falls City, however, were not content with a simple hospital room. A couple of his visits took him into what could have passed for luxury suites in a resort hotel. In each of the two suites he visited with some of the Falls City aristocracy, there was either a uniformed black male or female attendant. They were not a part of the hospital staff. No, they were in the employ of the family. Their task was to stay with the patients and take care of their every need.

Steele noticed that the nursing staff came into the rooms of the two aristocratic members in pairs like sojourners on a dangerous voyage in need of mutual support. They cast knowing looks at each other and escaped the rooms as quickly as possible. It was not until he passed the nurse's station and overheard them talking about one of the aristocrats that he understood.

"I tell you if she rings that bell one more time I am going to go down there and tell her that her doctor has ordered an enema. Can you imagine her constant complaints: 'My room is too hot, too cold; my soup is too salty, my pillows need fluffing, and the halls are too noisy?' There is no end to it. If she were in here for an illness, that would be one thing, but she is here for her fifth, or is it her sixth face-lift. I do feel sorry for her that the complications with this one landed her in the hospital. But I swear if they tighten her face any more, her boobs are going to be sitting on top of her shoulders." And with that the entire station found some relief in laughter.

As Steele exited the elevator on the Pediatric Floor he noticed a young couple standing in the hallway holding each other. They were crying. The husband met Steele's eyes and a look of recognition came over him.

"Reverend Austin—is that you? You are Reverend Austin?"

"Yes, I'm Steele Austin. Are you members of First Church?"

"No, we're not members, but we've been attending the past few weeks. We really enjoy your sermons."

"Thanks for telling me. And you are?"

"Oh, I am Bob Larson and this is my wife Leslie."

"You look upset. Can I help?"

"It's our daughter Molly. She's in here. She has leukemia. She's only four years old and had been taking some treatments that appeared to be working. Now she's developed toxicity to the medication and has an infection in her esophagus. She's having a difficult time breathing. They're going to take her to surgery at noon to do a tracheotomy."

"That's a relatively simple procedure, isn't it?"

"Ordinarily, but her body's been through so much. She's fought so hard. Now she's very, very weak. The doctors are telling us not to get our hopes up." With that the two of them broke down again. Steele put his arms around them.

"Can I see her?"

"Sure," the man looked at his wife. "Do you want to wait here?" She wiped her eyes with a well-used tissue and shook her head. "No, Reverend Austin, will you pray for her?"

Steele was not prepared for just how tiny and frail the little girl would look in the crib. She looked like the pictures he had seen of starving children in refugee camps. Even though she was receiving oxygen she was struggling for breath. There would be long deep gasps followed by silence as they stood there listening for her to struggle for the next.

Steele felt the tears in his own eyes. He tried to speak to her but his own voice quivered. He could not get the words to come out. He took a deep breath and tried to compose himself. He watched the parents dissolve into each other's arms. Steele's entire body hurt. He knew he was absorbing their pain. A lump filled his throat. He reached up and wiped the moisture from his own face.

He just stood there for the longest time. He managed an encouraging smile and held the little girl's hand. He wiped her forehead with a damp cloth. Then, when he felt his voice would not forsake him, he spoke to the parents.

"I have a wedding at twelve noon back at the church. I have to go do the wedding, but just as soon as it is over, I'll be back." He then took the little girl's hand in both of his and he began to pray. As he did, the quiver in his voice returned.

"Lord Jesus Christ, You called the little children to Yourself so that You could bless them. Take Molly in Your arms at this time and bless her. She is so tired and so weak, and she has fought so valiantly. Give new strength to her little body. Give her the power she needs to fight off this disease for the final time. Send Your holy angels to this place. Comfort her parents. Guide the hands of the surgeons and the nurses. Restore her to health and wellness."

Then Steele took the oil stock from his pocket. He made the sign of the cross on her forehead and anointed her in the name of the Lord Jesus Christ who is the giver of all life and all health. Steele bent over and kissed Molly on the cheek. In her ear he whispered, "Molly, you are not alone. Jesus loves you and He is going to help you get well."

Steele hated to leave the hospital, but he knew he had a bride and groom waiting on him at the church. On the drive to the church downtown he could not get Molly out of his mind. "Dear God," he prayed, "if I am to be granted but one miracle in this life, give it to that little girl."

When Steele arrived at the church he had a sudden impulse that he knew he would have to act upon. Almeda Alexander was the Altar Guild person on duty.

"Miss Almeda, I want you to gather all the bridal party in the undercroft. I want all the Altar Guild people present; I want the organist, the ushers, and the sextons. I want everyone having anything to do with this wedding to meet me in the undercroft in five minutes."

"What on earth for? We have a wedding to put on. This is highly irregular. Besides, the groom can't see the bride before the wedding."

"Almeda, leave the groom and the best man in the Sacristy, but you get every living person in this building into that undercroft in five minutes. Do you hear me?"

"I'll do it, but you're just bringing more trouble on yourself. Just wait until the rest of the Altar Guild hears about this."

Steele went down to the undercroft to discover that it was full of people nervously moving about.

"Ladies and gentlemen, can I have your attention? Just a few minutes ago I left the hospital where there is a little four year old girl fighting for her life. She is scheduled to have a tracheotomy at exactly the same time this wedding is to begin. I have to tell you that only a miracle can save her. I have called you here because I believe in miracles...."

Almeda interrupted again, "Mistuh Austin, how are we going to pray for a miracle? We can't go up to the church because the wedding guests are arriving. We don't have any Prayer Books down here..."

The mother of the bride chuckled. "You're going to have to excuse her, Reverend Austin. I've known Almeda for years. She thinks that you can't pray without a Book of Common Prayer in your hands. Take her Prayer Book away from her and the only prayer she knows by heart is *"Now I Lay Me Down to Sleep."*

With that Almeda relaxed and joined the nervous laughter that filled the room. Steele continued, "Can we all just stand in a big circle? Let's hold hands while I offer a prayer for this little girl. Her name is Molly."

They began to form a big circle and take hold of each other's hands. Miss Almeda Alexander folded both of her arms across her chest. Steele then prayed again for Molly, for her doctors and nurses, for her parents. He concluded by praying for the bride and groom, for a beautiful wedding, and a wonderful life for the happy couple. When he concluded, he looked up and saw that there were tears in the eyes of several of the bridesmaids. The mother of the bride looked at Steele Austin, "That was beautiful. Thank you for including us."

After the wedding, Steele rushed back down to the hospital. When he got off the elevator on the Pediatric Floor he prepared himself for the worst. As he started down the hall, he noticed that the area outside of Molly's room was packed with people. He edged himself through the crowd in the hallway only to be met by an even larger crowd of hospital personnel in her room. He maneuvered himself up to her bed. There he saw Molly sitting up in the hospital bed breathing completely on her own. Someone had blown up a surgical glove and tied a knot in the end of it. Molly was hitting it to the various people in the room who joyfully slapped it back to her.

Steele looked over at her surgeon who was still in his scrubs standing next to her beaming parents. "What happened?"

The surgeon smiled, "We took her down to do the tracheotomy. We were scheduled to begin at noon. At about fifteen minutes before noon we started getting her ready. Her throat relaxed and she began breathing on her own. We kept her there for an hour or so and she just kept getting better. So we brought her back to her room. Now you know as much as we do."

Molly's mother smiled. "No, Doctor, I think Reverend Austin knows something that we are just learning. Steele, we asked God to save our Molly. He did. Will you now help us thank Him?"

Her comment brought total silence to the room and to those in the hallway. Even Molly quit playing with her hand balloon and stared up at Steele like she understood. Tears flooded Steele Austin's eyes. With a quivering voice he asked everyone present to join hands. He took Molly's hand in his and he thanked God for His goodness and His love and for the miracle He had granted Molly. When he finished the loudest "Amen" in the room came from her surgeon. There was applause. The hospital staff began to disperse. Steele stayed with them for the rest of the afternoon. That night, he gathered his own child in his arms and cuddled with him long after he had fallen asleep.

CHAPTER 9

Steele Austin climbed the eight steps into the old First Church pulpit. He had never preached from a pulpit so highly elevated above the congregation. When he first arrived at First Church he had wanted to preach from the choir steps using his lapel microphone. This caused a tremendous uproar. The overwhelming complaint was that he looked too much like a television preacher. "It just isn't Episcopalian. Sermons in the Episcopal Church are supposed to be preached from the 'pull-pit'!"

It was hard not to take notice of the increase in attendance at Sunday worship. On his first few Sundays at First Church the nave had only been about half full. Now it was packed. There were people standing in the rear of the church. Steele was uncertain as to whether the increased attendance was the result of a genuine spiritual renewal in the congregation or was it simply the curiosity seekers coming out to see the new monkey perform.

He had been successful in his efforts to improve the music program. The warbling soprano was gone. He had attempted to explain to her the need to blend her voice to those of the rest of the choir. Her response was one of righteous indignation and she announced to him and all that she could find that she was canceling her pledge and leaving First Church until such time as there was a change in Rectors. She asked that her membership letter be transferred to a neighboring parish, but a search of the records showed that she had never joined First Church. In fact, she was not even a confirmed Episcopalian. Further, she had never made a pledge for the business manager to cancel and had no record of ever giving anything to the financial support of First Church. The organist was now Steele's new very best friend and strongest supporter for resolving the "soprano problem" for him. Since her leaving, the choir had doubled in size as people came forward to volunteer to be a part of a much better sound. Steele had reassured the organist before meeting with the woman that sometimes you have to lose a few to gain the many.

Steele began his sermon by talking about miracles. He stated clearly that he believed in a God of mystery. He related some of the times in his life that he had prayed for a person to be healed and they died. He also related those times when he had prayed for a healing and the miracle was granted. He admitted that he did not always understand how the Almighty chose to dispense miracles. He noted that he did not believe that it was our task to strive to be successful or attempt to manipulate God. He asserted that it was our task to simply be faithful.

Having laid that groundwork, Steele then told of the miracle that had been granted to Molly. He told how he had gathered the bridal party, the Altar Guild present, and the other wedding volunteers in the undercroft yesterday to pray for Molly. He shared the drama of walking back into her hospital room and discovering that she began breathing freely at exactly the same time that they were praying for her in the undercroft.

Steele could sense that the vast majority of the congregation was listening with great interest. He also noted that some had doubtful, or even questioning looks on their faces. He caught one couple rolling their eyes at each other. And he could not help but notice that a few had folded their arms across their chests as though they really did not want to hear this story.

Steele Austin was not to be discouraged. He brought his part of the story to a conclusion and then walked out of the pulpit to the steps of the choir. He looked out over the congregation and then announced, "Molly is still in the hospital, but she will be going home this afternoon. She will be able to continue her treatments and we will continue to pray that her leukemia will go into complete remission."

He continued, "While Molly cannot be at our church service this morning, her parents are here and they want to talk with you."

With those words there was a hush of anxiety that swept over the congregation. Several of the more disapproving visibly punched one another. Those that had been reading their bulletins or otherwise disengaged from Steele's remarks all looked up. He heard someone say, "Oh no, what is he going to do now?"

Molly's parents came to the choir steps. Steele handed them a portable microphone. Bob Larson began speaking first, "Yesterday, we thought our little Molly was going to die." Great tears came to his eyes and he had to stop to compose himself. "As a father I felt absolutely helpless standing there watching my little girl struggle for breath. We men are supposed to be able to protect our children. I guess I am just macho enough to think that there isn't anything I wouldn't do to keep my children healthy and safe. There is no enemy I would not fight. I would literally fight to the death to make sure that nothing would happen to my little Molly."

Again, he had to stop talking. His voice was shaking and he had to wipe the tears out of his eyes and off his face. He stood quiet for a few minutes and then reached out and put his arm around his weeping wife. "Can you imagine how painful it is for two parents to make funeral plans for one of their children? Our Molly has known nothing but needles and tubes and pills and pain for the past two years. She has been too weak to play like other children. We have known her pain. Her hurt has been our hurt. We really believed that this morning instead of being in this church we would be at the mortuary picking out a casket..." With that he broke down completely.

His wife Leslie took the microphone from him as he stood there continuing to sob. Steele felt the tears running down his own cheeks. He looked out at the congregation and saw a sea of white handkerchiefs.

Leslie spoke, "But we are not at the mortuary today. We are in the House of God among God's People. We are here to give thanks to the Lord for granting our Molly a miracle. Yesterday, God sent us an angel. Oh, he doesn't think of himself as an angel. He may not even know he is an angel. If the gossip I hear around Falls City is true, I know that some of you don't think he is much of an angel either." With that there was an uncomfortable chuckle through the congregation.

Molly continued, "Just when all our hope was gone, God sent us Steele Austin. He stood with us at Molly's bed. He held her hand. He anointed her with oil. He prayed for her healing. He kissed her on the cheek and he whispered the love of Jesus into her ear. And then he came back over here to this church and asked a bridal party to become prayer warriors on Molly's behalf."

She managed a big smile. Bob and Leslie walked over to where Steele was standing. They stood on either side of him and put their arms around him. "Father Austin," she said, "God is at work in you. Because you and the people in this church cared enough to pray for our Molly, we get to take her home today. Father Austin, today is the first day of Molly's healing." With that, she stretched up on her toes and kissed Steele on the cheek.

It began in the back of the church and then like a great wave crashing on the beach, a thunderous roar of applause washed over the congregation. It was deafening. The congregation rose to their feet. Steele looked out on the impromptu sight with disbelief. The tears of joy could be seen on most every face. He thought the congregation would not stop applauding. When the applause did begin to settle he heard the great organ begin the familiar doxology and the congregation sang like he had never heard them sing, *"Praise God from whom all blessings flow, Praise him all creatures here below, Praise him above ye heavenly host, Praise Father, Son, and Holy Ghost."* When the hymn ended there was yet more applause.

Steele stood looking out at the sea of faces. For the first time since he had come to this place he felt hopeful. He was beginning to think that maybe he had done the right thing in coming to First Church. He believed that just maybe -- just maybe, God would bring life to the dry bones he had encountered in Falls City.

CHAPTER 10
THE SAVANNAH NEWS
FOUNDATION OF OLD CHURCH SHAKING

The tremors coming out of Falls City have been felt all the way to this reporter's office here in Savannah. Ordinarily, even the calling of a new Rector to a prestigious Episcopal pulpit in one of our Southern cities would be relegated to a note on the religion page. It appears that the response to the calling of The Reverend Steele Austin to historic old First Church in Falls City warrants more than a passing note of interest.

After being without a Rector for nearly two years, the First Church Search Committee traveled to a small town in Northeastern Oklahoma. There they found a thirty-five year old priest who has distinguished himself on the streets of Falls City by wearing his black clerical shirt with blue jeans and western boots. He notes, "With the proper jacket this attire would be described as a Texas Tuxedo."

Old First Church is known as the Church of the elite in Falls City. It is the hallmark of conservatism, status quo, wealth, tradition, and prestige. The movers and shakers in Falls City see First Church as a sleeping giant that should not be awakened. The giant has been deep in slumber for several years with no overt attempt to wake up. The address of the church is not even included in the advertisements in the local paper or the telephone directory.

The Reverend Austin is a man deeply devoted to teaching the Scriptures and an evangelical approach to ministry. He asserts, "The Episcopal Church can no longer be 'the frozen chosen'. It's time for a change and a reordering of priorities."

Steele Austin hopes that First Church will become more than just the church to belong to when you have arrived professionally in Falls City. He hopes that the Vestry (the governing board) of the church will be more than just community service time for young attorneys wanting to make partner in their law firms.

Mister Austin has a different vision for community service ministries. At the top of his list is starting a soup kitchen for the poor and transient. He also hopes to form a closer partnership with the other congregations in the city, especially the black congregations. "One of the ways for people of different races to begin to celebrate their similarities is to worship and work together in the same church."

This reporter decided to make the journey to Falls City this past Sunday just to see for himself the man who is said to be literally shaking the very foundation stones of old First Church. Even though I arrived a full twenty minutes before the service was to begin, I discovered a full church with not an empty pew in sight. I ended up standing with several others in the rear of the church.

When young Reverend Austin climbed into the First Church pulpit his boyish looks gave him the appearance of a teenager who had just climbed an apple tree. However, when he opens his mouth to speak there is a wisdom that comes forth that is far beyond his years. Whether by accident or on purpose, the people of First Church may have just called the best preacher in Georgia. His reputation is turning some of the pulpit committees up in Atlanta green with envy.

Last Sunday Steele Austin spoke of his belief in miracles. He did not stop there. He then reported on a miracle that he had witnessed the previous day in the Falls City Hospital. He reported that a little girl dying of complications associated with leukemia experienced a miraculous reversal. He credited the reversal to a prayer session that he had organized with a bridal party Saturday right before he conducted their wedding ceremony at First Church.

The Reverend Mister Austin was not content to leave the account of the miracle to his own reporting. The parents of the little girl were present. He introduced them to the congregation. They told the story again in their own words. While I did not expect to hear such revelations in an Episcopal Church I would be less than honest if I did not tell you that this reporter was deeply moved. I, too, joined in the thunderous applause that swept over the congregation, who then concluded the service by singing a traditional hymn of praise to God with great gusto.

In spite of the emotion and the tears experienced by many that morning, I discovered through some selective interviews at the parish coffee hour that not everyone was excited about what they heard and saw.

One lady in a very proper hat and gloves stated, "I'm very disappointed in what that young man is doing to our church. Why, I felt like I was in the Oral Roberts television studio. But then, he did come from Oklahoma."

A man in an Augusta Green golfing jacket proclaimed, "That is the first time in our one hundred and ninety year history that we have had clapping in the church. It was absolutely disgraceful! I'm just glad my dear old mother is dead so that she didn't have to hear such goings on in our beloved church. To hear people clapping in church like they were at a football rally—well—it would have killed her! I tell you she would have died on the spot."

Another woman literally bent over with arthritis pointed her finger at me and stated, "You can put this in every newspaper in the land if you're so inclined, but that Okie is not moving my altar away from that wall. If I have to sit on it all day and sleep on top of it every night the rest of my life, that altar's staying put!"

A woman who was clearly agitated volunteered, "This talk of a soup kitchen is ridiculous! I never --- can you imagine what would happen if we started a soup kitchen in First Church? Why, all sorts and conditions of humanity will begin thinking that they can come here. If we start handing out free food we'll only attract the undesirables from other places to move to Falls City. I wouldn't be surprised if the criminal element in Florida moved their operations here."

When I asked Mr. Austin if he realized that not all of his congregation were happy about his vision for their future he replied quietly, "I think about sixty percent of the folks are with me. Of course, that means that forty percent are not. But then God did not bring me here to be successful. My job is to be faithful."

In this reporter's view, the eyes of all Georgia will be watching as old First Church faces this new challenge.

CHAPTER 11

The governing board of First Church, known as the Vestry, was all male. By Steele's count there were eight attorneys, two owners of construction companies, two physicians, two bankers, and a law enforcement chief. The President of the Women of the Church was an ex-officio member of the Vestry. Most of the members were twice Steele's age. Four of the attorneys were junior members of prominent law firms and the sons or grandsons of long term members of First Church.

After only a few meetings, Steele Austin had learned that a few prayers and a couple of stiff drinks was the best way for him to prepare for a Vestry meeting. It took his every effort to be upbeat and stay above the small-mindedness that characterized every Vestry meeting since his arrival.

Steele knew that the agenda was never the agenda. Usually, sooner rather than later in the meeting someone would say, "I don't know about the rest of you guys, but I've been getting a lot of phone calls...." One of the favorite leads was, "I've been talking with quite a number in the congregation and they are quite concerned..." Steele Austin hated the First Church Vestry meetings. He dreaded hearing about more anonymous "concerns." Tonight was no exception.

One of the junior attorneys began, "Mistuh Austin, there are quite a number of people who are concerned about this talk of a soup kitchen. I don't mind telling you that I'm not happy about it either. I just find it hard to believe that Falls City has the need of a soup kitchen. Everyone I know has more than enough to eat. Isn't the Light House Mission still in operation? I know the Salvation Army takes good care of the poor people. It seems to me we don't need to duplicate what is already being done. Besides, I think that we might just be sending an engraved invitation to the street people in Atlanta and Savannah to come on over to Falls City for a free meal."

Steele listened patiently, "Did everyone read the statistical studies that were done by the Black Minister's Fellowship and the Health and

Human Services Commission for the state of Georgia? I put them in your Vestry packet."

There were a few shrugs of the shoulders and then the lawyer replied, "Now Mistuh Austin, you can't expect us to take the numbers done by a bunch of bleeding heart liberals seriously."

Steele took a deep breath, "Gentlemen, out of my Discretionary Fund I have personally bought meals for men, women, teenagers, and families with small children who came to my office looking for help. Just the other day one of our staff members saw a man going through the church dumpster looking for something to eat. All of the studies show that Falls City does have a need for a soup kitchen. In fact, it is long overdue."

Chief Joe Sparks leaned across the table toward Steele. Chief Sparks had been Chief of Police in Falls City for close to three decades. He was highly respected for running a clean department. He was one of the first chiefs in the south to integrate his force and to bring on women officers. Steele had gotten to know him over the past few months and really liked him. Steele respected him as a man of faith, vision, and common sense. "Gentlemen, we in law enforcement are very aware of the homeless problem we have here in Falls City. It just could be that if we could give them one square meal a day, it might cut back on some of the crimes we catch them committing."

Several at the table shot Chief Sparks a cold look. Then Stone Clemons leaned forward across the table imitating the posture that Chief Sparks had taken. Stone Clemons was a third generation member of First Church. He was well into his seventies and was considered a wise patriarch in the community. His grandfather was a founding partner in one of the most prestigious law firms in the state. Steele had learned that he was a silent partner in several business ventures throughout the South. He was well read and kept himself fit and trim by making sure that his work was liberally interrupted with fishing and hunting expeditions. The congregation had elected him Senior Warden, or President of the Vestry. "I think the Chief makes an excellent point. The Rector may have just come up with a plan that will not only allow us to do some good for some folks down on their luck, but we'll be able to fight crime in the process."

In spite of the nervous laughter that followed his remarks, most everyone kept their eyes glued to the table. There was more silence. Steele felt like they had been talking to a wall. In exasperation he asked, "Do you mean to tell me by your silence that most everyone at this table is opposed to starting this soup kitchen?"

There was more silence. A few of them shot knowing looks at each other. Both Chief Sparks and Stone Clemons leaned back in their chairs and shrugged their shoulders.

Another one of the young lawyers spoke, "Father Austin, how would you propose to control who eats in the kitchen? What is to keep me and my friends at the law firm from coming to the soup kitchen for a free meal?"

With that the room resounded with laughter. Steele felt his face growing red.

"It's my hope that you will come to the soup kitchen to eat. Only I hope that before you eat you will help us make the soup and sandwiches. I hope you will serve them and walk around the tables to make sure that our guests have plenty of coffee or water. I would like you to sit down at the table and talk with the people. Share your faith with them and see what you can do to help them."

The lawyer looked at Steele with disbelief, "You really expect us to wait on those people? You expect us to talk with them?"

Steele nodded his head.

The young lawyer lifted his hands in the air and then sat back in his seat with a total look of amazement on his face. Others at the table simply dropped their heads and began to shake them.

The disappointment swept over Steele Austin. He sat looking at them in silence. No one said a word.

After a while he broke the silence. He asked very quietly, "Is there no one here who will make the motion to fund the soup kitchen?"

Chief Sparks spoke, "Mistuh Austin, I would be happy to make the motion and I believe my good friend Stone here would second it, but I just don't think there are enough votes at the table to pass it."

There was more silence.

Howard Dexter finally broke the silence, "Mistuh Austin, it's not that we are against helping poor people. It's just that we believe there are other organizations that are already doing a good job and they don't need our help. Beyond that, Mistuh Austin, we aren't a wealthy parish. We simply do not have the money to do everything. We have to take care of business here at home first."

If he had been standing, Steele really believed that his legs would have gone out from under him. He composed himself and then asked, "Would anyone object if I tried to raise the money in the community and from some of our other members sympathetic to this project? We could set up a separate 501C3 with its own board of directors."

Again, Howard Dexter spoke, "Mistuh Austin, you can do whatever you want to do on your own time as long as it isn't immoral or illegal, but you need to understand that this Vestry does not see this as a part of your job description."

Steele again sat in stunned silence.

Chief Joe Sparks broke the silence. "Are we ready to move on to another matter?" There was a general nod of agreement.

"My wife was talking with some of the other women at a luncheon the other day," he began. "It seems that Mr. Austin and his family were under the impression that we were going to do certain things to the Rectory before they moved in. It is my understanding that some of those things still have not been done." The Chief glanced over at Howard Dexter. He was shaking his head. He then met Steele's eyes, "Is it true that a rat actually ran across your baby's face while he was lying on the floor of the Rectory?" Steele nodded. There was an audible gasp in the room. The Chief then looked back at Howard. "I believe you were in charge of that project, weren't you Howard?"

Howard Dexter nodded, "Yes, Chief, I was in charge of the Rectory remodeling and what you say is true. But gentlemen, as we explained to Mistuh Austin, we ran out of the allotted funds for this particular project before we could get everything done. The work was simply more expensive than we originally projected. Perhaps as money becomes available over the next few years we can revisit the punch list and do some of that which the Rector and his wife had hoped we would do."

The Chief looked over at the Rector, "Are you in agreement with that, Steele?"

"No, Chief," he asserted. "We really aren't. We owned our own home in Oklahoma. We sold that house and moved a thousand miles into the Rectory and to this parish because we thought we had an agreement. I kept my part of the deal by relocating my family."

"Mistuh Austin!" Howard Dexter was clearly agitated. "I told you that this is not a matter of honor, so don't raise that question. I have told you before and I will tell you again, it is not that the church did not want to do the work. Sir, we simply do not have the money. Now surely you can understand that?"

Before Steele could reply, Stone Clemons interrupted, "Howard, what about the property fund?" Howard Dexter looked at Stone and shook his head. Stone continued, "The last time I saw that statement it had well over a million dollars in it. If I recall correctly, Howard, we keep all the church funds in your bank. Now the work on the Rectory couldn't cost more than five or six thousand dollars. Surely, your bank could afford to let the church have a little bit of the money that we allow you to keep for us?"

Again, Howard Dexter appeared agitated; "Now Stone, your family and my family have been friends for three generations. It was your granddaddy and my granddaddy who served on the Vestry that set up the property fund. Gosh, they were hunting buddies. One of your nephews married my daughter. That almost makes us relation. Our wives like to go on the theatre trips together and you and I have played more than just a few rounds of golf. But Stone, we're just not going to agree on this one. The money in the property fund was set up to maintain and repair the church, not the Rectory. You are just going to have to allow me to keep my own counsel on this one."

It was obvious that Stone Clemons was not going to be deterred. "Howard, now I believe that you and the rest of the Vestry will agree with me that we wanted a committee to welcome the new Rector and his family to the Rectory, but we didn't intend it to be led by rats." His comment was met with some uncomfortable laughter around the table. "Howard, if memory serves me correctly the property fund was set up to maintain all the church property, not just the church itself. We have a million dollars in that fund and we have it in your bank. I think it would be prudent to do the work on the Rectory that we promised this young man we would do. Now it is in that spirit that I make the motion that we complete the work on the Rectory as per the Rector's Letter of Agreement."

Chief Sparks spoke very quickly, "And I second the motion."

There was no further discussion and the motion just barely passed.

After the meeting Stone Clemons and Chief Sparks came up to Steele. Stone spoke, "Father, let's just stand here until the rest of these guys leave. The Chief and I have a little ritual we want to share with you."

The young attorney who had objected to the soup kitchen came up to where the three of them were standing; he extended his hand to Steele, "Mr. Austin if you are going to try to save these two old reprobate's souls, you are struggling with a lost cause."

They all chuckled just a bit and then the Chief responded, "You got one thing right. He may be trying to save our souls, but we're trying to save his ass!" Again, they all laughed.

When the room had cleared and it was just the three of them left, Stone spoke, "Father, you just can't let these boys get you down. Hell, Howard Dexter is the biggest tightwad in the Confederacy. If you put any money in his bank and then try to draw it out, he'll come out to the lobby and try to talk you out of doing so. I have known the man my entire life and he is constantly finding new ways to tick me off."

The Chief joined in, "I couldn't agree more. That's why Stone and I came up with this little ritual we are about to share with you. Come on Father, follow us."

"Where are we going?" Steele asked.

Stone Clemons motioned for Steele to follow, "We're going out to have a drink of whiskey on Howard Dexter's grave! The Chief and I came up with this little ritual a couple of years ago. Most Vestry meetings can drive a man to drink. A Vestry meeting with Howard Dexter requires a drink."

In just a few minutes they were standing in the churchyard in the middle of the Dexter family plot. Stone Clemons reached inside his coat pocket and brought out a flask of brandy. "Here, boys, this will take the chill off!"

After Stone Clemons took a big slug from the flask he passed it around. They stood there drinking out of the flask, sharing their frustrations from the Vestry meeting, telling jokes, and laughing for well over an hour.

"Father, you're from Oklahoma aren't you?" Stone Clemons asked.

"Yes, I am," Steele Austin shuddered in the cold night air.

Stone Clemons continued, "Two Okies were having lunch at their favorite restaurant when they noticed a young woman at the next table having trouble breathing. One of the Okies got up, walked to her table, took her face in his big rough hands and asked, 'Kin you swaller?'

She shook her head, 'No.'

'Kin ya breathe?'

Again, she shakes her head 'No'.

The Okie grabs her around the waist and with one of his hands turns her over, pulls up her shirt, pulls down her panties and licks her right on the bottom. Of course, the young woman was so shocked that she coughed, causing the food to dislodge. The big Okie then pulls up her panties, pulls down her shirt, turns her right side up, tips his hat and returns to his seat. His companion is sitting there stunned. 'I have never seen anything like that in my whole life!'

"Yeah, I tell 'ya, that hind lick maneuver works every time!!!"

After another good laugh the Chief spoke, "Boys, we're going to have to make that the last word. I've got to be getting on home."

As they walked out of the churchyard to the parking lot, Steele was reassured by the strength and wisdom of these two men. He was grateful that they had shared their ritual with him. He believed that they were two people he could depend on. After tonight's Vestry meeting and his very first meeting with the Altar Guild, Steele realized he was going to need some friends in this place.

CHAPTER 12

Chadsworth tried to make it to the gym at least three times a week. He preferred going early in the morning or in the early evening. Those seemed to be the favorite times for the serious body builders. Chadsworth found that his own workout would go faster if he could spot a young hunk to focus on during his own exercises.

He had used a personal trainer in the past at this particular gym. Of course, when he went to Atlanta, Earl always put him through a good routine. Earl also had given him some good pointers, especially when it came to using the free weights.

Eventually, Chadsworth had settled into a comfortable routine that seemed to be working for him. His body was tight and firm. He could easily pass for a man much younger if it were not for his gray hair. Chadsworth had not found the gray hair to be a disadvantage in the gay community. In fact, it seemed to be a real "boy magnet." A lot of the young men he had dated invariably complimented his hair. "Oh Daddy," they would say, "I love your beautiful gray hair."

On this particular morning he chose to stay with his familiar routine. First, he would do his waist exercises. He hated those most so Earl told him to always do them first while he was fresh. Then he would work his chest on some of the Nautilus machines. He especially liked working the butterfly machine. His pecs would begin to swell underneath his tee shirt. Then he went over to the free weights. He continued to work his chest, then his arms. He loved to watch his own biceps in the mirror. The blood vessels would fill and swell to the surface.

After he had completed his exercises he would finish off in the whirlpool. This was his favorite part of the workout. He liked the whirlpool because the warm water felt good. He really liked the whirlpool because the men removed all their clothes before getting into the whirlpool. It was a voyeur's delight. There were times when a particularly gorgeous guy would get into the whirlpool with him. On those occasions, he would stay a bit longer than usual.

This particular day his workout took on a little something extra. He spotted what was undoubtedly one of the most handsome men he had ever seen. The man was working his chest on the incline bench. He was absolutely incredible. He had dark black curly hair and the bluest eyes. He was wearing a muscle shirt that hung loosely on his chest. When he extended the weights, Chadsworth could see that he was hairless, but more, he was well defined. He could not stop staring at him.

Chadsworth struck up a conversation with the man. They talked about training and diet and the dangers of the sun. That led them to sharing ideas on supplements and vitamins. They shared a couple of jokes. Chadsworth was disappointed that the man's joke preferences were heterosexual. Still, when Chadsworth attempted some gay humor on the guy he laughed. Chadsworth put "the look" on the fellow when they were finishing up their weight training. The man returned his gaze, looking deep into Chadsworth's eyes. He felt himself stirring.

"Are you going to the whirlpool?" Chadsworth asked.

"I usually finish off in the steam room, but I guess I can do the whirlpool. Sure, why not?"

Chadsworth walked into the locker room, undressed and put his workout clothes in his locker. He wrapped a towel around his waist. He was aware that he was already becoming aroused so he hurried into the whirlpool. The other man was not yet there so he placed his towel on the rack and climbed into the water. One other man was in the pool. He was sitting with his eyes closed. He opened them briefly as Chadsworth waded into the water. The man nodded and he nodded in return and walked to the far end of the pool. Chadsworth sat facing the entrance so that he would have a good view of the young Adonis when he entered. He waited, feeling himself get more excited.

Soon the man walked in. He had a towel tied around his waist. His body was even more beautiful than he had imagined. Chadsworth had to force himself to keep breathing. Then the man dropped the towel. Again, Chadsworth's breath escaped him.

The man came into the water and walked toward Chadsworth and sat down on the underwater seat about three feet away. He looked over at Chadsworth. Chadsworth returned his look. They made some small talk about the temperature of the water. The other man in the pool stood and walked out of the pool to an adjacent room where the showers were located. Chadsworth looked around. Except for the sound of the shower running he could not see or hear any indication that anyone else was in the locker room. Chadsworth's heart was pounding in his chest. He kept looking at the man. It was now or never. He could hardly restrain himself. He knew that he had to make his move.

Chadsworth stared into the man's eyes. The man did not look away. Chadsworth stood up and began walking toward the man. In a hushed voice he spoke, "Except for the guy in the shower, I think we're all alone. We'll know when he turns off the shower. We'll be able to hear if anyone is coming." Chadsworth came up next to the man, bent over and whispered in his ear, "There's something that I just have to do." With that Chadsworth came face to face with the man and looked deep into his eyes. He leaned over and kissed the man on the lips. As he did, he reached between the man's legs...

The man reached under the water and took hold of Chadsworth's wrists. He looked into Chadsworth's eyes and gave him a deep smile. The man grabbed Chadsworth's wrists and squeezed with all his strength. Chadsworth cried out in pain. Then the man came up out of the water, twisting Chadsworth's arms up behind his back. He spun Chadsworth around and pulled both his hands together behind his back, and then he heard the man shout, "Mark, bring me my cuffs...Sir, you are under arrest for lewd behavior in a public place. You have the right to remain silent..."

Chadsworth was so humiliated. He learned later that it was a sting. The police department had planted this guy in the club. The management had received complaints about the queers. They allowed Chadsworth to dress. He was put in the back seat of the patrol car. At the police station he was booked, fingerprinted, and photographed. He was then allowed to make his one phone call.

"Father Austin," his secretary announced through the intercom, "Mr. Chadsworth Purcell Alexander is on the telephone. He says that it's an emergency."

Steele picked up the line, "Chadsworth, what's wrong?"

"Steele, what I am going to tell you may surprise, even shock you, but I have to demand that you keep it in the strictest of confidence." Chadsworth's voice was shaky.

"Of course, Chadsworth, whatever you tell me will be a pastoral confidence and I won't reveal it to anyone. Are you in trouble?"

"Steele, I am in jail."

"You are where? Chadsworth, have you been arrested? What on earth for?" Steele could hardly believe that he was in jail.

"I am in jail for lewd conduct."

Steele Austin almost dropped the telephone. "Chadworth, what did you do?"

"I propositioned an undercover officer." Steele could hear his voice breaking. He knew that he was crying.

"Chadsworth," Steele took a breath, "I have to know. Was the officer a female?"

"No," Chadsworth sobbed.

"What do I need to do?"

"Can you bring five thousand dollars down here and bail me out?"

"Gosh, Chadsworth, I just don't have that much money. I guess I could borrow it..."

"No, no," he interrupted, "Use your Discretionary Fund. Just write a check on your Discretionary Fund to a bail bondsman and I will make it good just as soon as I can get to my bank. I'll give you five thousand dollars in cash so there will be no paper trail coming back to me."

"Sure," Steele thought, "I guess I can do that. Sure, I'll get my checkbook and I'll be down in about twenty minutes."

When Steele got down to the police station he did as Chadsworth had instructed. He then waited in the lobby until an officer brought him out. By the look on Chadsworth's face he knew that he'd been completely humiliated.

"Let's get out of here," he snorted, quickly walking past Steele.

Once they were in Steele's car Chadsworth asked, "Can you take me to my bank first? We'll put the money in your Discretionary Fund before the Gestapo discovers you just wrote them a hot check. Then let's go get a drink. I owe you an explanation. Then, I'll need you to take me to pick up my car."

Chadsworth directed Steele to a quiet little bar on the edge of town. Except for the bartender it was deserted. Chadsworth ordered a double. When the bartender brought it, he turned it up and then quickly ordered another. He took a long look at Steele Austin.

"I have lived with this all my life. No one knows. No one in the church knows, not even my wife. No one in Falls City knows. I have been arrested twice before, but never in Falls City. The other two times I was arrested in Atlanta." He sat looking into his drink. Tears ran down his face.

"I guess you don't think very much of me right now, do you, Steele?"

Steele reached out and put his hand on his arm, "Chadsworth, you are in a lot of pain right now. You are hurting. I'm not here to judge you. I know a little bit about living with a secret. I can only imagine how difficult this is for you."

"We have to keep it out of the newspaper." Chadsworth was now pleading. "Can you talk to the Chief and ask him to keep it out of the newspaper? Please, Steele, this could ruin me. No one must ever know, please."

Steele Austin shrugged his shoulders, "I know Chief Sparks. I like him and I think he likes me, but I don't know if he can or will."

"You have to try, damn it, you have to try. Please." And then he broke down in sobs.

Steele put his arm around his shoulders. "Okay, I'll see what I can do."

Chadsworth wiped his eyes with the bar napkin, "Thanks. Thank you. And my secret...my secret, is it safe with you?"

Steele nodded. "Your secret is safe with me, but I really have to encourage you to at least talk to Almeda. Does she suspect that you are living a double life?"

He shook his head, "I don't think she suspects a thing."

"Chadsworth, it will be devastating if she were to read this in the newspaper. It would be best if it came from you. My best counsel is that you talk to her. You need to tell her yourself."

Again, his eyes filled with tears. His lips trembled, "If we can't keep it out of the newspapers then I will tell her. I promise."

Steele patted him on the back. "Even if we are able to keep it out of the newspaper, you've got to talk to her. You are living a very dangerous charade. Sooner or later she is going to find out." Steele paused to see if Chadsworth was going to be able to hear the direct counsel he wanted to give him. He made the decision to continue. "Chadsworth, I don't believe that you can help being who you are, but I do believe you have choices. Right now, the choices you are making are putting your wife's happiness in jeopardy. Your marriage is at risk...your reputation...and Chadsworth, you are living in a prison of your own construction. You cannot keep living your life this way. You have other choices."

Chadsworth shook his head. "It's not that simple. It just isn't as easy as you make it sound. I don't have the options that you might think I have."

Steele put both of his hands on Chadsworth's shoulders and looked directly into his face. "I want to listen. I want to understand. I want to help you, but Almeda has to be your first consideration.

"I know. Right now, let's just focus on keeping this out of the newspaper."

After he took Chadsworth to pick up his car, Steele began the drive home. He had only been a priest for twelve years, yet his memory bank was already clogged with other people's secrets. This was not the first secret he had been given to carry and he knew it would not be the last.

CHAPTER 13

Chadsworth was relieved that Almeda was not there when he got home. He really didn't want to face anyone right now. He just needed to calm down. The bar was just off the entrance hall. He filled the glass with Jack Daniels and then dropped some ice cubes in the glass that he took from the icemaker underneath the bar sink.

Out in the sunroom Chadsworth settled back in an easy chair and shut his eyes. He cursed himself for feeling the way he did. Why couldn't he be like other men? His entire life he had been attracted to men. A beautiful woman couldn't get as much as a second look from him. "Women are a complete waste," he thought to himself. But let a handsome man come within view and his heart would skip a beat every time.

Chadsworth knew about Almeda's flings. On more than one occasion he had her followed when she went out of town. He had the pictures, the videos, names, addresses, and phone numbers. He had everything he needed on her. If she ever gave him any trouble he would use it. The state of Georgia does not look kindly on adulterers. It can be plenty tough on a man who is caught. But an adulterous wife doesn't have a prayer.

The only real disappointment Chadsworth had was Almeda's choice in men. My God, Chadsworth even knew a couple of the men she would rendezvous with in a New York City hotel. Two of them were from Falls City. One was a skinny musician with a monstrous snout for a nose; he was nothing but skin and bones. Chadsworth bet that when he was a kid, he was the type everyone on the school ground wanted to beat up. Chadsworth didn't necessarily put him in the ugly category, but he was close. Chadsworth did know an ugly man when he saw one.

The second one that Almeda chose to have a fling with from Falls City was just as big a loser. He was a real redneck. He worked as a construction worker. Chadsworth had the detective run a back-ground check on him and discovered that he had rotten credit and not a penny to his name. He was as dumb as they come. Just what was Almeda thinking? Chadsworth figured she must have a really low opinion of herself to dip down into the dregs of society for a screw.

He smiled at himself to think that she thought she had covered her tracks. He knew the very first time she cheated on him, and they hadn't been married very long. He just knew she was up to something. He had a full box of photos, tapes, videos, and detective reports on her liaisons. One he kept in a large safe deposit box in Atlanta. Then he kept copies in a gay lawyer's office that he had once dated up in Augusta. He had given the lawyer authorization that if he should die and Almeda tried to scandalize him or misbehave in any way, the files were to be made available to the local Falls City newspapers. Almeda wouldn't be able to show her face anywhere in the south. She would have to slink back to some obscure trailer park. Chadsworth reasoned that if this does become public and she refuses to stand by my side I can always use the stuff I have on her to balance the scales.

There had been times when he thought about making the information he had on her public. It would be a good way to get rid of her and then he could live permanently with Earl. Deep down, however, he knew he would not do that and that he and Earl would never live together as life partners. He just had too much to lose. He had spent a lifetime building up his image and reputation in the community. He was well known in all the influential circles in the state as a man of character. He was the poster boy for the responsible, heterosexual, family man. He could not throw it all away. Not even for Earl. His choices were just not as easy and simple as Steele Austin tried to make them appear. He was a married queer living in the closet in Falls City, Georgia. He had no other choices.

Chadsworth walked back to the bar and poured himself another drink. Suddenly, the young detective's body flashed across his mind. Chadsworth felt himself grow weak in the knees. He let his thoughts linger over the sight of the detective walking toward the whirlpool with the towel wrapped around his tight waist. Chadsworth felt himself stir as he remembered what the man looked liked when he dropped the towel.

The ringing of a telephone interrupted his thoughts. He walked back to the telephone in the sun room. Chadsworth answered it with a weak, "Hello."

"Chadsworth, it's Steele."

"Yes, Steele," Chadsworth whispered.

"Are you all right?" Steele inquired. "I know that you've been through a lot today."

Chadsworth sat down in the chair next to the telephone, "Thanks so much, Steele. Thanks for not judging me. Thanks for helping me."

"Chadsworth, I might have some bad news for you," Steele Austin paused.

Chadsworth felt his stomach tie up in knots. His heart was beating rapidly. A cold sweat broke out on his forehead. He felt like he was not going to be able to breathe. "What is it, Steele?"

"Well, I couldn't get in touch with Chief Sparks. He's out of town. I did find out that your paperwork had already been released to the press. It is over at the newspaper office even as we speak...."

Chadsworth interrupted, "Oh my God, I...I...I've got to throw up." Chadsworth just barely made it to the powder room on the other side of the entrance hall. When he was finished, he washed his face with cold water and walked back to the telephone on the sun porch. He had tossed the receiver onto the floor. He picked it up.

"Reverend Austin, are you still there?"

"Yes," Steele reassured him, "I am still here. Do you want me to come over?"

"No, no, don't do that." Chadsworth swallowed the vile taste in his mouth. "Is there anything we can do?"

"That's where I need your help, Chadsworth." Steele waited.

"Anything...anything at all. Money, do you need money? My God, I'll be ruined. We have to keep this out of the papers. Please Reverend Austin, please, I'm begging you." Chadworth sobbed.

Steele waited until Chadsworth had regained his composure. I talked to the Chief's secretary. She is a member of First Church. Don't worry, I didn't use your name. I just explained to her what I was attempting to do. She suggested that I speak with an Officer Forrester, Steve Forrester. Do you know him?"

"No, I don't think so."

"Well, this Officer Forrester suggested that I talk to one of the men over at the newspaper who is also a member of First Church. I honestly don't know what this fellow does for sure, but Officer Forrester suggested that the man might be willing to help us kill the story. I need your permission to go talk to him. That means that he will know your secret."

"What do you know about him?" Chadsworth asked.

Steele swallowed hard this time. "That's the tough part. I baptized his son a couple of weeks ago and then went over to his house for a reception afterwards. He seems like an amiable guy so I am willing to talk to him."

"Christ!" Chadsworth exploded. "Why did that police officer, uh, Forrester, think he would help us?"

"I don't know. I just know that he suggested that this man might have some influence at the newspaper and that he believed that he would be inclined to help us."

"Is that it?"

"No—Chadsworth, there is something else", Steele blurted out.

"What?" Chadsworth was on the verge of tears again.

Steele spoke in a calm clear voice, "the officer I talked to over at the station tells me that this newspaper man is in their file."

"File? What kind of file?"

Steele took a deep breath, "It seems that they keep a file down at the Law Enforcement Center on all the men that are known homosexuals. From time to time they get pressure from the community to run stings on gays who frequent the department store restrooms, city parks, and roadside rest stops looking for tricks. The officer said that it makes it easier for them to run a sting by simply following some of the known offenders to their meeting places."

"What?" Chadsworth could not believe what he was hearing. "What kind of sick police department would do such a thing?"

"I reacted in the same way," Steele tried to reassure him. "Officer Forrester assured me that it is a pretty common practice in communities that consider homosexuality a crime. Vice squads keep the lists to expedite their sting operations. They have similar lists for prostitutes and Johns."

"Am I in the file?"

Again, Steele tried to speak with a calm voice. "They keep the file in three categories. In the first are the people that they know are gay because they have arrested them. The second category is for those that the first have outed, but have never been arrested. In the third category are the ones who have been identified as possibilities by those they have arrested or outed."

"Jesus, Joseph and Mary," Chadsworth shouted, "What kind of Gestapo tactics are they using down there?"

Steele did not reply.

Chadsworth took a deep breath, "Was my name in the file?"

"The officer tells me that you were in category three. They had heard from several informants that you were gay, but they had no proof until today."

"Did they set me up at the gym?" Chadsworth asked angrily.

"They had been working that gym for several days. It seems several of the customers had complained to management about the gay guys hitting on them." Steele paused, "Chadsworth, the fellow at the newspaper is also in the file. He is in category three. They don't know if he is gay, but several informants have told them so. If you let me talk to him, he just may be sympathetic. He may be in a position to kill the story."

"Call him. Call him right now. Anything, anything you can do, Steele, will really be appreciated. I will never forget you for this," Chadworth started sobbing again.

When he had calmed down, Steele Austin asked, "So I have your permission?"

"Hell, Reverend, as soon as he sees the police blotter he's going to know anyway. We don't have any choice. I guess it is better for one more man to know if it will keep the entire town from finding out." Chadsworth started feeling sick again just thinking about that possibility.

"Try to stay calm," Steele reassured him. "I'm on my way over to the newspaper office right now. I'll do my best. But Chadsworth, you've got to promise me that you're going to talk to Almeda. Sooner or later she is going to find out. It would be best if it came from you. Chadsworth, it's the only way that you are going to be set free from all the torment that you live with."

Chadsworth whispered, "I know, I promise I'll give it serious consideration."

"Then God bless you, Chadsworth. God give you some peace."

Chadsworth heard the priest hang up the telephone. He sat quietly in the chair for a few minutes and then began to shout at himself. "I was so stupid to make a move on that guy at the gym. What's wrong with me?"

Shaking, Chadsworth punched in Earl's number on the telephone next to his chair. When Earl answered the phone, Chadsworth lost his composure. His voice was shaking. He could hardly speak.

"Chadsworth, is that you?" Earl panicked. "What's wrong? What has happened? Are you all right? Talk to me!"

Chadsworth told Earl all the ugly details and then giant sobs swept over him yet one more time. He begged, "Earl, can you forgive me? I am so sorry that I was going to be unfaithful to you. Please, please, forgive me. I love you and I don't want anything to destroy what we have."

"Chadsworth, honey, it ain't no big thing," Earl tried to calm him. "We've never promised each other that we would be exclusive. And by your description of your young detective hunk I think ol' Earl might just have been tempted to do the same thing."

"God, Earl," Chadsworth chuckled, "that's the worst part. I can't get him out of my mind. I love you to death, but I can't stop thinking about him."

They both laughed. Chadsworth was feeling a little better.

"I'm telling you Earl, there's no crazy like queer crazy." They laughed some more.

Chadsworth took a deep breath. "Earl, can you believe this? The man almost broke my arms, cuffed me, arrested me, and took me off to jail. He obviously is so hetero that he wouldn't be aroused by his own mirror image. I had to call my priest to bail me out of jail and now the entire mess may be in the morning papers. I'll be ruined forever if it happens, but I'm so queer crazy the only thing I can think about is that cop standing there naked in that whirlpool."

"Uhmm, Uhmm, he really must have been something."

Chadsworth was silent for a long time. The tears rolled down his cheeks. "I hate myself, Earl. I have fought these feelings all my life. I really don't want to be a queer. God help me! I despise these feelings. I can't keep living this way. I'm so tired."

"Now listen to me you closeted faggot!" Earl interrupted. "Either God created you to be queer or you are an aberration...a mistake. The God I worship doesn't make mistakes. Does your Episcopalian God make cruel mistakes, Chadsworth? Get a grip. You don't choose your feelings. They are your God given emotions. Now accept them and walk out of that closet you have been living in for six decades. There is only one handle on the door and it is on your side. Set yourself free, white boy." Earl began coughing hard.

When he had stopped his coughing Chadsworth asked, "Are you all right, Earl?"

"I'm fine. I think my bronchitis has turned into the flu. I have really been sick the past couple of weeks."

"Why didn't you call me?" Chadsworth chided.

"I didn't want to worry you. I've gotten better. It's just that I don't have my strength back yet."

"I'm going to come up and take care of you," Chadsworth insisted.

"No, please don't come. I may still be contagious. There's no reason for us both to get sick. You stay there and take care of yourself. In a week or so, I'll be back to my old self and we can have a romantic weekend together." Earl started coughing again.

Chadsworth relented, "I suppose you're right."

Just then another call came in. "Earl, let me see if that's the priest."

"Hello, Steele is that you?" Chadsworth could not keep his voice from shaking.

"It's taken care of, Chadsworth. The story is killed. For now your secret is safe."

Chadsworth felt relief wash over him. "Thanks so much, Steele. God bless you. If you ever need anything—if you ever need me to kick some butt for you in this town, just let me know."

"Just take care of yourself, Chadsworth. And remember your promise to me. Talk to Almeda. If you need me to be there when you talk to her just call me. I want to help you, Chadsworth. Please let me help both you and Almeda." Steele hung up the phone.

"Earl—Earl, are you still there?"

"Yes, I'm here. Was that the priest?"

"Yes, it's taken care of. I won't be in the newspaper." Chadsworth laid the phone down so that he could wipe his eyes and blow his nose. "Earl, I really want to see you. I love you. I need to be with you. Call me just as soon as you feel better."

"I promise," Earl wheezed. "I promise. I love you too."

CHAPTER 14

Two hours before the Falls City Soup Kitchen was to open, a line of people formed at the door. The line wrapped around the block. The people stood patiently. Steele's heart broke as he caught a glimpse of the number of elderly and children. Their eyes were vacant. For the most part they were dressed in what would best be described as rags. He made a point of looking at each one of them and saying, "Good morning. We're glad that you're here. We'll open the doors soon. You'll be able to eat all you want."

With the assistance of the Black Minister's Association, a grant from the Methodist Church, and some money that he raised from a few sympathetic people at First Church, Steele Austin's dream of a Soup Kitchen was being realized. A small black church in the warehouse section of Falls City had agreed to allow him to use their parish hall and kitchen. He put the money he raised in his Discretionary Fund until such time as he could set up a separate account with a separate tax ID number. Some of the members of the black church and a few from First Church agreed to volunteer to work in the Kitchen.

Steele had asked his youth group to distribute copies of a notice to the homeless on the streets. The notice read simply, "No Sermons—No Saving—Just Soup and Sandwiches—Monday—Friday, 11:00 a.m. to 1:00 p.m. Gethsemane Baptist Church Parish Hall."

Steele had convinced a couple of the local markets to donate food. For opening day, they had been overwhelmed with a donation of calves' liver. The kitchen committee decided to make pâté sandwiches.

Just before 11:00 a.m., everything was ready. Steele called all the volunteers together. He thanked them for coming. He then asked if they could join hands for a prayer. After a moment of silence, Steele verbalized what was on his heart. "Lord Jesus, you washed the feet of your disciples. You call us to follow your example. You reached out to the lepers and the outcasts. You call us to follow your example. You took fish and loaves and multiplied them so that hungry men, women, and children could be fed. You call us to follow your example. You came among us to serve the least of these our brothers and sisters. We pray your blessing on us as we strive to do the same." With that, there was a resounding "Amen" from all in the circle. There was a group hug, pats on the back, smiles, and the doors were open.

There was an air of disbelief on the faces of the people who approached the serving window. Each was greeted warmly. Each was told that they could have all they wanted to eat and that they could come back as often as they wanted, but they could not take food out of the building. It would have to be eaten here. There were genuine nods of sincere thanks by each client as they were served.

The tables in the parish hall had bright colored tablecloths on them. There were fresh flowers on each table. Brightly covered napkins waited at each place. There were close to one hundred people in the hall, but there was an eerie silence in the room. There were only the sounds of clinking glasses. Occasionally, a baby would whimper or a child would cry, but otherwise, the room was silent. The volunteers moved among the tables refilling coffee cups, water glasses, and milk glasses. They tried to make conversation with the clients, but no one responded. Steele stood looking at the scene. "God," he prayed, "make this a welcoming place for these your people." He stood silently searching his mind for something to say or do.

At the far corner of the room he noticed a man dressed in an old overcoat stand and move toward the stage. His coat was in threads and his shoes had been wrapped with duct tape. Even though the hall was well heated he kept his stocking cap on his head. He obviously had not shaved or bathed in weeks or maybe even months. The man walked up onto the stage. Steele and one of the other male volunteers made eye contact. They both moved toward the stage not knowing what was on the man's mind. The man walked over to the piano. He opened the lid and stared at the keys for a long moment. Then, the man masterfully began to play. It was a magical moment. Every eye in the room looked toward the stage. When the man finished his first concerto, the entire room exploded with applause. The man stood and took his bow. He sat back down and began to play more quietly. Conversation rose up among the clients. The volunteers and the clients began to freely converse.

Steele looked over at the other volunteer standing at the steps leading up to the stage. The man smiled and slapped Steele across the back. "Pâté and Chopin...Father Austin, you Episcopal priests really know how to open a Soup Kitchen!" With that, Steele relaxed, and the two men hugged each other as they were rocked with the joy of laughter.

When the man finished playing he returned to his table and resumed eating. Steele sat down opposite him. "My name is Steele Austin." He extended his hand. The man shook Steele's hand and replied, "I'm Duke."

"Do you have a last name, Duke?" Steele inquired.

"It doesn't matter. Just call me Duke," he responded.

Steele attempted to engage the man in conversation, "Where did you learn to play the piano, Duke?"

The man put his spoon down and took a long look at Steele. He stared into his eyes for a cold moment. "How much do you know about us?"

Steele was taken back, "What do you mean—us? Who are you talking about?"

"Us...Us...Us..." The man made a great sweeping motion with his hands around the room. "Us, the people you call the homeless. Well, we're not homeless. We're houseless. We have homes. The streets are our homes. We have families. We know each other. We're a family. Now how much do you know about us?"

A flash of embarrassment swept across Steele's face. "I know that I want to help you."

"Why? Why do you want to help us?" the man shot back.

"Because you are my brothers and sisters in Christ. You are a part of my family." Steele thought he sounded preachy and tried to think of a way to regroup.

The man was on the verge of anger, "Are you sure you don't want to fix us? Are you sure you just don't want to get your spiritual jollies by feeding us so that you'll feel better about yourself?"

Steele lowered his voice and looked deeply into the man's eyes. "I care. I care about all of you. I care about you, Duke. Tell me how I can help."

The man once again took a deep look into Steele Austin's eyes. After a long moment, the man stated emphatically, "Then start by trying to learn who we are."

Steele nodded, "Fair enough. Duke, who are you? Help me to know you. Tell me who you are."

Duke lowered his head and lifted a spoonful of soup to his lips. He remained silent. Steele sat watching him. "You have to know that we weren't born on the streets. Many of us come from loving homes. Oh, not all of us, some of these people's parents were abusive or drunks or disowned them. Many of us went to college. You'd be amazed to know the number of people with professional degrees I meet on the streets. Some of us had families of our own, careers, money in the bank. Some of us had it all."

Steele's intuition kicked in, "Were you one of those people, Duke?"

Again, there was a long silence. Duke sipped his coffee. Steele sat silently watching the man. He so wanted to help him. Something inside Steele told him not to ask any more questions. Still, he wanted to break the silence. He wanted the man to know that he could trust him. Steele was about to give up. He was pretty sure that it was useless to wait any longer. Just as he was about to move on to another client, the man broke the silence. "My two year old son drowned in our swimming pool. It was a terrible accident. My wife was eaten up with grief. She was never quite the same again. She moved around the house like a zombie. She just couldn't function. She wouldn't talk to me. She shut everyone out. No one was able to break through to her. One morning after I went to work, she went out to the cemetery. She lay down next to his grave. She cut her wrists. That's where the caretakers found her. I had her buried next to him."

Steele reached across the table and put his hand on Duke's arm. "My God, Duke, I am so sorry. I can't even begin to understand the pain that you must live with."

Duke pushed his chair back from the table. He turned himself sideways to the table and to Steele. He stared off into space. They sat silently together. Most of the other clients had left the parish hall, and the volunteers were taking down the tables and chairs.

"It started simply enough," he reflected. "After they were both gone, I would come home at night...the house was so empty. It was so quiet. I just couldn't sit still to read or watch television, play the piano, or anything. I couldn't sleep or eat. I didn't want to be around people. I tried to get some help, but nothing took away the emptiness. The booze at least numbed the pain. First, a few drinks, and then I would drink until I fell asleep wherever I was sitting."

Something told Steele not to respond. He sat silently looking at the man. He leaned toward him so that he would know that he was listening. The man interrupted the silence, "After awhile I started mixing the booze with some prescription drugs the shrink gave me. I missed work. Sometimes I would miss days at a time. One of my co-workers must have picked up on my addiction. She introduced me to the needle. It got expensive. I had to sell everything. I lost my house, I lost my job, I lost my friends, and I'm too ashamed to contact my family. I hit the rails and tried to stay ahead of the weather. I guess my family thinks I'm dead. Now....." He stopped. He dropped his head.

"Now?" Steele whispered.

Duke turned in his chair to face Steele. He slowly removed his stocking cap. He pointed to a lesion on his forehead. "Now...now this."

Steele had seen similar lesions before. He knew what they indicated. "Have you been diagnosed?"

"No," Duke shook his head. "No, I don't have to be diagnosed. I know that I have it. I shared needles with anyone who would share with me. I still do. I have to have my fix. I don't suppose you can understand that, can you?"

This time it was Steele's turn to shake his head, "No, Duke, I really don't. How can I help you? What can I do for you?"

"I am just another homeless man with AIDS. Why would you want to do anything for me? Soon I'll be dead. When I'm gone you will have one less mouth to feed at your Kitchen. The streets will be just a little cleaner. Help me? Why in God's name would you want to help me?"

Again Steele put his hand on the man's arms, "Duke, I don't know the answer. I have to rely on you to help me find the answer. How can we help you and the other people on the street just like you? Please, Duke, God wants us to help you. Duke, I want to help you."

Duke stared for a long moment at Steele Austin. He put the stocking cap back on his forehead. He stood up and took another long look in Steele's eyes. He started walking toward the door. Duke stopped, turned around and looked back at Steele. "You going to be here tomorrow?"

"Yes," Steele replied, "yes, I'll be here tomorrow."

Duke nodded and walked out the door. Steele stayed to help the volunteers clean the hall. The room was filled with happy conversation. All were in agreement that the Soup Kitchen was meeting a real need. Even those that had volunteered more out of curiosity than anything else were now convinced that the Soup Kitchen was needed.

Steele's thoughts were not on the Kitchen, but on his conversation with Duke. He had been touched by his story. The room had been filled with people. He wondered just how many stories there were just like Duke's? How would he be able to help those that still questioned the ministry of the Soup Kitchen understand that those who came here were not lazy, criminals, or the dregs of society? How would he ever be able to help them understand that these unfortunate souls were their brothers and sisters? To feed them is to feed Christ Himself. He knew they had heard the words, but just how would he ever be able to help them understand?

CHAPTER 15

Steele's wife Randi was on his cell phone. "Steele, will you stop over at the Oldsmobile dealership? I was there this morning. I took a test drive in the prettiest little car. I really like it."

Randi and Steele had been looking at new cars before they left Oklahoma. Her old station wagon had just about made its last carpool. They had agreed that once they got to Falls City they would purchase a new set of wheels for her.

"Randi," Steele asked, "can we afford it?"

"Daddy said that we could use some of my trust fund for it. We can pay cash for the whole thing." She sounded so excited, "Please, Steele, can't you stop off and have a look at it? I want to know what you think."

Steele Austin could say "no" to a lot of people, but Randi Austin was not one of them. He loved her desperately and would do anything for her. "Sure, honey, I'll swing by. Did you talk to anyone in particular?"

"Her name is Dolly Stuart. She'll be expecting you."

"You mean they have a female car salesman in Falls City?" he quirked.

"Yes, and she's a real knockout," Randi quipped, "So be on your best behavior; I already told her that you're a priest."

"Now just how do you know that doesn't increase my magnetism?" he chuckled.

"Down boy, get your ego in place. You are going there to look at my car, not get your kicks by flirting with the blonde sales woman."

"A blonde…are you sure you want me to go by myself?" he waited.

"Just go and tell me what you think, okay?"

"Okay, I am pulling into the dealership right now. Randi, I love you." Steele started to hang up the phone.

"And I love you too. If you like my car as much as I do, I'll show you just how much when you get home."

It was not hard to find Dolly. She was about twenty-six years old with fluffed up blonde hair. Randi had described her correctly. She was absolutely gorgeous.

Dolly was very accommodating. She was outgoing with a bright smile and a bubbling personality. Steele was not surprised to see her featured on the showroom wall as the "Salesman of the Month."

Steele took a test drive in the car with Dolly. He approved of Randi's choice. He was excited for her. On his way down to the office, he called Randi to share his excitement over the new car. They would have it ready for Randi to pick up later that night.

Back at his office, Steele discovered a well-dressed black man and an equally well-groomed white man waiting for him in his office. The black man introduced himself as David Drummond, the head of the Georgia Black Clergy Association. The young man was the director of the Falls City AIDS Fund. His name was Duncan Hill. Steele invited both into his office.

"Reverend Austin," David Drummond began, "My office is in Savannah, but we have heard about your ministry here at First Church. I read with great interest the article that was printed about you in our state newspaper."

Steele chuckled, "I'm afraid that article has not been very well received by my congregation. If I had my druthers, I wish that it had never been written."

Duncan interrupted, "Father Austin, if you are the type of priest that we hear you are, then that article is pretty accurate."

"What kind of priest do you hear I am?" Steele questioned.

David responded, "May we call you Steele?"

Steele nodded.

"Steele, there has never been an AIDS Walk or an AIDS Healing Service in Falls City. We had one in Atlanta and we had one in Savannah, but there has never been one in Falls City. We think that you are the man who can change that. Are you?"

Steele sat quietly. The conversation he had with Duke at the Soup Kitchen flashed across his mind. God does work in strange ways His wonders to perform. Is this one of the ways that he could help Duke and the other people like him?

He glanced back at his two visitors. "What did you have in mind?"

Duncan was quick to answer, "We already have the support of the black clergy in Falls City. They're willing to sponsor the march and a healing service, but Steele, that could only serve to perpetuate the myth."

"The myth?" Steele questioned.

"Yes, the myth that AIDS is a disease of black drug users. As you know, AIDS does not discriminate. You are the Rector of the most influential church in Falls City. Your church sits right on the Main Street. If we could have the healing service in your church it would make a statement that cannot be ignored." Duncan was breathless.

David picked up where Duncan left off. "Steele, we only need the use of your church. Of course, we want you to participate. If you can get any of the other white clergy to participate that would be great. Otherwise, we'll pull in some of the white people from the AIDS Fund and from the gay community. Parents and Friends of Lesbians and Gays would also like to be a part of the service. We can have a candlelight march down Main Street. The march can end with the service of healing right here at First Church."

Steele sat silent. He felt called to do this. He knew in his heart that it was the right thing to do. His stomach, on the other hand, was churning. He knew that the service would not sit well with the "old guard." Still, it was the right thing to do. It is what God would want him to do. It was exactly what Jesus would do.

Steele looked back at his visitors, "Gentlemen, let's plan a healing service."

The three men gathered around the conference table in Steele's office. They planned the march, the service, and a reception in the parish hall afterwards. Steele called his secretary over the intercom and had her reserve the building for the chosen date. He heard the hesitancy in her voice, "Father Austin, are you sure?"

"Yes, I'm sure."

The candlelight march would begin with prayers. Steele would lead the prayers, and then along with the black clergy and any white clergy he could get to participate, they would lead the march down Main Street. At the church there would be a combined black gospel choir made up of all the participating black churches in Falls City. They would also invite the Gay Men's Chorus from Atlanta to sing. Members of Parents and Friends of Lesbians and Gays would read the scriptures. Men, women, and children who were living with AIDS would lead the prayers. There would be no sermon. There would be opportunity for all to come to the altar rail to be anointed with oil by healing teams and receive prayers for themselves, friends, or family members. It would be a magnificent event for the community.

Steele Austin was excited. He had asked Duke what he could do to help. God had given him an answer. He knew he had to obey, but then, there was that queasy feeling in his stomach.

Steele escorted his guests to the front door. As he was coming back into his office, his secretary ran up to him. "Father Austin, we just found out that Willie is in the hospital."

"What's wrong with Willie? How long has he been there?" Why didn't we know he was sick?" Steele was perturbed.

"I don't know, Father. Sometimes Willie just disappears for a few days and then he shows back up. He has been one of the janitors at this church since he was a teenager. He has a lot of freedom." His secretary continued, "His wife called a few minutes ago. She said Willie has cancer. Father Austin, she said he's dying."

Steele turned on his heels and headed toward the hospital. He got Willie's room number from the reception desk and took the elevator to the fourth floor. The room took Steele aback. Unlike the private rooms that most of his members had occupied when he visited them, there were four beds in this room. An elderly black man occupied each bed.

Steele spotted Willie in the bed by the window. There was an elderly woman sitting in the chair next to his bed. Her gray hair was tightly bound in a bun at the back of her wrinkled face. She was holding Willie's hand. Both of them had been crying.

Steele walked up to them. "Reverend Austin, you much too busy to be calling on ol' Willie. You shouldn't have come."

Steele was genuinely moved by the man's humility. "I'll bet this beautiful lady is your wife, Willie. I had heard that you had married above yourself. Now I know it is true."

Willie forced a smile and then gushed, "Yes sir, God gave me a good woman. The Bible say that a faithful wife be more precious than a jewel of any price. Yes sir, God sure been good to me."

"Now you just hush talking like that in front of the preacher. He can see right through yer sweet talkin' and so can I." She extended her hand, "Willie talk about you all the time, Reverend. He say you just what ol' First Church has needed for years. He say you a true man of God and that Jesus is your companion. My name's Grace, I have longed to lay eyes on you."

The woman's eyes filled with tears. "Reverend, it's gonna take some powerful prayin' to get us out of this. Willie's awful sick. The doctors say Willie not gonna get well. They say there's nothing they can do for him." She began to sob. Steele reached out and put his arm around her. He looked over at Willie and took his hand. The tears rolled down Willie's cheeks.

It was all Steele could do to keep from breaking down himself. That damn lump had returned to his throat. It was so familiar to him in situations like this. He knew that if he tried to say anything his voice would quiver. He felt his own eyes fill with tears. His heart went out to Willie and Grace. He just stood there, holding her with one arm while she cried. With the other arm he held Willies' hand.

Finally, he was able to speak. "The Almighty and I have been known to broker a deal or two. Let's see what we can do for you and Willie."

Steele reached into his pocket and pulled out his oil stock. "Willie, I am going to anoint you with oil and I am going to lay hands on you and pray for your healing."

"Jest like it say to do in the Book of James," Willie murmured.

"Yes, just like it says to do in the Book of James." Steele anointed Willie with the oil, made the sign of the cross on his forehead, laid his hands on his head and prayed for him. While he was praying, he heard Grace uttering her own prayers at the same time.

"Before you leave, Revr'nd Steele, can I ask you somthin'?"

"Sure, Willie, whatever you need. Just ask."

With that, Willie looked over at his wife. "Give it to him, honey." His wife walked over to the table next to Willie's bed. She opened a drawer and took out her purse. From her purse she pulled out the biggest wad of money Steele Austin had ever seen. It was held together by a rubber band. She reached out to give it to Steele.

"What's this, Willie?" Steele was astonished. "What do you want me to do with this?"

Willie beamed, "We want you to use it to buy us two graves in the First Church Cemetery. We've been savin' most all our lives so that we could be buried in that beautiful ol' cemetery. I been takin' care those graves for nigh onto sixty years. I know every marker in that graveyard. I want to be buried there. I want Grace to be at my side when she comes to join me. There's nigh onto three thousand dollars there. It should be enough. Ever time I try to buy a plot in the past, Mr. Howard Dexter tells me the price has jus' gone up. I asked Mr. Smith, the Business Manger, the other day how much they sellin' for now. He tells me. This is more than enough."

Steele looked at the couple. "Why the First Church Cemetery?"

"'Cuz that my home, Revr'nd Austin. I spend my whole life at that church. I know they ain't got no black folks at that church, but every one treat me just like family. Now we want to be buried with our family. Will you get the graves for us?"

Grace extended the money yet one more time. She wanted Steele to take it. Steele held up his hand. "Grace, is this all the money you have? Do you have any other money?"

She shook her head.

"Grace, what will you live on when Willie is gone? You need that money."

Grace retorted, "God will take care ol' Grace. Me'n Willie need a restin' place. We want that place to be at First Church." Again, she extended the money to Steele.

Steele stood silent looking at the two of them. "No, you keep your money. I think I can find a way to buy those graves for you. They'll be a gift to you from the church. You'll have your resting place, Willie, and I'll make sure that there is one for Grace. Put your money in the bank, Grace. Save it. You'll need it to take care of yourself."

Steele waved at the two of them. He turned and walked toward the door. He stopped and looked back at them. He left them just as he had found them. Grace was sitting by Willie's bed. They were staring into each other's eyes. They were holding hands.

CHAPTER 16

Steele had hoped the meeting of the Vestry this month would be a celebration. He presided over the set agenda with some excitement. All the numbers were up. The church was full at both services on Sunday mornings. He and the staff had been talking about adding an additional service. The Sunday School Director reported with great pride that all the classes were full and that additional cribs and attendants were needed in the nursery to handle the babies of all the new young families. The Choir Director was gushing as well. Not only had the Chancel Choir doubled in size, but they now had two Children's Choirs. He was thinking of starting a Handbell Choir. The Business Manager presented the financial statement. Year-to-date plate offerings had exceeded all expectations. He beamed, "Gentlemen, since Steele Austin became our Rector, our offering plates overflow."

Steele's excitement and that of the staff's was met with no verbal response on the part of the Vestry. All listened patiently to the reports. Each person nodded their head. There were some polite smiles, but for the most part the Vestry members kept their eyes fixed on the table in front of them. Steele tried his best to get eye contact with the members in his direct line of vision. He even asked several of them direct questions. "Ed, isn't your daughter in the new Children's Choir?" Ed nodded, "Why yes, we are proud to see her singing in the Children's Choir. It is a good thing." But there was no further enthusiasm displayed beyond these polite courtesies. It all seemed surreal. Steele just couldn't wrap his mind around the dynamics in the room. For the last decade the church had been on the decline. Attendance, giving, everything indicated a dying church. The congregation itself had grown old. For the first few months he had been with them he looked out on a sea of gray hair. Now young families were filling the pews.

Where was the celebration? He wasn't looking for a commendation. Surely, however, the elected leadership could commend the staff for all their success. A dying congregation was coming back to life, but the elected leadership received the reports in polite silence. Steele made a couple more attempts at getting a positive response.

"I think we should commend the staff and their volunteers for all their hard work."

Nothing. Just more nods of heads, but no verbal assent.

"It is really exciting to be a part of a church that is growing and reaching out to new people," he continued in the face of the stony silence. "God is doing wonderful things in this congregation. Don't you all agree?" More nods and yet more silence.

Steele looked around the table at his staff. Each had a puzzled look on their face. They were just as confused by the behavior of the Vestry as he was. Since the published agenda had been concluded, Steele was about to close with a prayer.

Howard Dexter interrupted, "Mistuh Austin, I would like to call for an executive session of the Vestry. I would like to ask all the staff to leave the room." With that the staff each gave Steele an even more puzzled look, stood, and left the room.

Howard Dexter closed the conference room door behind them. When he returned to his seat he made eye contact with Steele and began, "Mistuh Austin, this is not easy for me to say, but I have to let you know that there is a lot of unhappiness with you in this congregation. I have been receiving a lot of phone calls about you. I believe that the other members of the Vestry have also been receiving a lot of phone calls from displeased parishioners. Many of our members are sharing their concerns with us."

With that there was a general nodding of heads and a few murmurs of agreement around the table. Steele felt as though the entire group had just pissed all over the sacred fire that he and the staff had tried to build.

Howard Dexter invited comments from other members of the Vestry. "Gentlemen, I think it important that the Rector hear some of the concerns that are being expressed by members of the congregation. I think that we can do so without showing any disrespect for the Rector or his leadership, but it is important that he hear the concerns of the people who pay his salary." Again, there were more murmurs of agreement.

Mr. William Mudd spoke first, "Yes, Howard, while the numbers on the parochial report are important, it is more important that the congregation be satisfied with the direction of this parish. Reverend Austin, there are a lot of us who don't approve of your leadership style. Quite frankly we don't like what we see happening to our church. If you continue in the direction that you are headed, I for one will not be able to support you. In fact, I think you are in danger of losing the support of a large segment of this congregation."

Surreal—surreal, Steele just could not believe his ears. Who were they talking about, he asked himself? Aren't they here on Sunday mornings? Don't they hear the excitement in the pews and the full classrooms in the Sunday school? My God, they even applauded the choir anthem last week. Where am I? I must be dreaming! This really can't be happening.

William Mudd's mouth continued to move, but Steele could not make out what he was saying. He felt his eyes filling with tears and his heart sank. He knew William Mudd was a fourth generation member of the congregation. He knew he was a graduate of The Citadel and the University of Virginia Law School. Mudd was the senior partner at a law firm specializing in labor law. He was married to a rather puffy little woman and two equally puffy and prissy little girls.

"I think it is my responsibility to begin by passing on the concerns of the ladies of this congregation," Mudd continued to pontificate. "Reverend Austin, the ladies are quite offended by the foil wallpaper that you have put in the dining room at the Rectory. Every year the Altar Guild has held their Valentine Tea in the Rectory. That has been going on for fifty years, but Reverend Austin, the ladies are not going to hold their tea in the Rectory this year if you don't agree to take down that wallpaper."

Steele gulped. His voice was shaking, "Is that what this is about? Is this about foil wallpaper?"

"Among other things," Mudd responded.

"Randi chose that wallpaper. The Rectory is our home. We had that same wallpaper in our house in Oklahoma. As you know we owned our house there. That wallpaper was one of the things that she thought would help her get over having to sell our house in order to move here."

Henry Mudd rebutted, "Reverend Austin, the Rectory is not your home. That is our house. That house belongs to this church. We allow you to live there as long as you are the Rector. The ladies of this congregation take great pride in the Rectory. It needs to be a place that they can show off to the community. It should not be an embarrassment. That wallpaper is an embarrassment!"

"But..." Steele started to respond.

"There is no but, Mr. Austin. That is our house and you should not plant so much as one petunia up there without talking to us first."

Steele felt his mouth drop open.

Howard Dexter picked up the litany, "Gentlemen, I agree that the Rectory is a hot button for a lot of the ladies in the congregation, but we need to advise the Rector of other concerns." He paused for more nods and murmurs of agreement before continuing, "I know that you are pleased with all the new people you are bringing into this congregation, but frankly, Mistuh Austin, not all of us share your excitement. Just who are these new people and where do you find them? Frankly, I don't think they are our kind of people. I don't believe they belong at First Church."

"Howard," Steele looked for words, "Howard, these are the people that God is sending to us. It is our responsibility to welcome them to God's House and God's Family."

William Mudd's voice exploded, "Can't you get them to dress properly? Real gentlemen know that they are supposed to wear a jacket and tie to a house of worship. My wife reported at the Altar Guild meeting that she actually saw women wearing slacks at the 9:15 service. Now my family is always properly attired and it is your responsibility to advise the new people to dress appropriately as well."

It was hard for Steele to hide the disbelief in his voice, "Do you really think God cares about what people wear to church?"

William Mudd shot back, "Yes suh, He does. If it is important to us then it is important to the Almighty!"

Steele swallowed the laughter that was swelling up in his throat. He thought—"they are serious."

Howard Dexter continued the interrogation, "Reverend Austin, why do we need all these new people? We are big enough. We don't need to add another service. Let me tell you how big we have gotten. I don't know who you have answering the telephone down here, but I called down here last week. Whoever was answering the telephone didn't know who I was! Now, that's unforgivable. That is a sign that we are just getting too big."

"I can go you one better than that," William Mudd interrupted.

"My wife and daughters were at the Corner Market the other evening and ran into your wife, Reverend Austin. She didn't speak to them. Can you gentlemen imagine that? The Rector's wife snubbed my wife and daughters."

Again, the heads began to shake and the murmurs of disapproval rose up. Steele countered, "I'm sure Randi didn't see them. I know that she knows your wife and daughters. She has commented to me on how your wife always dresses them so nicely. I will advise her that your wife's feelings were hurt. I know Randi will want to make it up to her."

William Mudd shook his head, "I think this is beyond repair. Tell your wife to save her voice. Gentlemen, I just think this is one more indication of the fact that this church is getting too big."

"But I thought you wanted me to grow the parish?" Steele inquired, "That's one of the reasons that you called me here."

"Yes, you are right, that is one of the reasons that we called you here," Howard Dexter commented. "But Mistuh Austin, we meant for you to bring the *right kind of people* into this church. The people we see you bringing in are simply not our kind of people. They don't belong here. They don't fit in. They will never fit in."

With that Steele pushed his chair back away from the table. "Is there anything else?"

Howard continued, "Yes, I regret to tell you that there is more— much more. Since the hour is growing late and with the concurrence of my fellow Vestrymen, I am going to limit my remarks to one more glaring offense that must be addressed before it's too late."

Steele thought this nightmare would never end.

"This Vestry wants you to cancel the service that you have planned for the HOMO—SEXuals. You are not to have that service at First Church. We want nothing to do with it. Do you hear us, Mistuh Austin? You are to cancel it!"

"No sir, I will not." Steele rose up in his chair. He pushed it back from the table, leaned across it and looked directly into Howard Dexter's eyes. "AIDS is a deadly disease...

"God's punishment on queers!" William Mudd shouted.

"No sir, you are wrong. The God I believe in does not willingly inflict suffering on His children. Beyond that, I believe you are greatly misinformed about the disease." Steele pleaded.

Howard Dexter slapped his fist on the table, "Now listen to me, young man. You are not having a gay rights service in our church!"

Steele's temper kicked in. "It's not a gay rights service. It's a healing service. Gentlemen, I believe the Canons of the Church give me the authority to use our church for services of worship and the Vestry is prohibited by Church Law from interfering with my priestly duty."

Mudd shouted back, "Let me explain this to you one more time, preacher. This is our church! I had to help the last two Rectors understand that and by God I'm going to make you understand it as well. Since you seem to be upholding your reputation as an Okie, let me repeat this very slowly. This is our church...our church...this is our church! It is not your church! You are here to do as we tell you to do!"

Steele knew that he must not respond. The words that were forming in his mind and grabbing at his tongue were neither priestly nor kind. He looked around the table at all the hostile looks that were being shot at him. There was not one iota of support in the room. He really wished that Chadsworth were there, but he was in Atlanta on business. Stone Clemons and Chief Sparks were together on a fishing trip. He had no support in the room.

"Gentlemen," Steele's voice was shaking, "it is clear that we are not going to agree on this matter. The Prayer Book and Church Laws both give me the authority to hold such a service, but beyond that, gentlemen, I ask you to examine your consciences. It's the right thing to do. It's exactly what Jesus would do."

Howard Dexter began to chuckle, "Come now, Mistuh Austin, the Bible is quite clear about homosexuality. It is wrong. It is a sin. It is anathema. Queers are going to burn in hell. AIDS is but a call to repentance."

Steele was exhausted, "Howard, I think we need to have this discussion on homosexuality and AIDS at a time when our tempers are not so raw. I'm tired. I really don't want to hear any more. I'm going to adjourn this meeting."

"Before you do," Howard Dexter stared back at Steele, "I'm going to give you a warning that you had better take to heart. If you have that service, Henry Mudd and I will be sitting out in front of the church in my car. We are going to be watching the men go into our church. If we see any men holding hands or walking into our church with their arms around each other, we're going to report you to the Bishop."

This time Steele could not control himself. "Now let me get this straight. You and Henry are going to be sitting out in front of the church in the dark in a dark car?"

"Yes," Howard nodded.

"Two men sitting in the dark of night in a dark car? Just the two of you?" Steele continued to bait him.

"Yes, I've already made that clear to you," Howard nodded again.

"Then, Howard, who's going to be watching the two of you?"

With that Howard Dexter exploded. He stood up and shouted, "Mistuh Austin, I think you had better adjourn this meeting now and not say another word."

Steele stood and met his stare; "Meeting adjourned."

With that the Vestry began filing out of the room. No words were spoken. There were just angry glances at Steele and one another. Most left shaking their heads.

Steele sat quietly in the room looking at the empty conference table. He lowered his face into the palms of his hands. He felt so alone. "Jesus," he prayed. "I am trying to do the right thing. I am trying to reach out to new people, to the sick and the suffering. What am I doing wrong?" He sat quietly waiting on an answer. None came.

CHAPTER 17

The first thing that you need to know about Charleston, South Carolina," Stone Clemons sneered, "is that the people there like to live by the sea, eat rice, and worship their ancestors. Otherwise, have a great weekend. You and Randi have more than earned it. There is a great little hotel right on Front Street. It is owned by one of my clients. Since you are my Rector he is going to comp the room for two nights. You'll only have to pay for one night. It's quite lavish, so enjoy it."

Steele was really looking forward to a weekend away with Randi. He felt pretty beat up. In the past when he had gotten down, some alone time with Randi had been the perfect prescription. The first time he ever laid eyes on her he thought she was the most beautiful woman he had ever seen. Her big black eyes intrigued him. The fact that she was a blonde surprised him. He had always been attracted to brunettes. After all, Dawn had been a brunette, but Randi was a blonde.

They hit it off on their very first date. They went for drinks and then to dinner with some of his friends. They all approved of Randi instantly. When he took her home they sat in the car in front of her house talking. They talked the rest of the evening and into the early light of dawn. The energy flowed so easily between them. They had so much in common. Driving back to his apartment he recognized that Randi was a very special woman. They could talk about nothing or they could easily share their most intimate secrets with one another. Sometimes they would just sit in the same room together. She would needlepoint and he would read. They could sit together for hours and not say a word, yet if one of them left the room it just wasn't the same. Steele considered Randi to be his best friend. There wasn't anything in this world he wouldn't do for her. He quite literally worshipped her.

They both loved the sun and could lie at the pool or on the beach for days at a time. They loved to antique together or rummage through bookstores. In the winter, their joy was to head for the Colorado Mountains and ski together.

It sounded like Charleston would be the perfect place for a great weekend. They would sleep, make love, walk around the city, and lay by the pool. If past experience were any indication, it would renew Steele's heart and refresh his soul.

Randi's new Oldsmobile drove like a dream. When they arrived at the hotel, they were both taken aback. It was pure luxury. Stone Clemons had given them a tremendous gift. When they got settled in their room a basket of fruit with a bottle of wine was delivered. The card was from Stone Clemons. Already, Steele was beginning to feel a little better about First Church.

St. Philip's Episcopal Church Bell Tower could be seen from their hotel. Hand in hand they walked to the historic old church. A woman dressed in an 18th century costume came up to them a short distance from the church and "for a tip" offered to tell them some stories about the Church. Steele handed her five dollars. "There are many stories about St. Philip's Church, but my absolute favorite," her Southern accent was exaggerated. "My absolute favorite is about Vice President Calhoun. You all will notice that our historic cemetery is divided into two sections. The one portion—over there—is for native South Carolinians who are also members of St. Philips Church. The part of our cemetery—there—is for members of St. Philips Church who aren't native South Carolinians."

She continued, "Now during the war of Northern Aggression or, as we also refer to it, the War for Southern Independence, we became quite concerned about the Yankees desecrating the graves of our loved ones. A prime target would be the grave of the Vice President. Now, since he was not a native South Carolinian he had been buried in the St. Philips Members Section of the cemetery. His wife however, was a South Carolinian by birth. She was appropriately buried on the proper side of the Church. When that awful man Sherman began his destructive campaign through our beautiful state, city leaders felt that we needed to protect the Vice President's grave from desecration. So they dug up the Vice President's body and reburied it in the section of the cemetery reserved for native South Carolinians. They knew very well that the Yankees would never think of looking for his grave in that section of the cemetery."

She stopped and looked into their listener's faces. She took the handkerchief she was holding in her hand and touched her eyes as though wiping away a tear. Then she fanned her face with the handkerchief. "Of course," she continued, "when the war was over they dug him up and put him back where he belonged."

Steele and Randi both snickered. The woman gave them a stern look; "You all aren't from around here, are you?"

"No," Steele said apologetically.

"If you want to learn more about our glorious Southern heritage, please go on into the Church. A docent can give you more information." Steele and Randi entered the church and asked a docent for a tour.

When the tour was over, Steele suggested that they take a carriage ride. The carriage driver shared some equally pretentious stories as they rode around the waterfront. Steele was beginning to relax. He was beginning to feel like himself again. He sat back in the carriage and put his arm around Randi. The sun felt warm and healing on his face. Just as they rounded the corner, he felt Randi stiffen.

"What is it?" He asked.

She whispered, "Over there...oh my God, it's too late."

Standing on the curb with most disapproving looks on their faces were William and Virginia Mudd. Their two puffy little daughters were standing with them. William was dressed in a seersucker suit with a bow tie and a straw hat. Mother and daughters were all dressed in matching white outfits. Their jaws dropped at the sight of Steele and Randi in the carriage. Steele could feel their disapproval. He was in shorts and a tee shirt. Randi was in shorts and a halter-top. Her shoulders were bare. Steele managed a wave as the carriage passed them. William tipped his straw hat.

Randi started chuckling, "They looked like they were dressed up for the Fourth of July parade."

Steele chuckled as well, but he felt a shiver run through him. "There must be a devil in hell assigned to me full time," he uttered. "Of all the people to be in Charleston at the same time that I am trying to forget First Church and get some rest."

Randi patted his arm. "Let's go get a drink. It has to be five o'clock somewhere."

They walked down the street toward the Mills House. They walked into the garden and took a seat at one of the tables near the fountain. Steele took Randi's hand and looked into her eyes. He whispered in her ear, "When we finish our drinks let's go back to the hotel. I have something I want to give you."

"Steele Austin," she smiled, "You have some of the best ideas."

Steele saw Randi glance over his shoulder. Her eyes widened with a look of recognition. "Who is it, honey...The Mudds?"

"No," she shook her head. "Steele, I'd swear I just saw Chadsworth Alexander at the bar."

"Oh, really?" Steele turned to look.

Randi grabbed his arm. "Don't look. Steele, he was with this really good-looking black man."

Steele shrugged, "Maybe the man is a business associate."

She shook her head, "No Steele, I don't think so."

"What are you suggesting, Randi?" He asked.

"Oh, nothing...maybe it wasn't him at all." Then she wrinkled her forehead and began that reflective mood that was all too familiar to Steele. For Chadsworth's sake, he needed to get Randi to think about something else.

Their lovemaking was always more tender and less rushed when they were away from home. Steele would invariably feel closer to Randi after they had made love. His favorite thing to do next was to snuggle with her and take a short nap. He loved waking up next to Randi.

They dressed for dinner. Stone Clemons had told them about a fantastic restaurant across from the slave market. He had slipped Steele two hundred dollars and told him to spend every nickel on the dinner. "Go all the way for Randi. You buy her drinks, a nice bottle of wine, and a flaming dessert."

They had a great dinner. It was so romantic. Steele was really beginning to feel like himself again. He realized that he had been so preoccupied with all the problems at the church that he had been ignoring Randi. He apologized to her, "I am so sorry if you have felt lonely. It's just that everything that has been going on has been so overwhelming."

She took his hand. He just couldn't believe his good fortune. "You are so beautiful, Randi. I am the luckiest man in the world."

She smiled, "I love you Steele Austin. No one understands the challenges that you're facing better than me. You're not alone, buddy. We are in this together." They sat there in the candlelight of the restaurant holding hands, staring into each others eyes, and smiling. Just smiling like they had not been able to smile since coming to First Church. The waiter brought the bill. He placed the money Stone gave him on the tray and made a mental note that he would send him a thank you note on the hotel stationary. Steele Austin was floating on air. He was so happy. He helped Randi with her chair, kissed her on the cheek and put his arm around her as they walked toward the door. Just as they were walking out of the restaurant, Steele felt Randi stiffen. His own heart skipped a beat. There stood William and Virginia Mudd.

"Well, Reverend Austin," William held that same straw hat in his hands. "I see that not only do you have a fine taste in women, but in restaurants as well."

Steele shook his hand. He felt himself blush involuntarily. "Yes, we just had a wonderful meal. It was a splurge, but we enjoyed it."

Henry Mudd made no response. Steele could not figure why this one jerk had the power to make him feel like he had just been caught walking out of a brothel. Virginia Mudd did not say a word, but her disapproval was evident.

"Well, our table is waiting on us. I guess we will see you back in Falls City next Sunday." With that, the Mudds walked past them.

"They give me the creeps," Randi shuddered.

"I know." Steele took her hand. "Let's try to forget about them. Let's go back to the room. I have a novel I would like to start."

Steele did not tell Randi, but as they walked toward their hotel he had the eerie sense that someone was watching them or even following them. He glanced back over his shoulder a couple of times, but did not see anyone.

CHAPTER 18

S teele, this is Bishop Petersen." The voice on the other end of the telephone was firm.

"Yes, Bishop, what can I do for you?" Steele knew that this was a man who took being a Bishop very seriously. Perhaps he should have said, "Bishop Sir" or "My Lord Bishop."

"I need to see you," the Bishop continued. "I'm coming to your office tomorrow morning. I'll be there about 11:00 o'clock. Whatever you have scheduled, cancel it. I need about an hour of your time."

"Yes, sir...er, uh...Bishop," Steele fumbled for words. "Would you like me to make reservations for lunch?"

"Father Austin, I regret to tell you that this isn't a social visit." There was a long pause. Steele's heart jumped a beat and he felt his knees grow weak. The Bishop continued, "We need to talk. I've been receiving a lot of complaints about you."

Steele interrupted, "What kind of complaints?"

"We'll go into that tomorrow morning." Again, the Bishop paused. "Complaints I can handle. There's someone in every one of my congregations that is constantly complaining about their priest. For the most part I tell them to talk to their priest or I just choose to ignore them. This is different. I fear that there are some accusations that must be addressed."

"Accusations?" Steele asked in disbelief.

"Yes, accusations -- if proven true they could lead to the loss of your priesthood." The Bishop sounded angry.

"What kind of accusations?" Steele demanded.

The Bishop again took his time in answering. "I don't want to discuss them on the telephone. I will talk with you about them in your office tomorrow. I'm going to be bringing my Chancellor with me. Make sure your Business Manager is also available."

"Can't you give me some clue?" Steele pleaded.

"The fact that you need a clue is encouraging to me. We'll talk about it tomorrow." With that the Bishop hung up the telephone.

Steele didn't sleep well that night. He didn't tell Randi about the telephone call because he didn't want to upset her. All night long, Steele tried to think of possible allegations that could be made against him. He had not violated any of the Church Canons or his ordination vows. He knew that there was a very vocal group that did not support his ministry at First Church, but the overwhelming majority was with him. The numbers certainly proved that.

Steele had heard from the other clergy in the Diocese that Bishop Petersen was a very political animal. He literally won the Bishop's election by planting rumors among the convention delegates that each of the other candidates had questionable pasts. The clergy did not favor him, but the laity liked him. It took sixteen ballots to get a concurrent majority in both the clergy and lay ballots before he could be elected. Most of the clergy who opposed him saw that they were not going to win and simply left the convention rather than be forced to affirm his election. Their absence reduced the necessary number to get the required clergy majority.

He had a reputation as a real control freak. He tried to micro-manage the Diocese and every congregation in it including the personal lives of the clergy. The only ideas he tended to like were his own. The Bishop was known to have a violent temper. He used his anger to intimidate the mission clergy. All were obligated to obey his every whim if they had any hope of getting into a larger congregation or even moving out of the Diocese. There were plenty of stories among the clergy about priests who had gotten on the wrong side of the Bishop. They did not have happy endings.

The Bishop and his Chancellor arrived at exactly 11:00 a.m. They walked into Steele's office and closed the door. The Bishop walked immediately behind Steele's desk and sat down in the Rector's chair. He indicated for Steele and the Chancellor to sit on the other side. It was clear that the Bishop had not missed many meals. He was just about as wide as he was tall. The chair behind the desk towered over him. His feet just barely touched the floor. He took a long look at Steele. Steele felt himself grow very uncomfortable underneath the man's gaze.

Steele glanced over at the chancellor sitting next to him. He was not much taller than the Bishop, but was the polar opposite of the Bishop physically. He was quite thin and appeared almost anemic. He had a shock of red hair that ruled uncontrollably over his thin face. His black rimmed glasses kept sliding down his enormous nose that appeared even larger in profile. The chancellor glanced at Steele and then quickly looked away.

"You understand that Chancellor Hayes is my legal advisor?" The Bishop asked.

"Yes," Steele quietly replied.

"Chancellor Hayes will be taking notes on our conversation. It is imperative that you choose your words carefully. As I told you yesterday on the telephone, the accusations against you are quite serious. Do you understand?" The Bishop increased his gaze.

"Yes," Steele responded.

"Father Austin, the first accusation against you that I am here to investigate is an alleged act of adultery on your part..."

"What?" Steele couldn't keep himself from snickering, "That's absolutely ridiculous. I love my wife and we have a wonderful marriage. I would never do anything to hurt her."

"Adultery is grounds for dismissal as a priest," the Bishop leaned forward across the desk. "I have spoken with several people in your former Diocese. It seems there are rumors of your womanizing in your last parish."

"What? I don't believe anyone said anything like that!" This time Steele's voice was firm and emphatic. "I've never committed adultery with anyone. I am faithful to my wife because I love her and not because of my priesthood. My love for her would not allow me to do such a thing." Steele felt himself growing angry. "Who made these accusations? On what basis are they made? I demand that you give me the names of my accusers."

Bishop Petersen shrugged and motioned with his hands suggesting that Steele calm down. "You know that my sources have to remain confidential."

"No sir," Steele demanded, "Slander and character assassination are not confidential."

This time the Chancellor spoke. "Reverend Austin, you are accused of having a girlfriend right here in Falls City. Two of your parishioners have seen you with her. She is a young blonde girl by the name of Dolly Stuart. They followed her to her place of work; they know that she's..."

Steele interrupted, "She's a car salesman."

"So you don't deny knowing her?" The Chancellor looked at Steele over the top of his glasses.

"She sold Randi and me a car. She works at the Oldsmobile dealership. I've had exactly two conversations with her." Steele was both exasperated and relieved.

"Now listen here, Steele," the Bishop stood up. "The two of you were seen riding in a car together."

"Yes, that's correct. She took me on a test drive of Randi's car before I bought it. That is allowed, isn't it?" Steele stared back.

"Listen to me, young man!" The Bishop exploded, "you're not in a position to get smart with me." He began yelling at Steele at the top of his voice. His manner and his language were abusive. He clearly was a man out of control. He was attempting to control, intimidate, and humiliate Steele. During the Bishop's verbal rampage of several minutes he accused Steele of being an egotist, a materialist, disloyal to the Diocese, as well as one of the priests that was out to undermine his ministry as Bishop. His rampage had nothing at all to do with the accusations that had been made against Steele.

Steele could not believe what he was seeing or hearing. In his entire life he had never been subjected to such verbal abuse. He would have never expected it to come from any human being. The fact that he was watching a Bishop of the Church throw a temper tantrum that would have put a two year old in a romper room to shame, only added to his surprise. Finally, the Chancellor was able to calm the Bishop down and get him to try to compose himself.

Steele leaned back in his chair to watch the entire scene in utter disbelief. After several minutes the Bishop sat back down. Steele broke the tension. "Have you spoken with Ms. Stuart?"

"We wanted to hear your story first," the Bishop acknowledged.

Steele reached for the card file on his desk. He pulled out her business card and handed it to the Bishop. "I have every assurance that when you talk to her she'll confirm my story."

The Bishop handed the card to the Chancellor and motioned for him to make the call. Steele watched the Chancellor on the telephone. Now his anger had turned to embarrassment as the Chancellor asked Dolly Stuart about the nature of her relationship with Reverend Steele Austin. Steele's anger returned when he heard the Chancellor ask her if Reverend Austin had ever said or done anything inappropriate in her presence. When the Chancellor hung up the phone, he handed the card back to Steele and took his seat again. "That one checks out just as he says."

The Bishop looked disappointed as he stared at Steele. "Why on earth would you purchase an Oldsmobile?"

"It was the car my wife liked," Steel shot back.

"Don't you realize that you have people in your congregation who can't afford an Oldsmobile? Hell, boy, most of the clergy in this Diocese can't afford a new car of any kind. Just what were you thinking? There are a lot of people who think your choice of automobiles is in poor taste. Why didn't you choose a good second-hand Chevrolet or Ford? It is not fitting for a priest to drive such a fancy new car."

"I bought my wife the car she wanted and we did it with her money. I really don't think it's anyone's business." Steele was really trying to stay calm. "Is there anything else?" He wanted this Bishop and his so-called Chancellor out of his office.

Again, the Bishop leaned across the desk and took a long hard stare at Steele. "Ask your Business Manager to bring your Discretionary Fund records in here."

Steele walked over to the intercom and did as the Bishop asked. Soon the Business Manager was in his office with the file and checkbook.

"How does this checkbook work?" The Bishop asked the Business Manager.

"Father Austin makes check requests and we issue the checks out of the business office," he replied.

"Can the Rector write checks on his own?" the Chancellor inquired.

"Yes," the Business Manager responded, "but we reconcile the checkbook in the office so we're always aware of the activity."

"Have you seen any checks that have given you cause to believe that the Rector has been engaged in any wrongdoing?" the Chancellor asked.

"Absolutely not," the Business Manager looked equally exasperated. "I consider Discretionary Fund expenditures to be confidential and to be made entirely at the Rector's discretion."

The Bishop picked up the inquiry. "There are members of the congregation that are very suspicious of Father Austin's lifestyle. It has been reported that he has bought an expensive new car, that he has been seen staying in luxury hotels and eating in lavish restaurants. Would you know anything about this?"

"I know that the only checks that my office has issued to the Rector have been those that he is due and not one check out of this Discretionary Fund has ever gone to him," the Business Manager gave Steele a puzzled look.

"Bishop Petersen," Steele tried to stay calm. "My wife's father allowed us to buy her new car out of her trust fund. I assume the rumors of our extravagant life style come from our trip to Charleston last weekend. My Senior Warden, Stone Clemons, made arrangements for the hotel room and the restaurant. They cost us very little."

The Chancellor asked suspiciously, "And your Senior Warden would be willing to confirm that?"

"Of course," Steele shot back. "Do you want to call him as well?"

The Chancellor walked over to the telephone. "I have his number."

While the Chancellor was dialing the number, the Bishop excused the Business Manager, but kept the checkbook and the records open on the desk.

Once again, Steele was humiliated as the Chancellor had his story confirmed by Stone Clemons. The Chancellor then turned to Steele, "Mr. Clemons wants to talk to you."

"What the hell's going on over there, Steele?" Stone asked impatiently.

"The Bishop and his Chancellor are here in my office investigating some accusations that have been made against me," Steele heard his own voice shaking.

"Jesus!" Stone muttered, "Those bastards...I knew they were mean, but I had no idea. Tell that poor excuse for a Bishop that I'm coming right over."

"Bishop," Steele returned to his seat, "Mr. Clemons says he's on his way over."

The Bishop did not look happy. "We don't need him here. What does he think he can do?"

"He's my Senior Warden, Bishop," Steele could see that explanation didn't help.

The Bishop began thumbing through the checkbook and the cancelled checks. He pulled out two and handed them to the Chancellor. He circled one of the deposits on one of the statements and handed it to the Chancellor as well. Just then Steele's secretary interrupted them to announce that the Senior Warden had arrived.

Stone Clemons walked in with a full head of steam, "Just what the hell's going on here, Rufus? This man has done nothing wrong. The only mistake that he's made was accepting our call to come to this priest-eating hellhole. Now just what are you doing to him?"

The Bishop stood up. His anger was also apparent. He shouted back at Stone Clemons, "I didn't invite you here. I have no need of you. This does not concern you. This is between me and one of my priests. Now you can go back to your office. If I should have any need of you, I'll call you."

The tension between the two men exploded. Stone Clemons shouted back, "Now you listen to me you sanctimonious little phony, I am not one of your petrified clergy beholden to you for their next pay check. I didn't vote for you and I didn't sign your certificate of election. As far as I am concerned, you're nothing but a little bully in a purple shirt. As far as that goes, this is not just between you and one of your clergy. Steele's my Rector and I'm his Senior Warden. I've sworn to defend him against all enemies and if necessary that includes you! I'm staying. Do I make myself clear, Rufus?"

The Bishop pounded his fist on the desk. "Sir, I did not give you permission to call me by my first name. You are to address me as the Bishop."

Stone Clemons slapped his hand down on the desk right next to the Bishop's and just as forcefully. "The day you start acting like a Bishop, I'll call you Bishop. Until that day or the Second Coming, whichever arrives first, I'll call you Rufus."

The Bishop glared back at Stone Clemons. It was clear neither man was going to back down. Finally, the Bishop broke the silence. "All right then, Steele, can you explain this sizable check made out to a bail bondsmen and an identical cash deposit on this statement?"

Stone Clemons boiled, "It doesn't take a genius to figure that one out. Hell, the man bailed somebody out of jail and they reimbursed him. I can tell that just by looking at the account and I didn't even know he did it or for whom."

The Bishop's temper was unleashed, "Sir, I didn't ask you! I asked Steele! Now, if you can't stay quiet I'll call the police and have you removed from this office."

Stone Clemons placed both his hands on the desk and leaned across it. He put his face inches away from that of the Bishop. Through gritted teeth he gloated, "I believe before I call anyone, Rufus, I'd check the deed on this property." Stone Clemons smirked. "This parish predates the organization of the Diocese. We hold the deed to this property, not you. If anyone is trespassing, it's you, Sir -- not me."

Steele had heard that the two men hated each other, but he had no idea that it went this deep.

The Bishop looked back at Steele and demanded, "Who?"

"Who?" Steele was dumbfounded.

"Yes...who did you bail out?" the Bishop asked again.

"I'm sorry sir, that is confidential. It's priestly privilege. I can't tell you." Steele felt the Bishop grow even more tense.

"There's a difference between keeping something confidential and keeping secrets. Now, you tell us who you bailed out of jail," the Bishop pounded the table.

"Bishop, I don't make a distinction between secrets and confidentiality. To me they are one and the same. The only way I'll tell you who I bailed out is with the consent of the person involved." Steele waited for the Bishop to respond.

"Then get it," the Bishop sat back down behind the desk. "I suppose you can explain this check to the Cemetery Corporation for two graves."

"Yes, Bishop, I can." Steele swallowed hard, "I bought two graves for Willie and Grace Jones."

The Bishop rolled his eyes and threw his head back against the chair. "You did what? Boy, have you got a death wish? Don't you realize that this is an all-white cemetery?"

"Yes, Bishop, I know that," Steele looked for words to explain, "Willie is dying. I went to see him in the hospital. He's worked for this church since he was a teenager. He considers this church to be his family. His dying wish is that Grace and he be buried in this cemetery."

The Bishop took a deep breath, "Where did you get the money... twelve hundred dollars for two graves?"

"Randi and I made a donation to the Fund to pay for the graves. You will see the deposit on the December statement." Steele felt apologetic. He couldn't figure out why this Bishop was trying to make him feel guilty about making a donation to the Discretionary Fund to help someone in need.

"Okay, I'm beginning to get the picture," the Bishop was much calmer now. He turned in the chair to look out the window. He continued to speak without looking back, "Steele, you're dealing with some real mean-spirited people here. I know that you think you're preaching the gospel and doing good work, but you're challenging a way of life that has existed in these parts since the beginning of this nation. In time it will change some, but it won't change completely in our lifetimes."

The Bishop turned back around and looked at Steele, "I suppose there are some things that I could do to help you, but I'm not going to. It's evident to me that there are those in this congregation who are intent on getting rid of you. I think it's probably too late for me to do anything to help you anyway. I can get another priest for this congregation, but I can't get another congregation. The people here at First Church give me ten percent of my Diocesan Budget. Steele, I have to think about what's best for this Diocese. You have drawn the short end of the stick here, boy. You need to know that your time here has come. They're going to find a way and a reason to get rid of you. You had better start making plans for a move. Things are probably going to get pretty rough here before it's all over. Don't call me for help. You have made your bed—there is nothing I can do."

Stone Clemons started to speak, but the Bishop held up his hand, signaling him to halt. The Bishop and the Chancellor stood up. Steele started to shake the Bishop's hand, but the Bishop just looked at him and gave him a pathetic look. He and the Chancellor walked toward the door. The Bishop stopped at the door and looked back, "Father Austin, I know these people. They'll stop at nothing. They'll do whatever it takes to get rid of you. If I were you, I wouldn't let any grass grow under my feet." With that the two men turned again to walk out the door.

Stone charged toward the door. "Now you listen to me!" he shouted.

The Bishop just sneered at Stone. "Let it go. You're not going to win this one. I don't want to hear anything you have to say." The Bishop then reached for the door handle and closed the door behind him in Stone's face.

Stone Clemons was furious. He paced back and forth the full length of Steele's office. His ramblings were so angry as to be incoherent. When he ran out of steam, he sat down on the edge of Steele's desk and looked back at him. Steele had been staring out of the window. In his wildest nightmare, he had never dreamed that he would see a Bishop act the way this Bishop had just acted. Further, he could not believe that all of his venom had been directed at him.

Stone Clemons interrupted his thoughts. "Father, I want you to know that there are a lot of people in this parish who love you. I want you to know that I love you, but Father, I need to apologize to you. I am so sorry that we ever brought you to this place." Steele looked back at this gentle giant of a man. He was tough as nails, but he had the heart of Christ.

"I know," Steele nodded. "I know."

Rufus Petersen settled back in the soft leather seats of his new black Lincoln Continental. "What do you think, Hayes?"

"Well, it was pretty unpleasant, but at least we got the issues resolved that had been brought to your attention. It is good to know that they were without merit."

The Bishop reached into the storage compartment between the driver and passenger seats. He pulled out a silver flask of brandy. He put the flask to his lips and swallowed. "I don't like him, Hayes."

"There never has been any love loss between you and Clemons."

"Not Clemons, I hate that idiot. No, I mean young Austin. I don't like him. I've known pretty boys like him my entire life. Take away their looks and you have nothing left. I think we should help Howard Dexter and the boys get rid of him."

The Chancellor felt his face flush with embarrassment. "How? Do you think they really need our help? It appears to me that the Rector has pretty well done himself in. It's just a matter of time."

The Bishop pushed the accelerator as he drove up the entrance ramp onto the freeway. "Maybe, but I want to make sure. I want him out of my Diocese. Get to work on it, Hayes. Everyone has some skeletons in their closet. Make some phones calls, hire a private dick if you have to, do whatever it takes. Let's find out just what this frat boy is hiding."

CHAPTER 19

Howard, I simply can't stand anymore." Almeda had spent the last two days telephoning every member of First Church that she trusted. "I'm having a cottage meeting here at my house on Sunday evening. I believe that there will be about fifty of the leaders of the congregation present. Virginia Mudd is having a meeting at her house at the same time. She tells me that every single person she called on her list plans to attend. All together we will have over one hundred people present at the two meetings."

"What about Chadsworth? Is he going to be there?"

Almeda allowed a breath of exhaustion to exhale into the telephone. "No, he will be in Atlanta on business. I have not told him about the meetings nor do I plan to. For some strange reason he has developed an affection for the boy. He will not be happy with me when he finds out what I have done, but I only have the best interests of the church at heart."

"I know Almeda, God bless you for your courage." Howard tried not to sound patronizing. "Some of us men should have stepped up to do what you and Virginia are taking on yourselves. Nevertheless, I am with you."

"Then you will attend and help me lead the meeting?"

"Nothing could keep me away. I agree with you. Something has to be done. The Bishop seems to think his hands are tied right now, but he is willing to go along with whatever the leaders of the congregation want. He can't overstep his canonical bounds, but he will stand with us when it comes decision time. My wife and I will both be there. See you on Sunday evening."

Almeda spent all of Sunday afternoon preparing for the meeting. She employed her gardener to help her set up the folding chairs she rented from the local supply house. As the time for the meeting drew closer, she became more determined to do something about Steele Austin.

Howard Dexter and his wife were the first to arrive. His daughter and her husband came as well. While his son-in-law had not been to Church since his wedding, his daughter did attend on Christmas and Easter. They too were angry and wanted to do their part to save the Church. Soon Almeda's house was filled with clusters of people who stood around in hushed whispers shaking their heads and then nodding in agreement.

"I want to thank each of you for your attendance this evening. In order to get us started on the right foot I have asked Howard Dexter to lead us in a prayer. Will you all please find a seat?"

When everyone was seated, Howard held up his Prayer Book. "Normally I would read a prayer from the Prayer Book, but since this is an especially difficult situation facing the congregation I have written one of my own. Now you all know I'm not a priest, but here goes:

Lord, thou doest always watch over thy children when they are in trouble. Our beloved Church is in trouble. So, just as you guided the children of Israel through the waters of the Red Sea we now beseech thee to guide us through these turbulent times. For thine is the power and the glory.

The end of the prayer was marked with a resounding "Amen" from every person present. Almeda asked Howard to remain at the front of the room with her as she began to speak. "I simply cannot tell you how much it grieves me to have to invite you all into my home for this meeting." She waved her hand in front of her face in an attempt to get more air. She reached down and pulled a tissue from the box on the table in front of her and dabbed at her eyes. Her lips trembled as she continued. The list of concerns that I have about the current Rector and the concerns that have been brought to me by other members of the congregation appears to grow daily."

There was a general murmuring of agreement around the room. "You all are well aware of some of the most glaring. This man has invited people into First Church that simply do not belong there. He is doing work in the community that is not in keeping with the mission of our congregation." She made some gestures of frustration. "I mean, can you believe this Soup Kitchen he started? Awful, it's simply awful. And now he plans to have this homosexual service..."

Howard interrupted, "Almeda, what you say so far is true and it's certainly representative of the sentiments of my family and me, but the people here are entitled to know that these things have all occurred over the objections of the Vestry leadership. We have all tried to talk to this boy, but…but, I don't mean to sound disrespectful, but he is just bull headed. He insists on doing things his way. He is his own worst enemy."

A man sitting on the front row asked, "What about the Bishop? Has Bishop Petersen talked to him?"

Howard nodded, "It pains me to tell you that this priest appears to have no respect for his Bishop. Both the Bishop and his Chancellor tried to reason with the Rector, but he rebuffed their efforts by calling in the Senior Warden. We all know how Stone Clemons feels about our beloved Bishop, don't we?" Again, heads nodded as whispered conversation accelerated. Howard and Almeda gave each other a quick glance and a smile of satisfaction crossed their faces.

When the whispers began to quiet, Almeda spoke. "It is my understanding that at the service for the gays Mistuh Austin has invited the *Negara choir* to sing. Can you imagine that? But there is so much more. Howard, tell them about the Discretionary Fund."

Howard grimaced as he shook his head, "I wasn't going to bring that up Almeda, but perhaps the leaders of the congregation should be fully informed. Ladies and Gentlemen, I fear that the Rector just might be a thief!" Howard stood swallowing hard as though he were choking on the very words he was being forced to utter. "I have known since he arrived that he was a man who had an inordinate love of money. The conflict that he and I had over the money he wanted the Church to spend on the Rectory is well known to all of you. I love this parish just like all of you and I feel a special responsibility to make sure that the funds of the Church are not wasted. But let's put all that aside for the moment. Some of the most glaring evidence can be seen in the Rector's lifestyle. He and his wife appear to be living beyond their means. You all have seen the new car they bought. Well, there's more…oh, there's so much more."

"Like what?" a woman shouted.

"Almeda, you tell them. It just hurts me too much to have to report these matters to these good folks."

Almeda dabbed her eyes with a fresh tissue. "They have been seen dining in expensive restaurants that my Chadsworth and I only frequent on very special occasions. Beyond that, they have spent weekends in luxurious hotels in Charleston, Savannah, and Atlanta. God only knows where else. This all caused the Bishop and the Chancellor to do an audit of the Rector's funds."

"What did they find?" asked several people.

"Howard, will you answer that question?"

Shaking his head again while looking down at the floor Howard replied in a voice that was just barely audible, "I can only tell you that there is an ongoing investigation."

"What did he say? The Rector is under investigation for mismanagement of funds. Oh…no." The room exploded with anger. "Are our contributions safe? Are they being used for the purposes intended?"

Again, Howard answered in a soft voice. "The answers to all those questions will be answered when the investigation is complete."

A dark headed young man stood, "I am very active in the Coalition for Christian Values. I think that you need to know that one of my staff approached Reverend Austin about making our research on political candidates available to the congregation. Now mind you we are not a partisan group. We have simply determined where the various candidates stand on moral and political issues that are important to Christians. We believe it is our solemn duty to make this information available so that Christian voters can mark their ballots accordingly. Can you believe that Reverend Austin refused to let us simply lay the papers with the results of our research on a table at the entrance to the Church? He was absolute in forbidding us to distribute this valuable information that would only strengthen the work of Christ and His Church. It leads me to wonder if you have any evidence that he might be using Church funds to support a political party that might be more in keeping with his liberal bias?"

"Thanks for bringing that to our attention," Howard smiled. I was not aware that Mistuh Austin had forbidden your organization to make this extremely helpful information available to our voters. I will certainly advise the Bishop and encourage him to expand the boundaries of his investigation."

"Where can we get the results of your research?" several people asked.

"Oh, I have copies with me." The man quickly opened his briefcase and began passing the papers out.

Mrs. Gordon Smythe stood. "As you all know, I am the President of the Altar Guild. I am not comfortable with this meeting. What we are doing here does not strike me as being very Christian. I have had my disagreements with Mistuh Austin, but I have addressed them directly to him. He has responded one way or another and we continue to work together. The members of the Altar Guild take a vow to be loyal to the Rector whoever he might be. I believe that any issues we have with this Rector should be taken up with him personally and not in the context of a secret meeting. Howard, Almeda, just what do you expect us to do here tonight? What is the purpose of this meeting?"

Howard Dexter responded, "I'm not rightly sure just what we can do, but I know that we have to do something. I am convinced that this man is destroying our Church and I for one am not going to stand for it. His leadership style is not compatible with our way of doing things. I for one believe the man has to go."

Almeda walked up to Mrs. Smythe so she could look her directly in the eye. "Did you realize that the Rector plans to remove the Mudd Family Prayer Desks from the Church?"

She shook her head.

"Well, he does. Those desks were given in memory of Henry Mudd's great grandparents. Colonel Mudd was a decorated veteran in the war for Southern Independence. Those Prayer Desks have been sitting in their rightful place in the Church for almost one hundred years. Now, this new Rector wants to remove them in order to make more room for the choir. I understand he is even thinking about bringing in drums and horns to sit where our lovely Prayer Desks currently sit. Can you imagine such as that at First Church?"

Mrs. Gordon Smythe sat down.

A man standing in the back of the room by the front door spoke. "I have only been here a few minutes, but I have heard enough to turn my stomach. I want all of us to get in our cars right now and go over to the Rectory and simply tell the man he is fired."

"Well, it's not quite that simple," Howard Dexter responded. "Rectors cannot be fired. The Bishop can remove them if they are found guilty of sexual immorality, heresy, or some other canonical violation."

"Well?" the man shouted.

"Well what?" Howard asked.

"Is there any evidence of such? The man echoed.

Howard nodded, "I hope everyone present can understand just how difficult this is for both Almeda and me. As some of you know, the Mudds are hosting a concurrent meeting at their home at this very hour as well." He paused, "but to answer your question...there have been rumors of infidelity on the Rector's part. There have even been rumors that his wife is a bit of a loose woman."

There was an audible expression of shock and disgust around the room. Again, Howard shot Almeda a knowing glance. "It is worse though, much, much worse."

"It can't get any worse, Howard!" A woman with tears covering her cheeks stood shouting and shaking her fist.

"I wish that were true." Howard's eyes brightened knowingly. "Have you all noticed the Rector's affection for...well, uhh...for lack of a better way to say it? Have you all noticed the Rector's affection for members of the homosexual persuasion?"

"Disgusting!" The woman squealed. "You don't mean it. I will not have a gay priest teaching my children. It simply is not natural. It is a violation of God's law. If this priest is gay then the Bishop can get rid of him or we will!"

Again, there were general murmurs of agreement from all present.

Almeda gestured with her hands for all to calm down, "We are not accusing anyone of anything. We are just telling you that the Bishop is conducting an investigation and there is speculation fueled by rumors."

"I've heard enough," the man by the door shouted. "What do you want us to do?"

Almeda picked up a stack of papers and handed them to a couple of men to distribute. Howard held up one of the sheets. The ultimate answer will be found on this sheet. In the interim and until the Bishop concludes his investigation, I have set up an account at my bank to receive the donations you intend for First Church. I would suggest that you not put them in the offering plate or mail them to the Church Office. I would suggest that you send them to my bank. I will hold them in the designated account until such time these matters are resolved. At that time, I will then turn your deposited donations over to the Church."

"You can count on me," the man replied. "Do you have extra copies? I want to give them to some of my friends."

"Yes," Howard answered. "We can give each of you all the copies you need, but I would strongly suggest that you not publicize the plan outlined on this paper. Share it only with people you can trust. Our cause is not hopeless. First Church has been here a long time. With your help it will be here for hundreds of years in the future. Just remember that what we are going to do is absolutely necessary. We did not choose it. The Rector has forced our hand. We have no choice. I believe it is the only way we can save our beloved Church. We all want to do what is best for our Church. Now, are there any final questions? If not, Almeda is going to lead us in a closing prayer. I would suggest that we come out from our chairs and form one large circle in the room. I am not usually comfortable with this sort of thing, but I am going to suggest that we all hold hands as Almeda leads us in prayer. We need God's help and we need His blessing on this most important work that we are doing in His name. Christ has entrusted His Church to our care and care for it we must."

The people moved as Howard asked to form a large circle. Clearly they were uncomfortable holding hands. Some of the men moved so that they stood between two women. Almeda looked around the room, "Like Howard, I would normally read a prayer from the Prayer Book." Again she wiped the tears from her eyes. "But you are going to have to just allow me to read the words that are so heavy on my heart. I have written them on this piece of paper." She began,

Sweet Jesus, our beautiful Church has been here for almost two hundred years. It has been a happy place for baptisms and weddings. Our services have always been conducted with grace and dignity. Please, please God, help us to make it a place of grace and dignity again. Please help us make it a happy place.

Her prayer ended with many solemn and several tearful "Amens." Several of the women came to the tissue box in order to wipe the tears from their eyes. Some hugged each other. A heavy veil hung over the room. As the people started to leave there were general pats on the back for Howard and expressions of gratitude to Almeda. Howard caught Almeda's eye. She gave him a "thumbs-up."

CHAPTER 20

Outside old First Church the television camera crews ran their cables from the remote vans to inside the church. Steele had consented to have the service on television, but none of them wanted to broadcast the service in its entirety. They just wanted to be able to broadcast some live newsbreaks. Steele went into the Sacristy to put on his vestments. He and the other clergy had decided that they would vest for the candlelight vigil. That way they could lead the congregation into the church and begin the service as soon as all were inside.

"You've got a lot of guts, preacher," Steele turned to see Chief Sparks and a couple of uniformed officers standing in the Sacristy door.

"Then why are my knees shaking?" Steele returned to the vesting closet. "Do you think there is going to be any trouble, Chief?"

"I don't have to tell you that there are a lot of people that are real unhappy with you right now." The Chief looked back over his shoulder at the uniformed officers. "Get the dogs and do a sweep of the building. Once you've secured the building, station an officer at each door. Everyone is to enter through the front doors. No one comes in or out except through those doors. You two take your positions at the front. Frisk anyone who is acting suspicious. Once they are in the church, no one leaves until the service is over."

With that the two officers departed. "Steele, I'm not particularly excited about what you are doing tonight. I have some gay officers, but I really don't have a lot of tolerance for queers."

Steele interrupted, "Aw, Chief, not you too. This is a healing service for people who are very sick."

"Don't go getting your bowels in an uproar, Reverend," the Chief smiled. "I'm with you, but not for the reasons that you might want."

"Then why?" Steele inquired.

"Because you are doing something here tonight that most of the numb-skulls in this town can't see," the Chief patted Steele on the back. "You are bringing the black and white preachers in this town together.

I've lived in Falls City my entire life and in my thirty years as a police officer I've never seen the black ministers and white ministers even say one prayer together. Tonight, that's all going to change. Steele, every law enforcement officer in this town would have an easier job if the blacks and whites in this community could work closer together on worthwhile projects."

Steele was surprised, "Chief, I never realized that the black and white clergy associations have never done anything together."

"Hell, the churches in this town are more segregated than anything else." The Chief looked like he was looking for a place to spit and then thought better of it. I integrated the police force thirty years ago and no one said a word, but the churches are still segregated. "Damn it, even the dead are segregated in this town. Look at the graves in your own churchyard."

"Yes," Steele snickered, "I was reminded of that rather forcefully just yesterday."

Steele finished putting on his vestments and then picked up his Prayer Book. He turned full face to look at Chief Sparks. "Are we in danger? Do you think anyone will try to disrupt our service?"

"There is no way I can tell you for sure." The Chief shrugged, "The unhappiness over this project tonight is not confined to this church. It's now community-wide. I fear it might be statewide. We're ready for whatever might happen. Let's just hope that everyone stays calm."

"Thanks, Chief," Steele shook his hand. "You know that I wouldn't be doing this if I didn't think it was the right thing to do."

The Chief nodded and together they walked into the church. A few people were taking their seats. Others were standing in the back talking. The two officers were stationed at the front door with a large dog. The Chief and Steele walked between them and out into the night air. They walked the four blocks to the plaza at the end of Main Street. Steele estimated there were about two hundred people gathered there. The march organizers had started to line the people up across the breadth of the street. Some were holding banners and posters they intended to carry. The news photographers and television cameras were moving about the crowd. A couple of reporters were doing on-camera interviews with some of the marchers.

The clergy all lined up at the front of the procession. The large clock in the Village Square struck the six o'clock hour. A silence fell over the crowd. Steele waited for the sixth ring of the clock chimes. He took the microphone and asked God's blessings on their march and their service. There were a few "Amens" both during his prayer and at its conclusion. Then they moved forward down the street toward the steeple of First Church.

The participants walked in silence. Not a word was spoken. The only sound was the shuffling of their feet on the brick pavers. A block or so down the street they encountered a group holding signs condemning homosexuality. Some of the signs had Bible quotes on them. Others proclaimed AIDS as God's punishment on homosexuals. There was some jeering from those on the sidewalks, but not a single participant in the march responded.

The parade continued another block and then another. Out of the corner of his eye, Steele spotted Duke leaning against a lamp pole. Steele looked straight at Duke and made eye contact. He gave Duke a slight wave of his hand. Duke just stared back. No wave, no nod of the head, he just stood there staring at Steele.

First Church was just one block away. Steele rehearsed again the words of welcome he would use to open the service once everyone was inside. Then he felt a change in the atmosphere around him. The black ministers on either side of him stiffened. He felt an even greater hush fall over the already silent marchers. Then the black minister on his left whispered, "Just keep your eyes forward. Don't look at them. Don't pay them any attention." For just a few seconds Steele was confused about what was happening. His mind just couldn't wrap around all the tension he was sensing in the marchers. Then, he saw them. There they were, standing on the sidewalk dressed in white robes. Their faces were covered. One of them was holding the Confederate Flag. There must have been thirty or forty of them. Steele had seen pictures. He had even seen them on the nightly news, but never had he seen them in person.

The Klan members did not say a word. They just stood there. Steele could feel their piercing stares right through their hoods. As he and the other clergy passed them, several of them stepped off the sidewalk and into the street. Steele's heart jumped a beat. The adrenaline kicked in. He knew beyond a shadow of a doubt that he was about to confront some people who really wanted to harm him and all those around him.

"Don't look at them, Reverend Austin," the minister on his left whispered firmly. He kept his eyes forward. "They aren't going to come over here. They just want to scare us and get a closer look at us."

Suddenly several police officers appeared. They walked between the marchers and the Klan members. The Klan members returned to the sidewalk. No words were spoken.

As the front of the procession walked through the front gates of First Church, Steele saw Howard Dexter's silver Mercedes parked on the street opposite the church. "Well, he said he was going to be here." Steele thought to himself. "Hope the bigot gets his eyes full."

There were about two hundred people already in the church. With the addition of the two hundred marchers, the choirs, and the clergy, Steele estimated that about five hundred people would be present for the service.

As the service unfolded, Steele was struck by the fact that well over half the congregation were people of color. In addition, there were some colorful people. There were those who had just about every visible body part pierced. There was every color of dyed hair one could want. Three or four very large women particularly amused Steele. Of course, Steele knew they were not women, but he couldn't help but think to himself, "The First Church Altar Guild would be so proud."

When it came time for people to come to the altar rail to be anointed with oil and have prayers offered for themselves or a loved one, the emotions in the room reached a peak. Steele was having a hard time keeping his composure. A nice looking middle aged couple came to the rail. They were holding hands. They looked up at Steele, "Please Father, pray for our son Duncan. He has AIDS. He is dying." Together, they dissolved into tears. They laid their heads on the altar rail. They put their arms around each other. Their bodies were shaking with great sobs. Steele knelt down on the floor in front of them. He fought back his own tears and that damn familiar lump in his throat. He knelt there quietly waiting for their tears to calm. The black gospel choir and the Gay Men's Chorus were singing "Amazing Grace" in the background. Steele lifted each of their faces so that he could look in their eyes. He put his thumb in his oil stock and made the sign of the cross on each of their foreheads. He managed an encouraging smile. Steele laid his hands on their heads and prayed, "For your beloved son Duncan, I now anoint you with oil asking God Almighty to relieve Duncan of all his pain and sickness and to restore him the blessings of health."

"Thank you, Father." They stood and put their arms around each other again. They leaned across the rail and together gave Steele a hug. He returned their embrace. "Thank you, Father. God bless you, Father."

Steele stood there watching them walk away. Then he heard a child ask, "Why are we here, Mama? What is this place? I want to go home. No -- let's go home."

A young girl of about nineteen or twenty was kneeling at the rail in front of Steele. She had dyed her hair a strange shade of orange. Steele noticed that her nose and lips were both pierced. Her right ear was pierced from top to bottom. She was holding a little girl with the brightest blue eyes. Her mother had braided her blonde hair. She looked up at Steele. He looked at both of them, puzzled.

"We both have it. Will you pray for both of us?" Tears dropped down the young woman's cheeks.

"Why are you crying, Mama? Are you sad, Mama? Please, Mama, let's go home!" The little girl buried her face on her mother's shoulder.

The tears flooded out of Steele's eyes. He tasted the saltiness. His vision was blurry. He could hardly see. He tried to speak, but couldn't, so he just nodded his head. Steele wiped his face on the sleeve of his robe. Once again, he knelt down before the little girl and her mother. He put his thumb in the oil stock and made the sign of the cross on each of them. He put his hands on them and began to pray, "Lord Jesus Christ, you gathered little children in your arms and blessed them. Put your arms around this mother and this child. Bless them. Remove the sickness from their bodies. Grant them the blessing of health."

Steele leaned forward and kissed the little girl on the cheek. "He kissed me, Mama. Is he a nice man, Mama?"

The woman nodded. The little girl stretched out her arms and hugged Steele. Then she planted a big kiss on Steele's lips."

"Thank you, Father," the mother whispered.

"Thank you, Father," the little girl squealed with laughter.

One by one they came. Virtually every person in the congregation came forward asking prayers for themselves or a loved one. This part of the service lasted for almost an hour. The choirs continued to sing through it all. No one left. Every member of the congregation stayed for the final blessing.

Steele and the other clergy returned to the Sacristy. No one said anything. Each found a place to sit. When all the chairs were taken the remainder of the clergy just sat down on the floor. They sat in silence together. They did not look at each other. Those in the chairs leaned forward, burying their faces in their hands. Those on the floor wrapped their arms around their legs and hid their faces in their knees. Then one by one they broke down. One by one these men of prayer let out their own pain and suffering. The sound of great sobs filled the little room. Their bodies shook. Together, they cried. And in their crying, they gave each other strength.

CHAPTER 21

Steele and Randi were the last people to leave the church. The parking lot was deserted, but then so were the streets around the church. Steele took Randi's hand as they walked to the parking lot, "I didn't realize just how late it had gotten."

They pulled out of the church parking lot and started south on Main Street toward home. Just as they were crossing over the bridge above the falls, a car pulled up beside them. The car swerved toward them. Steele honked his horn at the car. Randi shouted, "Steele, that guy doesn't have his lights on."

Steele honked his horn all the more and flashed his own lights, but to no avail. The car pulled ahead just a bit and then swerved toward their front fender. Steele had to pull toward the bridge railing in order to keep from being hit by the car. The driver of the other car persisted. Steele pulled even closer to the bridge railing. It was at that point that his left tires were now up on the curb and the rail was but inches away. The car continued to swerve toward them. It was evident that the driver intended to run them off the bridge. Randi screamed, "He's trying to kill us!"

In one desperate move just as the car swerved at them for the final time, Steele put on his brakes and brought his car to a stop. The other car pulled ahead of them and then stopped. The driver turned on his inside dome light. He yelled some profanities at them out his window while saluting them with his middle finger. Steele saw the now familiar Klan robe lying over the back of the passenger seat. Randi started screaming and crying. She was hysterical. Another car came up over the bridge and the other driver sped off. Steele tried to memorize the license plate while trying to calm Randi.

He picked up his car phone and called Chief Sparks. "Chief, someone just tried to run us off the Main Street Bridge over the falls."

"Are you sure?" the Chief asked.

"Positive!"

"Did you get the plate numbers?"

Steele repeated the numbers he had memorized.

"Where are you now?"

"We're on our way home."

"I'll run the plates. Call me after you get home." With that the Chief hung up the telephone.

They pulled into the driveway of the Rectory. "Honey, do you think we're going to be safe here tonight?" Randi looked terrified.

"I think so." Steele tried to reassure his wife and himself. "I think it was just a crackpot trying to scare us."

When they walked into the house the telephone was ringing. Randi picked it up. She began crying and became hysterical again. Steele walked over and took the phone from her. The voice on the end was spouting forth an entire string of profanities. "Who are you? What do you want?" Steele demanded.

"Oh, it's you, nigger lover." The voice was disgusting. "Do you know the only thing worse than a nigger lover?"

Steele shouted back into the phone, "Leave us alone!"

He was about to hang up the phone when he heard the voice continue, "The only thing worse than a nigger lover is nigger queer lover. You don't deserve to live."

"Are you threatening me?" Steele was really getting angry.

"This is no threat. You're a dead man! You hear me? You're a dead man! That's not a threat. It's a promise!" Then the phone went silent.

Now both Steele and Randi were shaking. Steele walked through the house to make sure all the doors and windows were locked. He then went over to the bar and poured both of them a drink. They went into the living room. Randi was still crying and shaking. Steele put his arm around her and continued to try to calm her. It was difficult since he was shaking as much as she was. Just then they heard a window break out in the dining room. It was followed by a big thud. Randi screamed. Steele jumped up and ran to the dining room. He turned on the lights to discover that a brick had been thrown through the window. He looked out the window and saw a white pickup truck pull down the driveway. There were two men in Klan robes standing in the back of the truck giving a rebel yell. Just then he heard a gun go off. Steele hit the floor. Randi screamed from the other room, "Was that a gunshot? Steele, are you all right?"

Steele shouted back, "Stay where you are!" He remained on the floor until the sound of the truck and the men yelling had disappeared. Then he crawled back into the living room. Steele called the Chief to tell him about the phone call, the brick, and the gunshot.

"I'm going to send one of my men over there right now. He'll check on things and then spend the night in front of your house." The Chief was reassuring. "We'll catch them, Steele. Tell Randi not to worry."

In just a matter of two or three minutes a black and white pulled into the driveway. The young officer walked around the house and then rang the doorbell. Steele showed him the window in the dining room and recounted the events. The officer told them to go on to bed. He would keep an eye on things.

They went to bed, but they were both so anxious it was clear they were going to have a difficult time sleeping. Randi pleaded, "Steele, I think I'm going to need something to help me. I need a sleeping pill or an anti-anxiety agent or something." Then she began to cry and shake again.

Steele called the primary care physician with their HMO. "No, I can't prescribe any medicine for you. I will have to see you in my office. Call the appointment number tomorrow morning and they'll get you in."

Steele tried to explain the urgency of their situation again, but the physician would not relent. Steele then called the Chief again to see if he knew a doctor who would give Randi something to help her through the night.

"Ol' Doc Walker will do it. I'll call him and explain your need." The Chief hung up the phone. Five minutes later he called back. "Doc Walker is on his way over to your house. I have radioed the officer in front of your house. He'll be looking for the Doc."

"Thanks, Chief. Thanks so much. You're a good friend."

"Just tell Randi she is safe. We'll catch these guys." With that, the Chief bid them a good night.

Doc Walker came and gave Randi something to help her sleep. He gave Steele a package of samples that they both could use. He told them they were for anxiety. It wasn't long until Randi was asleep. Steele took one of the pills and lay down in the bed next to her. He couldn't help but wonder just what he had gotten her into in this so-called church. He was feeling really guilty for bringing her here.

Steele awoke first the next morning. He looked out their bedroom window and saw that that the police cruiser was still there. He went downstairs and walked out to the officer's car. "How about coming in for a cup of coffee?"

"That would be great, Reverend Austin. I have to confess that I wouldn't mind getting out of the car and stretching my legs."

Steele was struck by just how young the officer was. Steele made the coffee while he used the guest bathroom to freshen up. They sat opposite one another at the breakfast table in the sunroom. "That was a great thing that you did for us last night, Reverend Austin."

Steele was puzzled, "Us?"

"Yes, I'm gay." The officer looked for a reaction on Steele's face.

"Does the Chief know?" Steele inquired.

"Yes, there are about a half-dozen of us on the force. The Chief has told us that as long as we don't flaunt it and we stay out of trouble we have his support." The officer smiled and took a sip of his coffee.

"We've talked before haven't we?"

"Yes, I am Steve Forrester. I helped you with a newspaper problem."

"Now, I remember. I'm sorry I didn't recognize your voice last night."

The telephone rang and Steele picked it up. It was the voice again. "Listen you nigger lover. We missed you last night on purpose. Next time we won't miss." Then the line went dead again.

Steele stood there with the phone in his hand. Officer Forrester came over, took it from him, and put it to his ear. He then hung it up. "What did they say?"

Steele repeated the message. The officer dialed a number. No response. Then he dialed the Chief. "Then Chief said to tell you that he will be here in just a few minutes."

When Chief Sparks arrived he looked at the broken glass and brick on the dining room floor. He then walked into the kitchen. Steele poured him a cup of coffee. He gave Steele a long look.

"We ran the plates. They belong to a newspaper reporter. He has an alibi for last night." The Chief sipped his coffee and then leaned back against the kitchen counter. With your permission, we can put a wire on your telephone and try to trace the calls. My hunch, though, is that they're using a pay phone. He looked over at Officer Forrester. "Did you dial Star 69?" The officer nodded his head.

The chief thought for a moment. "Where's Randi?"

"Still sleeping. The doctor gave her something to help her sleep last night. It knocked her right out." Steele sounded relieved.

"I can put a body guard on both you and Randi for a couple of days, but I don't have the personnel to keep a cruiser in the driveway." The Chief paused for a long moment. "Steele, we're dealing with some real mean-spirited people here. They like being in control and you aren't doing things their way."

The Chief began to sound remorseful, "I can't guarantee your safety. I can't guarantee anyone's safety, but I don't think these people are going to be stopped. They've decided that you have to go. You need to know that I have every confidence that they will do whatever they have to do to get rid of you."

Steele tried to absorb what the Chief was saying. It was as though he was talking about someone else. He didn't see himself as a threat. And Randi was certainly no threat. She is so sweet. She would never harm anyone. This isn't real. He just didn't want to believe that the Chief was talking about him. He had to be talking about someone else.

"Who do you think they are, Chief? Are any of them members of First Church?" Steele did not want to believe that any of his own church members would do such a thing, but he already knew how angry some of them were with him.

The Chief looked at the young officer. "Steve, what do you think?"

"Clearly the Klan is involved," the officer responded. "I don't know if any of them belong to First Church."

The Chief shot back, "We've always suspected that there were some connections between the Klan and some of the big wheels in your church. There have just been too many instances of Klan violence against someone who had crossed one of the VIP's at First Church. I've always suspected that little jerk Howard Dexter used the Klan to settle his accounts. I just haven't been able to prove it."

Steele poured himself another cup of coffee. He stood there looking at the Chief and Steve Forrester. "What are you guys trying to tell me?"

"Son," the Chief walked over and put both his hands on Steele's shoulders. He looked him directly in the eye. "For your family's sake...for

Randi's sake...for your own safety...shake the dust of this place off your feet and leave this city."

Steele could not hold back the tears running down his cheeks, "How soon? How much time do I have to look for another job?"

The Chief thought for a moment and then shrugged, "If I were you I would put Falls City in my rearview mirror just as soon as possible."

CHAPTER 22

The Creekwood Christian Church was filled to capacity. A strong aroma of carnations and mums filled the air. The floral tribute surrounding Willie's open casket was indeed impressive. On a small table near the casket was a silver-framed picture of Willie and Grace taken at their last wedding anniversary.

Willie's body was dressed in a dark blue suit. He was wearing a maroon tie on his crisp new white shirt. Grace wanted to make sure that Willie was put to rest in proper style. She had bought Willie a new suit.

Creekwood Church was well kept by the congregation. The white frame structure was freshly painted. There was a well-maintained red carpet throughout the building. The windows were colored glass, alternating panes of gold, violet, and green. The only stained glass window was a rose window above the front entry to the church. The windows, while attractive, paled in comparison to the Tiffany window above the altar at First Church.

Steele Austin sat in one of the three oversized chairs directly behind the large wood pulpit and in front of the choir. The two pastors of Creekwood Christian Church sat on either side of him. His traditional surplice and cassock was subdued next to the colorful robes worn by the two clergy. Their robes had a definite African influence; the colors were bright and uplifting.

The choir was filled to overflowing as well. On one side of the chancel there was a grand piano. On the opposite side there was an electronic organ. Below on the floor of the church, but off to the side, a small orchestra had been assembled. There was a set of trap drums, a couple of guitars, a bass, and a synthesizer. The combination of the music moved the congregation to utter words of praise. A few would lift their hands while others were content to sit in their pews and simply sway to the beat of the music with their eyes shut.

Surprisingly, the first four pews directly opposite the family were filled with white faces. Sitting prominently on the first pew across from Grace were Mr. and Mrs. Howard Dexter. The entire First Church Vestry and their spouses accompanied them. Almeda Alexander was dressed in black. She was wearing a full black picture hat that framed her face. The brief veil hanging down over her eyes could give a passerby the impression that she was the fashionably dressed widow in mourning.

The funeral liturgy began with the piano, organ, synthesizer and orchestra building on each other to a sound that was both stirring and deafening. The choir rose to its feet and began to clap and sing. "Jesus --- Jeee----sus, Jesus is here right now." The congregation then rose to its feet and began to clap and sing with the choir. The first four rows of white faces all politely, but uncomfortably stood. The music and the entire atmosphere moved Steele. The three clergy remained seated until the Senior Pastor stood to go to the pulpit. The younger Associate Pastor next to Steele stood. He lifted Steele up by the arm. The young associate held up one of his hands in an act of praise. He put the other arm around Steele's waist. They began to sway in time to the music.

The Senior Pastor sang into the microphone, "Jesus ----- Jeeesus, wrap your arms around your child Willie." With that the music became even louder than Steele thought possible. The choir echoed the words of the Senior Pastor. The congregation exploded with shouts and rhythmic clapping. Steele had heard of a church rocking, but he had never experienced it for himself. The emotion in the room was cathartic. He happened to glance down at the four rows of white faces. Every one of them was looking at him.

Steele was invited to say a few words about Willie. He spoke of Willie's lifetime of faithful service to First Church. He told them about visiting Willie and Grace in the hospital and their desire to be buried in the First Church Cemetery. He repeated Willie's words that he felt like the people at First Church had treated him like family all these years. He wanted to be buried with his family. Steele concluded, "Today Willie is in that place where the saints suffer with only one affliction." He paused and looked directly at the members of his congregation occupying the first four rows. "In Heaven there is only one disease—one ailment— one disability that afflicts all the saints." He paused again for effect. "In heaven," he concluded, "everyone is color blind!"

A thunder of applause rose up from the congregation and the people all came to their feet with shouts of praise. The organ and the piano softly played a gospel rendition of "Jesus Loves the Little Children." The choir rose to its feet and shouted out alternately "red and yellow—black—and—white—precious, yes, precious, O Lawd they are precious—precious, precious in yo' sight."

The Senior Pastor delivered the eulogy. All the time that he was speaking, the organ played quietly in the background. At particularly significant moments the organ would get louder and the choir, piano, and orchestra would interrupt the sermon with chords of approval. Sometimes the Senior Pastor spoke, sometimes he whispered, sometimes he shouted, and sometimes he sang. Steele sat in complete admiration of just how well this Pastor had mastered black, southern oratory.

The Senior Pastor spoke of Willie's faithfulness to the church. He visited the sick and the elderly. He did repair work on elderly people's houses. He and Grace had led a Bible Study in their home for young people for well over thirty years. Steele was not surprised to hear that Willie was a tither. The Pastor emphasized that Willie was a true ten percent tither!

Steele found the viewing of the body at the end of the service to be his undoing. The three clergy stood at the head of the casket as each person in the church filed by to view Willie's body. The last to come by was Grace. Her two grandsons held her up. They were identical twin boys. He guessed them to be about six feet four inches tall and two hundred pounds or more of solid muscle. They looked to be about seventeen years of age, but they let out great sobs as they helped their grandmother say a final farewell to her husband.

The service and the viewing had lasted well over an hour and a half. It took another half an hour to get the very long funeral procession from Creekwood to the First Church Cemetery. Every mourner that was in the church filled the area around Willie's freshly dug grave. Every mourner, that is, with a black face. The only white faces in the entire crowd were Steele, his wife Randi, and the white police officer Chief Sparks had assigned to guard them.

Grace had instructed that the mortuary lower Willie's body into the grave while she was still there. She then took a shovel and tossed in the first few spades full of dirt. She handed the shovel to several members of her family to do the same. Steele had promised Grace that he would stay at the grave until the task was completed. She could then have every confidence that Willie was at rest in the First Church Cemetery.

As Grace was leaving the cemetery, she approached Steele and Randi and hugged both of their necks. She planted a big kiss on Steele's cheek. "I want you to meet my grandsons. They made their granddad so proud. He never missed one of their football games." Steele knew that the boys were local football heroes. "These boys are gonna be police officers. Chief Sparks already know that. He say he ready to have two fine officers."

Steele shook the young men's hands and told them how much he loved their grandfather. They both nodded.

Grace looked at Randi, "God sent your husband to this church. He jus' what we been needn.' The Lawd send him to this church and to this town. Yo' husband is a prophet. He be doin' what Jesus would do. Now we have to take care you so you can finish the job."

Grace then spoke to Steele, "Chief Sparks tell my Pastor that he don't have the manpower to protect you all the time. So my boys gonna do that. We already worked it all out. They gonna be in front of yo' house tonight. They stay there until the Chief can send his people to give them some relief. Don't you worry Revr'nd, we black folks grown tired of being afraid of the Klan. You gonna be safe here in Falls City 'til the Lawd decide to call you someplace else."

Steele really did not know how to respond. In the face of this little black woman's courage, he felt ashamed of the fears that had haunted him. He watched the frail little woman take each of her grandson's arms and walk toward the car. When they had driven away, Steele nodded to the funeral director. They fully lowered Willie's casket into the ground. Two men with shovels removed the artificial turf and began covering the casket with dirt. Steele stayed in place until the casket was completely covered and the squares of lawn that had been removed earlier were put back in place and padded into the loose soil. The funeral director placed a temporary marker in place and then shook Steele's hand before he left. Steele stood staring at Willie's grave. He then uttered one final prayer for the repose of his soul. Randi and one of the police officers had stayed at the grave with him after everyone else had left.

"I need to stop at my office for just a moment," he told the officer. "You go ahead and take Randi home. I'll be there in a few minutes." Randi and the officer protested, "No, it's okay. I'll be all right. I'll be home soon."

Steele walked through his office. The building was deserted. He picked up a book from his desk and walked down to the chapel. He knelt in one of the back pews. He buried his face in his hands. He was too tired to pray. He simply knelt there in the silence. When Steele lifted his face he realized that the chapel was now dark. The yard lights outside were now illuminating the stained glass windows. Steele sat back in the darkness. He studied the windows of the chapel. They each depicted an event out of Jesus' life. In one, Jesus was feeding the multitudes; in another Jesus was blessing the children; in another, He was changing water into wine. Then Steele rubbed his eyes as he strained to focus on the window directly across from where he was sitting. His mouth fell open in disbelief.

The window opposite him depicted the temptations of Jesus. There were two primary characters in the window. Jesus was lit with a white radiance. His blonde hair glistened. Steele strained to make sure his eyes were not deceiving him. He stood up and stumbled across the chapel in the darkness. He came right up to the window. His eyes had not deceived him. Satan was a black man! The artists had actually portrayed Satan as a black man. Here in the heart of Falls City, one of the greatest evils in human history had been blessed in a stained glass window in a Christian Church. "How did I miss seeing this?"

Steele was exhausted when he got back to the Rectory. The day's events had taken their toll on both Steele and Randi. They each had a difficult time going to sleep. Steele finally convinced Randi to take one of the blue pills that the doctor had prescribed. Soon after taking the pill she was sleeping. Steele picked up the book he had taken from his office and went downstairs to the den. As he passed by the front dining room window he glanced outside. There stood Grace's two grandsons leaning against their pickup truck. They were laughing and talking with a couple of other friends who had dropped by.

Steele Austin felt all alone. He had been ordained to preach the good news of the love of God for all people. He wanted to teach the gospel story. He wanted to visit the sick and comfort the dying and bereaved. He felt called to minister to the hungry, the prisoner, and the homeless. Such a ministry should not be a threat to anyone. Yet here he was, a white priest being guarded by two black high school football players. He did not know if he was being protected from strangers or members of his own congregation. Steele laid his head against the cool window glass. His voice quivered with emotion as he prayed, "God, how did I get to this place? What madness brought me here? Where did I go wrong?" Again, he listened for an answer.

CHAPTER 23

The rumors of secret meetings in the homes of parishioners at First Church were sweeping over Falls City. The staff at First Church became anxious not only for Steele, but for their own job security. The gossip was that the secret meetings had been called for the sole purpose of plotting a strategy for getting rid of Steele Austin. It was rumored that a slate of candidates was chosen to run for the Vestry. Howard Dexter would.be nominated as Senior Warden. Henry Mudd would be nominated as Junior Warden. Clearly, church law held these two offices up as the most powerful in the congregation. The Church Canons clearly directed the Senior and Junior Warden to report any misconduct of any kind on the part of the Rector to the Bishop. A Senior and Junior Warden could be a priest's greatest asset or their worst nightmare. If the Wardens supported the priest, they could run interference with members of the congregation who did not like the Rector. They could help communicate the vision of the Rector and build support in the congregation for the priest's ministry. On the other hand, the Wardens were also in the position to micro-manage the Rector's every move. They could pull the rug out from under a priest at every opportunity. In short, a Senior and Junior Warden antagonistic to the current administration could bring that Rector's ministry in the congregation to a conclusion.

In most congregations throughout the nation, the Rector always chose the Senior Warden. The Vestry elected the Junior Warden. In this way there could be balance and fairness. First Church had amended its By-laws long ago to insure that the congregation elected both Wardens at the annual meeting. The change followed a previous effort to get rid of a Rector. Some accused him of being a communist. Others accused him of being an alcoholic. There were rumors of adultery and rumors that he was molesting the acolytes. Special auditors were brought in to look over the church books, especially the funds administered by the Rector. At that time, the Senior Warden was appointed to office by the Rector. That particular Senior Warden was unyielding is his support of the Rector and was continually defending him. He threatened to expose the names of those who were leading the plot to unseat the Rector. The Junior Warden which had been elected by a particular segment of the congregation was malicious with his attacks and innuendo. The Bishop stepped in to preside at a called congregational meeting. The meeting itself went far into the morning hours. The Rector sat patiently as member after member stood up to accuse him of wrongdoing of every manner. There were a few who spoke on his behalf, but clearly the scene had been orchestrated. Shortly after two a.m. the Rector tendered his resignation. There was a burst of applause from those who wanted him out, and tears from the people who had tried to defend him.

The staff knew that this was a congregation who knew how to make a Rector's life miserable. They had tasted blood once, and the staff feared there were those who wanted Steele to bleed. It was rumored that there would be only the two nominations for Wardens. They would be elected by acclamation. They would have Steele Austin back in Oklahoma by Easter.

The parish hall began to fill a full hour before the annual meeting was to begin. One half hour before time to call the meeting to order, there was no wiggle-room in the hall. There was not room for one more person to get in the door. It was decided to move the meeting to the church. Still, people were standing along the walls and out into the narthex. Having gotten wind of the impending crucifixion, Steele's supporters were there in full force. Those on the inside, however, took no note of them. Howard Dexter was heard to smirk, "Just who do these people think they are? Don't they realize they don't matter? They don't mean a thing to the important people in this congregation. There's nothing they can do to stop us. Steele Austin is history."

Stone Clemons tried to head off the showdown by reasoning with Howard Dexter. "Just what has Steele Austin done, Howard? You know that you don't have any canonical grounds for getting rid of him."

"I don't need them." The venom flowed out of him. "He is the wrong man for this job. We don't like his style of leadership. We don't like his sermons. We don't like his vision for this parish. We don't think he is very spiritual. He seems more concerned about creature comforts than about the needs of the people of this parish."

"Who is we?" Stone persisted. "How many people here feel like you do? Do you think fifty per cent?"

"No, nothing at all like that," Howard shrugged.

"Well, how many then? Twenty percent?"

Howard Dexter chuckled, "no, it's not even that many."

"Well, then, how many, Howard?"

Laughter roared out of Howard Dexter. "You, sir, are just about to find out."

"Pull in your horns, Howard." Stone walked to the podium. "The good people in this parish are not going to let you tear this congregation apart."

As the current Senior Warden, Stone Clemons called the meeting to order. The first item of business was nominations for Junior and Senior Warden. Howard Dexter was nominated immediately for Senior Warden. There was an immediate call that nominations cease. A quick second, a call for the question followed. A motion and a second that he be nominated by acclamation was shouted followed instantly by a quick call for the question. A voice vote with an equally loud voice to the contrary, but since there were no other nominations Stone Clemons reluctantly announced the election. Within seconds Howard Dexter became Senior Warden and moved to the podium to take the gavel.

Steele could not help but notice Howard Dexter's chosen wardrobe for the occasion. He had on a pair of slacks that were absolutely littered with little green ducks. Steele chuckled to himself. They looked like a mattress cover from the Sierra Club. He had on an Augusta Green jacket as well. The green of the jacket clashed with the green ducks. His triple chin quivered with excitement. His little eyes bugged out under his bushy eyebrows. Steele thought he looked like the model for a Jeremy Fisher frog.

Mudd was elected just as quickly, as was the slate of four Vestrymen. Clearly, the entire thing was rehearsed and well executed. Steele looked over at Randi, who sat silent. He knew she was on the verge of tears. One-half of the Vestry had just been elected to run him out of town. Howard Dexter could not hold back the pleased look on his face. Finally, he was in control, and he was going to have things his way.

Stone Clemons came over to Steele and put his arm around him, "Don't you give up. We're not going to give in to these SOB's. They've declared war and we're going to fight back. This is not over until it's over."

Steele looked at this dear man and nodded, but in the face of the successful manipulations he had just witnessed, he had his doubts.

"Mr. Chairman, may I be recognized?" A tall lanky man in a seersucker suit with brown suede shoes was standing at the microphone. His skinny neck was accented by a red and blue bow tie. Steele had never seen the man before. Stone Clemons whispered into his ear, "Prepare yourself, that pin head only shows up here when there's trouble. His name is Ned Boone. You have never seen anyone who enjoys a fight more than that guy. He has single handedly gotten rid of two college presidents, a museum director, and the director of the Chamber of Commerce. He wears them all like scalps on a belt to cover up his skinny ass."

"Mr. Chairman, as a faithful member of this congregation, I have become greatly disturbed by the rumors that the Rector is mismanaging his Discretionary Funds. If what I hear is true then he is not only guilty of co-mingling personal funds with church funds, but using those funds for his own gain." He looked around the room as though looking for Steele, but not wanting to see him. "Mr. Chairman, I have always believed that where there's smoke there is fire. There has just been too much smoke for this congregation to ignore it. I would like to move that the Rector's Discretionary Funds be made a matter of public record. This congregation needs to know just who has been contributing money to his account and just how he has been spending it." There was a quick second and a call for the question. There was a sprinkling of yea votes. Howard Dexter did not call for contrary votes. He simply announced that the motion had passed.

Chadsworth rushed to the microphone. "Howard, you know that Clergy Discretionary Funds are confidential. The Canons and the By-laws of this parish prohibit revealing the names of the recipients. The funds can be audited by the auditors or the Bishop, but they cannot be made a matter of public record...."

"Sit down, Chadsworth!" Howard Dexter pounded the gavel. "This congregation has ruled...."

"I'll not sit down," Chadsworth interrupted. There was a loud burst of applause in support. "Let him speak," several members of the congregation began to shout. "What you have just attempted is highly illegal and the Bishop will not stand for it."

Howard Dexter leaned over the podium. He was slapping the gavel into his hand. With that same self-serving smirk on his face he looked right at Chadsworth, "The Bishop is not in charge here. I am!" With that, several in the congregation began to hiss and boo.

"Mr. Chairman," it was Ned Boone again. Steele thought his neck had gotten even longer in all of the excitement. His adam's apple was protruding over the bow tie. "If Mr. Chadsworth Purcell Alexander the Third is through interrupting these proceedings, I would like to continue." This was met by more hisses from the congregation.

"Mr. Chairman, I would like to propose the following resolution." He held up a sheet of paper and started reading:

"Whereas, First Church Cemetery is the oldest cemetery in Falls City,

And whereas, there are many of the honorable Sons of the South who gave their lives in the struggle for Southern independence buried in said Cemetery,

And whereas, First Church Cemetery is on the Registry of Historic Places,

And whereas, it has from its beginning been the final resting place for the leaders not only of this nation, but also of this state, this community, and this church,

Be it resolved, that any person desiring to be buried in this cemetery or any family desiring to have a loved one buried in this cemetery must first receive the unanimous approval of the Vestry of First Church. Mr. Chairman, I so move."

Again, there was the quick second, a call for the question, and a call for a vote. Those voting contrary were never asked.

"Do you have anything else, Mr. Boone?" Howard Dexter leered.

"Yes sir, I do have one final item of business." Ned Boone swallowed. His adam's apple disappeared up into his chin and then dropped again. "I, along with many faithful members of this congregation, are quite concerned about all the rumors surrounding the Rector's behavior. I believe that the good people in this church are entitled to know if there is any truth to these rumors. I shuddered when I heard the news that our Rector is an adulterer. Then, I hear that he may have homosexual leanings. This is all bad enough, but then when you couple these with the rumors of his misappropriation of church funds; it is just too much to be ignored."

It was as though the entire church began booing. Steele, Chadsworth, and Stone Clemons all started moving toward the microphone. Several others stood and started rushing toward the microphone with them. Clearly they were agitated and were not going to allow any of this to continue. Howard Dexter pounded the gavel, "I believe that Mr. Boone has the floor. Do you have a motion, Mr. Boone?"

"Yes sir, I would like to move that a court of inquiry be called immediately to investigate the fitness of Steele Austin to serve as our Rector. Said court of inquiry shall be composed of the two Wardens and the four newly elected members of the Vestry."

"Second!" Someone shouted.

"Call for the question!" Shouted another.

And true to form, Howard Dexter kept the train on the tracks, never calling for votes to the contrary and declaring that the motion had passed.

People were now coming up out of their seats. They were shouting and shaking their fists at Howard Dexter. Howard Dexter responded by pounding the gavel and declaring that all business had been concluded and the meeting was adjourned.

Steele looked over at Randi. She had the look of a deer staring into car headlights. He realized he probably didn't look much better. They both were surrounded by lots of people crowding up to pat them on the backs and give them hugs and words of encouragement. Steele knew he had the support of the majority of the people in this place. He just didn't know if that was going to be enough. They were not organized. The group that had controlled this meeting were not only well organized, but rehearsed. For the first time in his life, he felt like he was actually doing hand-to-hand combat with the devil. Steele stood on his toes to see if he could see Randi. Chief Sparks had his arm around her. There was a uniformed officer with them. He was escorting her out of the church. Just then, two officers came up on either side of Steele. One of them whispered into Steele's ear, "The Chief says we're to get you out of here—now! Let's go, Father." With that Steele began moving through the crowd and out the Sacristy door into the cool night air.

"The Chief is going to drive your wife home in your car. We'll take you in the cruiser." Once Steele was in the back seat of the squad car and the two officers were in the front, the one on the passenger side looked back at Steele. "Father Austin, we don't want you to be alarmed, but something happened over at the Rectory during your meeting."

"What...what happened?" Steele felt his throat go dry.

"We don't know if it was the Klan or just who, but someone burned a cross on your lawn."

Steele sat there in disbelief. "Are you all right?" The officer asked.

Steele nodded. "There wasn't any damage to your house. Some of your neighbors saw the cross burning and watered the lawn around it until it went out. We're going to stay with you tonight just in case they decide to come back."

The squad car rounded the corner and headed toward the driveway. Several of their neighbors were on the front lawn. The cross was still smoldering. The air smelled of kerosene. Randi was standing with Chief Sparks looking at the scene. His heart went out to her. He knew right then and there that he would have to get her away from this church and away from these people. He would get her out of this city. Steele Austin wanted to go home. It was time to call it quits. He would take Randi home to Oklahoma.

Howard Dexter was absolutely giddy. He could not control his excitement. His telephone had not stopped ringing since he got home. Caller ID helped him identify which calls to answer. His supporters spewed congratulations on him. "We've done it. That Okie is history. Great job, Howard! My hat is off to you." Howard knew to ignore the phone calls from those who were not in agreement with him.

The last call of the evening came from Bishop Petersen. "Give me a report." Howard filled the Bishop in on the meeting. "Well, clearly the boy has to go. I don't know if there is anything I can do to help you, but Hayes is working on it. It doesn't sound like you are going to need anything from me anyway. As soon as you get his resignation I'll sign off on it."

Howard Dexter had a difficult time going to sleep. He simply could not stop smiling. He had won. He had shown Austin, Stone, Chadsworth...all of them. It would be a long time before any of them tried to cross him again.

CHAPTER 24

Chadsworth pointed his Jaguar north towards Atlanta. He shouted at the top of his voice, "Damn that Howard Dexter. What a little piss ant. Just what the hell is he trying to accomplish?" Chadsworth was filled with both anger and anxiety. He simply could not believe that Howard and his gang called themselves Christians. He pondered the lack of Christian charity he witnessed in the parish meeting last night. He thought of all the good that Steele Austin had done for the church. Have they forgotten that before Austin came the church was dying? He recalled the number of priests that refused to be a part of their search process. He reasoned that if they successfully chased Steele out it would be two years before they would be able to get another priest to even talk to them.

His anger was replaced by anxiety. He knew he had to figure out a way to keep them from auditing that Discretionary Fund. He easily passed the semi that was immediately in front of him.

Chadsworth noticed that the kudzu was beginning to come back. The winter cold and frost had turned it brown. It was hanging like a ghostly web from the trees and shrubs. Now, spring was near. The redbuds were also springing into bloom. The tulip trees were blooming as well. In just a few weeks, the dogwoods and the azaleas would turn the entire south into a garden of beauty. Chadsworth hungered for spring.

He trusted Steele. He did not believe he would betray his secret. He had concluded that Steele was a man of integrity. He figured that he was the type of priest that would take the hit himself before he would betray a confidence. But an audit of the Discretionary Fund would lead them back to that bondsman. He feared that if that happened it wouldn't take much to match up the amount of the bail with the time, date, and name of the person the money was used to release. Chadsworth was desperate. He knew that his entire life, marriage, career, reputation, credibility— everything depended on his secret staying a secret.

He started pounding the steering wheel with his palms, "Damn,

damn, damn!" I can hear all those hypocrites now. Did you hear? Chadsworth Alexander is a queer. I can see them all snickering and raising their eyebrows whenever they see me. Oh yes, there would be pity to end all pity for Almeda. Poor Almeda, married to a queer. I hear he has a black boyfriend. Tsk, tsk, ain't it awful? It is just awful. Poor darling, we just have to pray for her.

They would grin at him at first, but then they would cut him off. First, he would not be re-elected to the board of the Country Club or the Magnolia Club. He and Almeda would not be invited to the Cotillion or the Debutante Ball. Then they would begin to exclude him from the business deals. He would not be included in the charity golf tournaments or the hunting trips. In their typical Southern fashion they would continue to be nice to his face, but behind his back—oh God, behind his back they would cut him up like a fish ready to be fried. He had to figure out a way to help Steele. He had to figure out a way to keep the Discretionary Fund from becoming public information. He just had to stop them.

Then it struck him. He knew what he had to do. He knew exactly how he could position himself to do something about Howard Dexter. He would get Stone Clemons to help him buy up shares in Dexter's bank. Stone was already a major shareholder. Chadsworth had never bought any shares when they were available because he didn't want to do business with Howard Dexter. But now he figured Stone and he could come close to being the majority shareholders. They would have enough votes to not only get Chadsworth elected to the board of directors, but elected as chair. Once he was chairman of the board of Howard Dexter's little bank, the playing field would be leveled. Howard would be a lot more willing to listen to both Stone and him. Then it came to him. The best way to insure the success of his plan would be to get Howard to cooperate with them. He would promise Howard that once he was a majority shareholder, he would deposit a large portion of his cash assets into Howard's bank. It would be the largest deposit Howard Dexter would ever receive into his little drive-through. Oh yes, he would appeal to Howard's greed. He would not be able to refuse the money.

The spring sun warmed his face through the sunroof. Chadsworth needed this trip to Atlanta. He looked forward to dancing with Earl at Hernando's Hideaway. There he could be himself. He could be gay and proud. He could be real.

Chadsworth took note of the speedometer. The car was only doing forty miles an hour. He had been completely lost in his thoughts. As he pushed down on the accelerator, he reflected on the fact that since his first sexual awakening he had lived his life as a lie. He had tried to be something that he simply was not. And now, he was exhausted. He was so tired of pretending. He ached to be free. He wanted to be himself all the time, yet he knew he could not. He must not.

On the horizon, the skyline of Atlanta appeared. The sun was shining brightly on the buildings. They glistened in the cool of the noonday. Atlanta has a beautiful skyline. Chadsworth thought that at this moment it resembled the New Jerusalem coming down from the heavens. It was beautiful. Chadsworth needed this visit to Atlanta. At this moment, Falls City seemed so far away. He wanted to forget Howard Dexter, Henry Mudd, First Church, the whole lot. He didn't want to think about any of them. For the next few days, he was going to lose himself in Earl's love. He was going to lose himself in the vastness of Atlanta. He was going to be free of all need for pretense. He was going to just be Chadsworth the queer and he was going to love every minute of it.

Chadsworth pulled into Buckhead and onto the street on which Earl's condo was located. Buckhead is a somewhat pretentious part of Atlanta. Chadsworth noted that South Georgia was several weeks ahead of Atlanta seasonally. In less than a couple of hundred miles to the north, the season was dramatically delayed.

The potted plants on the porch of Earl's condo had turned brown. The hanging basket near the wind chimes had shriveled from the lack of water. This is not like Earl. He always takes such care to see that his plants are well tended. Chadsworth reached into his pocket and brought out his key chain. He turned the key and opened the door. "Earl...Earl?" There was no response. Chadsworth wondered if he had stepped out for a minute. He went up the stairs to the bedroom. He would freshen up before Earl got home. He opened the bedroom door and was brought to an abrupt stop. Chadsworth could not believe his eyes. Earl was in the bed. He was asleep. Chadsworth stood there in disbelief. Earl, who had previously had no body fat at all, was now even thinner. The flu had really taken its toll on him.

Chadsworth sat down on the side of the bed and ran his fingers through Earl's hair. He bent over and kissed him on the cheek. "Wake up, sleepy head. Chadsworth is here."

Earl smiled and opened his eyes; he looked up at Chadsworth and put his arms around his neck. He squeezed him to the point that Chadsworth began to choke. Then he felt the moisture on Earl's cheek against his own. It was then he knew Earl was crying. He broke the embrace. "Earl, it's going to be all right. We'll get you well and then fatten you up. In no time you'll be yourself again. I'm here to take care of you and take care of you I will."

Earl shook his head and then covered his face with his hands. He began to sob all the more. "Chadsworth, it's not that simple."

"Now, now, Earl," Chadsworth chuckled, "Don't go getting gay dramatic on me. All you need is some bed rest and some good meals. I'll call the Meal Taxi People and have them bring us some food loaded with carbs and fat. Let's get you well. That is the first order of business."

Earl protested, "Please, Chadsworth, please listen to me."

The look on Earl's face caused a lump to form in Chadsworth's throat. He felt his stomach tie in knots. "Of course, honey, talk to me. I am all ears. What do you need to tell me?"

Earl took Chadworth's hand. "What we have is really special, don't you agree?"

"God, Earl, if it weren't for you and for what we have together, I would be in the mental hospital. My love for you and our time together is the only thing that keeps me going. Earl, you are my reason for living."

"Chadsworth, you know that I feel the same way." Earl looked away from Chadsworth as he continued to talk. "We never said that we were exclusive, did we, Chadsworth? I mean, was there any part of you that thought, well you know, that I never...I mean, even though we love each other we were free to..."

"No, Earl, I never thought we were exclusive. I knew that would be impossible. God, sometimes weeks would go by before we could see each other. That is too much to ask of any two healthy males as horny as you and me." Chadsworth chuckled.

Earl started sobbing again, "Chadsworth, there is no easy was to say this. There have been others."

Chadsworth put his fingers over Earl's lips, "Please, no confessions. I don't think I can handle that. Let's just focus on each other."

Earl removed Chadsworth's hand from his mouth, "It is not that easy. Please let me finish. Please for once in your life just sit there and let me finish. You have no idea how hard this is for me."

Chadsworth did not want to hear what Earl was going to say. He knew he was about to lose him. He knew the whole thing had been too good to be true. He had enjoyed the best of both worlds. In Falls City he had been the respectable, straight, married man. Here in Atlanta he had relished being loved by one of the best looking gay men he had ever laid his eyes on. Now it was going to come to an end. Even in the best of circumstances long distance relationships are hard to sustain. He had taken it all for granted. Deep down he knew it was going to have to come to an end. Earl was far too handsome and far too available to stay in a relationship with a married man. No, it was just a matter of time until he would find someone who could be his life partner. Chadsworth always knew that he could not be that person even though he so ached to be able to chuck it all and live happily ever after with Earl.

Chadsworth swallowed as he now fought back his own tears, "Who is he, Earl? Do I know him?"

A surprised look crossed Earl's face as he realized what Chadsworth had concluded. "No, Chadsworth, that's not it. There's no one else. I mean there have been others, but there's no one special. You're still the only man for me. That's not it."

Relief washed over Chadsworth. "Then what is it? Why are you so upset?"

Earl sat up in the bed. Again, he took Chadsworth by the hand and he looked him directly in the eye. "Chadsworth, I have AIDS."

Shaking his head, Chadsworth refused to believe what he was being told, "You have what?"

"I'm sick, Chadsworth. I'm really, really sick." Earl began coughing.

"Damn it Earl, weren't you careful? Didn't you use rubbers when you were with other men?" Now he was furious and he started to stomp about the room, "You say that you love me, then you go out and have unprotected sex with God only knows who. Damn it Earl, don't you read the newspapers? Why the hell do you think they have a bowl full of free condoms in the bathrooms of the gay bars? They're not party favors. They're life savers."

Earl began to sob. Chadsworth returned to the bed. He sat down and took Earl in his arms. He held him for a few minutes and rocked him back and forth. Then a startled feeling washed over him. He pushed Earl back so that he could look him in the face. After a long silence, he asked the question that was now fearfully weighing on his own heart, "Earl, could I have it?"

Earl broke eye contact and looked out the bedroom window. "You've got to be tested, Chadsworth. Get tested, and the sooner the better. Chadsworth, you could be infected."

CHAPTER 25

Rocky smothered Almeda's face with kisses. For well over three years Rocky had come to her house as her personal trainer. After a few minutes on the treadmill and some basic routines on the equipment in her home gym, she would lead him to the master bedroom. Every Monday, Wednesday, and Friday that Chadsworth was in Atlanta he would exercise her and then she would work him out. Not one time in three years had she even come close to being caught. Chadsworth had never met Rocky. In fact, she had made sure that not another soul knew about Rocky.

The telephone beside the bed started ringing. Rocky rolled off her so she could answer it. "Hello."

"Almeda, this is Chadsworth." The sound of his voice made her heart skip a beat. She reached down and pulled the sheet over her as she simultaneously sat up in the bed. Rocky shot her a look and she put her finger over her lips indicating the need for him to be silent.

"Chadsworth, where are you? Are you still in Atlanta?" She prayed that he was not anywhere near Falls City.

"Yes, I'm still here."

She fought back a sigh of relief, "When are you coming home, Chadsworth? I miss you."

"I need to stay here in Atlanta for at least the rest of the week...."

"A week, Chadsworth?" she interrupted, "I thought you were just going for the weekend. Why do you need to stay the week? I don't understand. Come on home, Chadsworth."

"Almeda, it's just not that simple." Chadsworth swallowed and took a deep breath, "Almeda, something's come up. I just have to stay here in Atlanta to see it through."

Rocky stood up and started putting on his sweat suit. Almeda could not help but admire his tight body and his really cute little posterior. He was a fine specimen of a man. Rocky blew her a kiss and waved at her as he left the room. She heard the outside door to the workout room close.

Then she remembered Chadsworth. She realized that he was still on the line but had been silent.

"Chadsworth, are you still there?"

"Yes, I'm here." Then there was more silence.

Almeda felt a strange, almost frightening sensation wash over her. "Chadsworth, is everything all right?" She had the sensation that he was crying. She listened carefully to see if that was in fact what he was doing.

"I'm all right, Almeda. I just have a lot on my mind." Again, there was silence.

"Is there anything I can do? I can come to Atlanta and help you if you need me to." She realized that she actually wanted to go. She really wanted to be with him.

"No...no...don't come up here. There's nothing that you can do. I need to take care of this myself." Then there was more silence.

Her heart went out to him. "Chadsworth, I could come and when you're not working we could spend some quality time together. It could be a romantic week. I can shop while you're working and then in the evenings we can have some romantic dinners. Chadsworth, it's been so long since we have had time together...just the two of us."

"I know," he uttered. "I wish that things could have been different for us."

Almeda began to plead, "They can be, Chadsworth. They can be different. We could start tonight. I can be at your hotel in just a few hours. We can start tonight. We can be together, Chadsworth, we can have a fresh start. I mean, Chadsworth, we need to be with each other. You know, to really be with each other."

"I'm sorry, Almeda. I am going to be occupied day and night. It just wouldn't work. I'm really sorry." His voice broke.

Almeda sat up and placed her feet on the floor beside the bed. She picked up the picture that was on the bedside table of the two of them. It was taken at the last Cotillion. Chadsworth looked so handsome in his tails and white gloves. She was so proud to be seen with him. "Chadsworth, I think I want to come just so that I can be near you. I miss you. I don't want to spend the week without you."

"Please, please, Almeda," Now it was Chadsworth who was pleading. "Please don't come up here. I need to be able to focus on this project. I need to get through this. I don't want to feel guilty about neglecting you."

"Would you, Chadsworth?" she queried.

"Would I what?"

"Would you feel guilty about neglecting me?" She wrapped her hand even more tightly around the telephone. She clutched the picture of the two of them next to her chest. She anticipated his answer. Again, she had the sensation that Chadsworth was crying.

"Chadsworth, is it the business? Are we in financial trouble? Should I be worried?" She put the picture back on the table and fearfully waited for his answer.

Chuckling, Chadsworth answered, "No Almeda, we're not in trouble financially. We have so damn much money right now that if...."

"If what, Chadsworth? If what?" She persisted.

"Almeda, you'll never have to worry about money. Neither of us will ever have to worry about money. We have enough money to do anything we want." Then he was silent again.

"Chadsworth," she tried not to sound worried, "I get the feeling that there's something that you're not telling me. Please talk to me, Chadsworth. Whatever it is, I can help. I want to help, but I can't help if you won't talk to me."

"Almeda, I promise you that there's nothing that you can do." His voice broke again, "Almeda..."

"Yes, I am listening." For the first time in a long time she actually felt that they were communicating. She felt as though she and her husband were bonded.

"Almeda, I just want you to know that I think you're a good wife. You've always taken good care of me. You took good care of our boys and I regret that it has turned out to be such a thankless job."

She interrupted, "I should have strangled both of them in their cribs when I had the chance."

"Oh, give them some time, Almeda. They'll grow up eventually. I still think they'll make us proud." He did not believe his own words, but he felt better for having said them.

"If you say so, Chadsworth. I just pray that you're right." She did not want this conversation to end. She relished feeling close to her husband. She had hungered for this feeling for so long.

"Almeda, I just want you to know that I'm proud of you. I have always thought you were a striking woman." She felt herself blush.

"Now Chadsworth, you can't go sweet talking me on one hand and then tell me to sleep in this bed by myself for the next week." She giggled like a schoolgirl.

After a long silence, Chadsworth spoke again. His voice was low and his words were carefully chosen. "Almeda, I'm sorry that I've not been a better husband to you."

"Oh, Chadsworth," she rebutted, "I don't have anything to complain about. I mean, I'm the envy of most every woman in Falls City. After all, I am married to the most handsome man in the entire state of Georgia."

"No, Almeda," he continued, "I don't want us to lie to each other. I've not been the kind of husband you deserve. I haven't been very attentive, or affectionate, or romantic. I really haven't appreciated you as another man might appreciate you. I just want you to know that I'm sorry. I really wish that things could've been different."

Tears streamed down Almeda's face and dropped onto her bare legs. She released several large sobs.

"I didn't mean to make you cry," Chadsworth's voice was shaking.

"Are you crying too? Chadsworth, it's okay to cry. I won't think less of you for it. I'm flattered that you can trust me with your tears." She waited for him to answer.

"I have to go, Almeda," he tried to sound matter of fact.

"Oh, Chadsworth, please don't hang up. Please don't end this conversation. Please reconsider...I really want to come to Atlanta. Please, Chadsworth, please..." she knew she was begging, but she could not stop herself.

"I'm sorry, Almeda. I'm really, really sorry. I am heartsick, Almeda. I'm so very sorry. I regret that I have let you down as a husband. I have no excuses. Just tell me that you forgive me." This time she knew beyond a doubt that he was crying.

"If it will make you feel better, Chadsworth," she whispered, "all is forgiven. Now just come home to me so that we can make a fresh start. Can we do that, Chadsworth? Can we make a new start? I mean...people at our age fall in love for the first time, so surely we can fall in love all over again. Can we, Chadsworth, I mean, can we give it a try?" Again she picked up the picture of the two of them and held it close to her chest.

"I pray so, Almeda; I pray so with all of my heart. I pray that God will let us do that very thing." He knew his voice was quivering.

"Why wouldn't God allow us to begin again? Come home, Chadsworth. Hurry up and get your business there taken care of and then come home to me." The tears would not stop flowing. "I'll be waiting for you. Please come home quickly. Don't wait until the end of the week, please. Chadsworth, please."

Chadsworth knew that there was nothing else to say. He started to hang up the telephone and then he stopped, "Almeda..."

"Yes."

"Almeda, I...er...uh...I love you."

Almeda began rocking back and forth on the bed. Her bare chest and legs were wet with her tears. She bit her lip and squeezed her eyes shut. "Oh, Chadsworth, I love you so very much."

There was a click and the phone went dead. Almeda opened her eyes and gently placed the receiver back on the cradle. She held the picture of the two of them in front of her. She wiped her eyes and tried to get the picture to focus through the blur. She looked at Chadsworth's smile. It was as though he was smiling directly at her. She again squeezed the picture to her chest. She lay down on the bed and pulled the sheet up over her naked body. A great smile came across her face. She would go shopping. She would buy a new outfit. She wanted to look her very best when Chadsworth came home. She would plan a romantic dinner for just the two of them. For the first time in years, Almeda felt wanted. She was a woman in love. Only this time, she was in love with her husband.

CHAPTER 26

Bishop Petersen stared out the window of his spacious office. The large magnolia trees on the front lawn kept vigilance over the old colonial house that he used for Diocesan Headquarters. Chancellor Robert Hayes sat in a purple wingback chair near the desk. The office was richly furnished in purple. Purple is the designated color for Bishops. Rufus Petersen wanted to make sure that when anyone walked into his office there would be no doubt in their mind that they were in a Bishop's office.

He had his certificate of consecration proudly displayed on the wall immediately near his desk. All the red wax seals of the Bishops who had participated in his ordination were spread around the document. His mahogany desk was imposing even in this large space. If he were not careful to sit up straight, the large desk chair would dwarf his body. In the middle of the room he had a latch-hook rug with the Seal of the Diocese on it. He had seen pictures of the Oval Office of the President of the United States. The rug with the presidential seal on it struck him. He had told himself if he were ever elected a Bishop—no—when he was elected a Bishop, he would have the seal of his Diocese put on a rug and placed in front of his desk.

"Hayes, what the hell are we going to do about that recalcitrant priest? He has that congregation in a total uproar. If we can get rid of him, things will settle down and get back to normal." He turned to look back at his Chancellor.

Just then his secretary entered the room. "Here is another stack for you. The fax machine cannot keep up with all the letters coming in. We have had to reload the paper twice." She was carrying a stack of letters nearly two inches thick. She placed them on the Bishop's desk on top of a pile of unopened envelopes, pink telephone slips, and yet more unread messages off the fax machine.

"Are they all the same?"

"Mm- hmm", she nodded. "Most of them want you to do something to get the wolves off Father Austin. Several are recounting the annual meeting and calling it a witch-hunt. All are concerned about the safety of the priest and his wife."

The Bishop glanced at his Chancellor with a look of desperation. "We have got to find a way to get rid of him. He has got to be stopped."

"Well, before you do anything, your royal holiness, you had better read this wire from the Governor." His secretary handed him an opened envelope.

"The Governor? The Governor?" Rufus Petersen stood straight up. "Why the hell is the Governor wiring me? What has he got to do with this?"

"Hold on to your mitre, Bishop," the secretary chuckled. "It seems the Governor likes young Mr. Austin."

"You are really enjoying this, aren't you?" The Bishop scolded her.

"Just save your bark for someone who is afraid of you. You don't scare me one bit. Besides, I like the man." She glared back at him.

"I don't pay you to like these clergy," he snarled. "I pay you to take care of my office."

"Now, I just told you, Rufus, save your bark." She put her hands on her hips and leaned over the desk to look at him. The Bishop sat back down and put his face in his hands and began to shake his head from side to side. "The Governor has been down to Falls City on several occasions to hear our boy preach. He likes what he has to say. He has also had Father and Mrs. Austin to the Governor's Mansion for parties and meals on several occasions."

The Bishop sat back down, shaking his head. "I have been a resident of this state for sixty years and not one time have I been invited to the Governor's Mansion. Hell, I am one of the Bishops in this state. Not one damn time have I ever been invited to the Governor's Mansion. Steele Austin gallops into Georgia and in a matter of months is a regular at the Governor's dinner table. How do you explain that, Hayes? Can you help me understand?"

Hayes stood up and walked over to the Bishop. The Chancellor patted the distraught Bishop on the arm. "Calm down, Rufus. You're as red as a beet. Now calm down before you have a stroke."

The Bishop glared at his secretary. He was furious with her. He knew that she was only relaying information, but he did not want to hear it. He particularly did not want to hear it from someone who was taking such delight in presenting it to him. Of course, he knew she couldn't help herself. She was having a really good time. She saw him as an old bully and he knew she really did like watching him burn.

He stood and pointed toward the door. "Please go and shut that door behind you. You already know too much of my business."

She turned and walked toward the door. She kept talking but did not look back. She knew what she had to say would knock his knees out from under him. He would be sitting on his fat ass again before the door even shut. "It seems that the legislature is considering awarding The Reverend Steele Austin the Magnolia Award for all of his community service work." She could not hold back the chuckle as she closed the door behind her. Sure enough, on hearing that bit of news the little fat man had fallen back in his chair.

The Bishop sat stunned. He was in total disbelief. He read the letter from the Governor asking him to intercede in what was obviously the work of a few malcontents in Falls City. The Governor noted that he was no stranger to the jealousy and contempt of those who disagreed with him. A strong leader like Reverend Austin would be a tempting target for those envious of his success. The Bishop sifted through the latest batch of faxes, flipped through the telephone messages, and then turned again in his chair to look out the window.

"What do we have on him, Hayes?" The Bishop whimpered. He was so upset he was barely audible.

The Chancellor's heart went out to this Bishop he had served for nearly ten years. He saw his pain. He knew that he was not going to help Steele Austin. It was going to be his job to figure out a way to get rid of this young priest. He had done it before. He knew he would have to do it this time and he most likely would have to do it again. If there was ever a choice between the lay leaders of the congregation and a priest, the Bishop always took the side of the laity. He had heard him say it so many times, 'I can always get another priest, but I can't get another congregation.' The Chancellor knew that it all boiled down to money. Without the contributions of the parishes and missions the Bishop would not be able to operate the Diocese. He could not afford to cross the lay leaders.

"Well?" The Bishop asked impatiently.

"Do you want to use the same maneuver that group did on the one down in Centerville a few years ago?" The Chancellor fought back a chill of conscience. Some of the congregation had wanted to get rid of that Rector because he had offended the wrong people in the parish. The priest would not apologize. He would not agree to look for another job. He would not resign. He and Rufus had suspected that a small group in the parish framed the priest, but they didn't have any proof. The rumor was that one of the "Big Wheels" had paid a couple of women in need of money to say the priest had propositioned them. The priest denied it, but in order to avoid an ecclesiastical trial and a lawsuit he agreed to resign. The last that they heard of him he was a car salesman in Atlanta.

The Bishop shook his head. "Everybody knows that Steele is really in love with Randi. I've seen them together myself. It's obvious the man worships the woman. No, that dog won't hunt. Bob, I don't think any rumors of sexual misconduct will stick. In this case, most people would see right through them."

The two men sat in silence for a long time. Then the Chancellor searched through what little conscience he had left and dared make a suggestion that he had been pondering. "What if we try to save him?"

The Bishop swung around in his chair to look at him. "Do what?"

"Now listen to me, Rufus. Just think about it for a minute." This time it was Chancellor Hayes who stood and began to pace around the office. "Maybe we can get with Howard Dexter and figure out a compromise. If Austin will agree to do some of Howard's bidding, maybe we can save the situation. Steele Austin can give up his radical customs. Maybe we can get him to agree to let Howard screen and supervise all of his future activities."

This Bishop opened his desk drawer and pulled out a large manila envelope. He tossed it to the Chancellor.

"What's this?"

"Open it." The Bishop stood and walked into his private bathroom. He didn't bother to shut the door. Above the sound of nature's call he shouted at the Chancellor. "It's from Howard Dexter. It's a list of all the mortgages his bank holds on the churches and priests in the Diocese. There are car loans, credit cards, balloon notes..." The Bishop flushed the toilet and came back into the room. "His damn little bank even holds the mortgage on my house, my car, this very office building."

The Bishop sat back down in his chair and looked directly at the Chancellor. "You see the ones that he has highlighted?"

The Chancellor nodded.

"Those are the ones that the bank can call on notice or are up for renegotiation. Now, tell me Bob, do you think Howard Dexter is going to compromise with me? He has this Diocese and me by the ying-yang. He wants Steele Austin out. We have to figure out a way to get him out." The Bishop put his feet up on his desk and leaned back in his chair. "Now, Mr. Chancellor, how are we going to do it?"

"We can always go to other banks and get all of these notes refinanced through them. Let's just pay off Dexter's bank; problem solved."

"Bob, it's not just about paying off the notes. Howard Dexter is a force to be dealt with in that parish and in this Diocese. We need him on our side. This list of bank notes is just his way of reminding us that it is to our advantage to play team ball with him." The Bishop stared at his Chancellor. "Now, one more time, what are we going to do?"

The Chancellor shrugged his shoulders, "We either use sex or money. If you don't think sex is an option, then we have to get him on some sort of fiscal mismanagement."

"We already checked that out. There wasn't anything there." The Bishop was exasperated. "His funds were all in order. He had all his receipts. He had everything documented."

The Chancellor lit up. "Receipts can disappear."

"What are you suggesting?" The Bishop leered at the Chancellor.

"You can call over to Falls City. Tell the Business Manager to bring you those files. Tell him we're going to keep them a few days and look them over." "The Chancellor smiled, "Receipts can disappear."

"I like it. I think you just might have hit on something." For the first time in weeks the Bishop felt pleased with himself. Then, he had a second thought. "I don't know, Hayes, I think that Business Manager up there is pretty efficient."

"So?"

"So, he will make a copy of everything before he sends us the originals." The Bishop began to thump his fingers on the desk.

"Then we'll surprise them. I'll just show up and take the files before he has a chance to copy them. I'll tell him that I am acting on your direct orders. We'll bring those files here; then we can do whatever the hell we want to do with them."

A big smile spread across the face of Chancellor Robert Hayes.

The Bishop stood up. He started clapping his hands together. He patted his Chancellor on the back. "Brilliant, Hayes! Absolutely brilliant, we will finally be able to bring some peace and order back to First Church."

The two men embraced as they continued to chuckle and pat each other on the back. "Why don't you go to Falls City right now? This is Friday. The Rector won't be in the office. I know that he takes Fridays off. Pick up the files. Bring them to me here in my office on Monday morning."

The two men shook hands and the Chancellor opened the door to leave. The Bishop's secretary walked back in with another stack of faxes, pink telephone message slips, and yet another stack of unopened mail. "More appeals to you from Steele Austin's fan club," she chuckled. "I expect a call from the White House any minute."

"Get out! Get out of my sight!" The Bishop shouted and then slammed the door behind her. His blood was boiling. He had visions of Steele Austin dining at the Governor's Mansion and his blood pressure shot even higher. The thought of that Okie receiving the prestigious Magnolia Award made his stomach roll. He just couldn't believe the injustice in this world. He reasoned that he was the Bishop. If anyone should be eating with the Governor it should be him. If anyone was to be recognized by the legislature it should be him. He was furious. He reached into his bottom drawer and pulled out the fifth of brandy he kept inside a tissue box. He unscrewed the top and turned up the bottle. He took a long drink and then allowed the liquid to slide down his throat.

Rufus Petersen sat quietly in his spacious office leaning back in his overstuffed chair. The warmth of the brandy was washing over him. He felt all alone. He fondled the large pectoral cross that was hanging around his neck. Walking across the room to the wall opposite his desk he stopped to study his certificate of ordination. Bishops from all over the country had attended his consecration and placed their red wax seals on his certificate. Several hundred people had filled the cathedral to witness his elevation. It was the best day of his life.

There were several photographs of his service of consecration. He stopped to study each one of them. He was particularly drawn to the photograph of him kneeling before the Presiding Bishop with all the other Bishops standing around him and laying their hands on his head. He mentally rehearsed the names of each Bishop that had come to his ordination. Every Bishop in the confederate states was present. The only non-Southerner was the Presiding Bishop. He was from one of the New England States. His accent was like a foreign tongue in Georgia.

He lifted his hand to take another drink from the bottle. As he did the Episcopal ring on his finger caught his eye. He sat the bottle down so he could study the amethyst stone set in the ring. He twisted the ring on his finger. The Bishop's ring was the symbol of his authority. In some Dioceses clergy and lay people were required to reverence the ring when greeting the Bishop. Maybe he should require the priests in this Diocese to do so and to teach the people to do so as well.

Thoughts of a short, fat little boy being ridiculed on the playground came into view. It was a familiar video. He had lived it. He had been rejected by boys and girls alike his entire life. Mocked, ridiculed, Rufus had always been chosen last for games and parties, if chosen at all. He had been the object of practical jokes all through his primary schooling into college and even in seminary. His classmates would roll their eyes when he entered the room. Even his teachers had picked on him. He lived his life constantly aware of the whispers, the sneers, but more painfully the feelings of being insignificant. He was not good enough. He had grown up to be a very lonely man. In the church however, he found that priests were awarded a level of respect he had never before known. He thrived on the deference that his clerical collar earned him.

He picked up the bottle of brandy and walked to the mirror in his private bathroom. He looked at his reflection. His purple shirt gave his face a glow. "But I've shown them. I've shown all the handsome frat boys just like Steele Austin. I have shown every one of them. I am a Bishop! I am somebody! I can do anything I want. That hillbilly is going to find out that I am in charge of this Diocese and not him."

Lifting the bottle into the air, he toasted his reflection in the mirror. "To you, Steele Austin. This is to your demise. I'll teach you to come into my Diocese and try to one-up this Bishop. Yes sir, you'll regret the day you met me."

CHAPTER 27

The Sisters of Mercy Care Center sits on a bluff in West Atlanta overlooking the Chattahoochee River. The well-manicured grounds are filled with beautiful tall pines, oaks, dogwoods, and magnolias. There is a small chapel and a refectory. The resident's rooms are situated around a beautifully landscaped quadrangle. Bird feeders are strategically located so that the care receivers can see the magnificent birds of every color imaginable. The cardinal, with his brilliant red feathers, is a special treat.

The building itself is brightly furnished and well lit. There are the sounds of fountains and man-made babbling brooks throughout the facility. The walls are covered with brightly painted pictures. Current and former residents had painted many of them. If the signs had not told a visitor otherwise, one would think that they were in an exclusive hotel.

Chadsworth stood looking out the window from Earl's room. The daffodils and the crocuses were now in bloom. The azaleas and dogwoods were coming into bud. The earth was in the process of renewing itself. Signs of birth and re-birth were abundant, but here in this place, life as the residents had known it was coming to an end.

It only took a couple of days for Chadsworth to realize that Earl was not going to be able to take care of himself. Earl had lived with HIV, but had been in denial. Chadsworth realized the thought that Earl might have it had passed through his mind on more than one occasion, but he didn't want to see it either. Even though he had continually encouraged Earl to go to the doctor, he would not allow himself to think the worst. Now the disease was full blown. Earl had AIDS and he was dying. Everyone that entered Earl's room had to wear a surgical mask, gown and gloves. Visitors were told not to touch Earl's bed.

Chadsworth stood berating himself. He could have put Earl in his car and taken him to a doctor long ago. Now Earl needed oxygen all the time. He was unable to hold down what little food and liquids he consumed. He was too weak to get out of the bed to take care of any of his needs. He slept most all of the time. Hospice was his only choice. At least they would know how to keep him comfortable, Chadsworth thought to himself. In this place he would be able to die with some dignity.

Earl had no family. When he came out of the closet in his teens, his parents threw him out of the house. He had not spoken to them or any of his relatives since. He did have a wide circle of friends here in Atlanta, primarily members of the gay community, and some from his work and neighborhood as well. Earl had given Chadsworth his Durable Power of Attorney several years ago. "Just in case anything should happen to me," he handed it to him over dinner one night in Beaver Creek, Colorado. They had enjoyed a wonderful week together skiing, making love, and just being with each other. Chadsworth still recalled the grin on Earl's face, "If I ever need anyone to take care of my affairs, I would just as soon have a rich white boy do it. At least I know you won't steal from me."

Through the years Chadsworth had given Earl some financial advice and guided his investments. He had done nicely for himself, but it was going to take it all now. After Chadsworth had the ambulance transport Earl to this hospice, he selected just a few of the more personal items to put in the room with him. He wanted Earl to be comforted by some familiar things on the wall and on the bedside table when he was awake. Then he invited their friends in to take whatever they wanted. Chadsworth wanted nothing for himself. He donated what was left to Goodwill.

It only took twenty-four hours to get an offer on the condominium. It was a cash offer. Chadsworth made arrangements for a quick closing. He put the money in a trust fund for Earl's care. He put some of his own money with it to make sure that there would be more than enough to meet all of Earl's expenses for as long as his dying took.

He had stayed in Atlanta now almost three weeks. Almeda was constantly calling for him to come home or for her to come to Atlanta. He had successfully convinced her that he was negotiating a deal of a lifetime and she needed to be patient with him. For the very first time he really did feel guilty about lying to her, but right now, Earl was his priority.

Chadsworth turned his gaze on his friend and lover. He was so thin. His once muscular body was literally skin and bone. He appeared far beyond his years. The bed swallowed him up. He looked so frail—so tiny. He slept soundly. Chadsworth was thankful for that.

Earl opened his eyes and a smile came to his dry lips, "Hey, white boy, who you looking at?"

Chadsworth moved to the side of the bed and sat down. He took Earl's bony hand and cupped it in both of his. "I was just watching the love of my life sleep."

"Well, I have looked better for you." Earl whispered.

"You have never looked better to me than you do right now," Chadsworth forced a smile.

Earl looked up at the ceiling. There was silence between them, and then Earl uttered what had been weighing on his heart. "Chadsworth, I don't want a funeral."

"Shh, let's don't talk like that," Chadsworth put his fingers over Earl's lips.

"No, I need to tell you some things." Earl was insistent. "And you need to hear them."

Chadsworth shook his head. Earl continued, "I don't want a funeral. When I go, have them take my body and have it cremated. You decide what to do with the ashes."

"Anything else?" Chadsworth had a large lump in his throat.

"If I have any money left, arrange a great party for all our friends at Hernandos' Hideaway." Earl gazed even deeper into Chadsworth's eyes. "Then I want you to divide the rest of my money between St. Paul's Catholic Cathedral and these wonderful sisters here at the hospice. I don't want you to give it to the hospice; I want the sisters to have it for their order."

Chadsworth shook his head again, "I'll take care of it."

"You know I only have one regret, Chadsworth." Earl had a pained expression on his face.

"What's that?"

"I regret that you never came out of the closet!" Earl softened his accusation with a smile.

"It has really been hard to live with this secret." Chadsworth soaked a damp cloth and put it on Earl's forehead. "The only time I have really felt alive is when I have been with you. I only existed when I was away from you. I only went through the motions of living. The only thing that kept me going was knowing that in a few days or a couple of weeks we would be together again."

"That's a terrible way to live." Earl studied Chadsworth's face. "It's too late for us, but it's not too late for you. Do it, Chadsworth—do it. Set yourself free! You're a fine looking man. There will be someone else. Just go where the boys are. You won't have to look for a new love. Love will find you."

Chadsworth shook his head, "No, if I can't have you, I don't want anyone. You're my love. If I can't have your love, then I would rather not have love at all."

"Those are the words of a fool!" Earl hurled his judgment at Chadsworth. "You're no fool. You're just too afraid of what people will think. To hell with what people think. Promise me, Chadsworth; promise me that you'll set yourself free."

Chadsworth sat in silence. He made no response.

Exasperated, Earl whispered, "Damn you, Closet Queen. Damn you. At least tell a dying man that you'll think about it like you have never thought about it before."

Chadsworth nodded.

Again there was silence between the two of them. A nun came into the room to check on Earl. They exchanged a few polite words. Then Earl made a request of the nun, "Sister, will you do something with my friend and me?"

"Of course, what would you like for me to do?"

"I would like for you to do something with us that we have never done before." Earl looked up at Chadsworth. "Will you pray with us?"

Chadsworth's eyes flooded with tears, the pain in his heart was so great he thought he was going to pass out. His entire body hurt.

The nun looked at Chadsworth. "Are you Catholic? Do you know any of our Catholic Prayers?"

Chadsworth tried to lighten the atmosphere in the room. "I'm Episcopalian. We're kind of Catholic Light. I think we're the Catholics who flunked Latin, but I've been in enough Catholic churches to keep up with you."

The nun took his hand and took Earl's hand. The two men tightened their grip on each other. "Let's pray to the Blessed Mother that she will give us all peace." Then the nun began:

"Hail Mary, Full of Grace
The Lord is with Thee,

Blessed art thou amongst women,
And blessed is the fruit of thy womb Jesus,"
Then Earl and Chadsworth joined in:
"Holy Mary, Mother of God,
Pray for us sinners now
And in the hour of our deaths."

Soon after the nun left, Earl went back to sleep. Chadsworth leaned over and kissed him on the cheek. He stood there watching him a long time. In his heart, he wished that things could have been different. He wished that he could have been like Earl—out, open, and free to be himself. He wished that they could have been that way together. Chadsworth slowly walked to the door. He stood quietly and took another look at Earl. The tears soaked into his surgical mask and dropped onto his gown. He quietly shut the door and removed the mask, gloves, and gown. He tossed them into the hamper by the door. He then leaned the weight of his body against the wall outside Earl's room. He knew he would never see the love of his life again. All his faint hopes of a future of any kind with Earl were now gone forever. His vision was blurred, but he was able to make his way to the parking lot. He sat in his car sobbing until he could cry no more. Then he drove back to his hotel. He knew just what he had to do next.

He arrived at the Ritz Carlton overlooking Phipps Shopping Center on one side and Lenox Square Shopping Center on the other. He turned his car in to the valet and took the elevator up to his room. He walked over to his desk to double check his *"To Do"* list. When his eyes fell on Howard Dexter's name, he recalled how warm and downright friendly Howard had sounded when he told him what he wanted to do. Howard could not have been more eager. His greed was undeniable. Chadsworth made sure, however, that he did not have any of his funds wired into Howard's bank until Howard had signed the contract specifying his terms of agreement and Chadsworth had a copy of it in his attorney's office. When Howard first learned that Stone Clemons and he were buying up shares in his bank, he resisted. When he learned that a large chunk of Chadsworth's fortune was also going to be deposited in his bank, he offered to sell them some of his own shares. Chadsworth concluded that Howard's greed would ultimately be his undoing.

Chadsworth opened the mini bar and took out a bottle of scotch.

He poured it into a glass and took a large sip from it. "God, forgive me, but I hate Howard Dexter. I feel like I have entered an agreement with Satan himself." Chadsworth knew that he had no other alternative. He owed Steele Austin and he wanted to make sure that snake Dexter would never be able to hurt the boy again. He shook his head and heard himself mutter, "But for the life of me Father, I don't know why you would want to stay at First Church?"

Chadsworth spoke to Earl's attorney and then faxed him a codicil to make sure that any funds left in Earl's trust would be distributed accordingly. He made himself a drink and sat staring out the window until a messenger arrived with the appropriate amendments. Chadsworth signed them and put a copy in a sealed file. He instructed that it be delivered to his Atlanta attorney. He looked down his list again. Everything had been accomplished. He searched his mind to see if there was anything else he needed to do. He could think of nothing. There was only one telephone call left for him to make.

After he made the call, he took another bottle of scotch out of the mini bar. This time he did not bother to put it in a glass. He turned the bottle up and let the liquid slide down his throat. He walked into the bathroom and undressed. He got into the shower and let the hot water wash over his face and down his body. Chadsworth was tired. He was really, really tired. His soul was drained. He had no energy left. He sat down on the shower floor and rested his head back against the marble wall. The warm water flowing down over his body made a soothing contrast to the cool marble he was both sitting on and leaning against.

Chadsworth thought of Earl. He thought of all the fun they had had together. He remembered their trips to New York, San Francisco, and of course, the apartment he secretly kept for them in Charleston. He remembered the gay cruise they had taken together in the Caribbean. He could hear Earl's contagious laughter that could always get him out of a bad mood. In just a matter of minutes, he would be laughing with him. He thought of all the late nights they lay awake in each other's arms talking about how things would have been different if he had not felt trapped into pretending to be a 'good ol' straight boy.' He remembered how Earl would chide him, "You are nothing but a gay man trapped in a heterosexual prison. Come on out! Set yourself free!"

Chadsworth had wanted nothing more in his entire life than to be free. He knew he could not. He had been born to wealth, privilege, and responsibility. He had been born in Falls City, Georgia. He was one of the leading citizens. If he had been born in San Francisco or Los Angeles or New York or for God's sake, even Atlanta, maybe folks would have understood. In a larger city with a significant gay population maybe he could have been free to be himself. There is no way that he could be open and out in Falls City. He just had too much baggage. He had been forced to settle. He had been forced to live a double life. He had no choice. No, he had a wife, two useless sons, and a sterling reputation. It was God's cruelest joke, only Chadsworth was not laughing.

Earl's muscular body entered Chadsworth's vision. Earl may very well be the most handsome man Chadsworth ever met in his life. His arms were well proportioned, his chest was magnificent, and his stomach was cut. He could just sit for hours and stare at him. Not only was he beautiful, but they were in love. And when they made love, nothing else in the world mattered.

He recalled the last time they made love. Then Chadsworth heard himself cry out, "Earl, Earl, I love you. I am so sorry, Earl. Please forgive me." He lowered his head to his chest. He continued to whimper. He continued to recite Earl's name over and over again. It became a mantra for him. "Earl...oh my God...Earl, I love you." And then, with all the strength he could muster...

CHAPTER 28

Steele reached his arm out and pulled Randi closer to him. She nestled her head on his chest. A faint smile crossed her sleeping face. Steele rubbed her bare back. The spring breeze through their open bedroom window washed over them. Steele lay quietly cuddling with his wife. He started to plan his day.

Randi ran her fingers through the hair on his chest. "You awake?" he asked.

"I'm getting there."

"Do you know that you are my favorite person in the whole world to wake up with?" He pulled her closer and gave her a kiss on the cheek.

She pretended to bristle, "And just how many people have you spent the night with, Steele Austin?"

"Only you," he chuckled, "just you. After waking up with you, anyone else would be such a disappointment I would have to take a vow of celibacy."

She lifted her head to look at her husband's face, "You see, right there. That's what gets you in trouble all the time. You are such a smooth talker that folks don't know whether to believe you or not. Sometimes you just come off sounding so clever. No wonder the Bishop called you a con man."

They giggled like school children. She put her head back down on his chest. They lay quietly together. He rubbed her shoulders. He had always loved her shoulders. They were so petite...so very, very fragile looking. At the same time, they were absolutely beautiful. She carried herself well. Head up, eyes straight ahead, shoulders back, chest out. She walked with such poise. She was such a lady.

He could hear the anxiety in her voice as she asked, "Steele, what are we going to do?"

"We're going to be all right," he tried to reassure her. "Even if I have to leave the church and take up some other kind of work we're going to be just fine."

She protested, "Steele, you were meant to be a priest. You're the best priest this church has to offer. You can't give up the ministry. You're doing the right thing and you can't let the people down. There are too many folks depending on priests just like you. You can't quit."

"And you, my darling, are prejudiced." He patted her on the back. "Thanks for believing in me, Randi. Thanks for sticking with me. Thanks for being my friend."

"Steele Austin, there's no way that you will be able to get away from me, so don't even think about it." She slapped his chest. "We're in this together. I'm with you for the long haul."

Steele was grateful that God had blessed him with a good and faithful wife. He had seen for himself the pain that a shrew could bring to her husband. He had listened to the grief of more than one husband who had discovered only too late that his wife was only using him. He knew that he loved Randi from the start. What he was never completely sure of was whether or not she loved him as completely. He had seen men look admiringly at her. What touched his insecurity and at the same time hurt him was to see her look back. Still, she had never done anything to cause him to question her fidelity to him. He knew that, in the long run, that was beyond his control. While he could not control the way she sometimes flirted with other men, he knew that the only thing under his control was himself. He knew beyond a shadow of a doubt that he would never betray her.

Probably the thing that surprised Steele the most about the ministry was the number of times he had been propositioned, most often by married women in his own congregation. Naively, he had thought that his ordination vows or his clerical collar or the combination of the two would clearly mark him as 'off limits.' He was surprised to discover just the opposite. It was as though he were a challenge to some of these women. He wondered if they simply wanted a secret trophy to carry in their hearts in order to bolster their egos. Perhaps if they could seduce that which was the most untouchable they could convince themselves that they were truly desirable, still attractive.

Randi interrupted his thoughts, "Did you call Bishop Powers in Oklahoma?"

"Yes, I did. He would really like for us to come home, but he doesn't have any parishes open right now. He has one small mission available out in the panhandle. We can have that, but it will be at a tremendous cut in salary."

Randi sat up in the bed, "Did he know of anything else?"

Steele sat up and leaned back against the headboard, "He named several congregations he knew in other Dioceses that were just starting their search process. He volunteered to give my name to the Search Committees with the highest of recommendations. But Randi, they are months, maybe even a year from calling a Rector and there are no guarantees."

"Will all of this at First Church hurt us?" she asked.

"It's not going to help." He threw his hands in the air, "It's clear that Bishop Petersen wants us out of this Diocese, but that doesn't mean he will help us get another job. If we do get in a process, or even get a call, I don't trust the man not to try to taint it. There's no telling what he may or may not tell the next Bishop or the next Search Committee. What's really sick is that whatever he says doesn't even have to be the truth. There's no way for us to know just what he says. After all, he's the Bishop. And everyone knows that a Bishop wouldn't lie; only priests and lay people do that. We're completely at his mercy."

He could sense that Randi was growing anxious again, "Listen to me, I'm going to spend the first part of this morning calling everyone I know in this church. I'm going to tell them what has happened here and just why we want to move. Something will break. There will be another parish for us out there somewhere."

She put her arms around his neck and kissed him, "You betcha' there will be something for us. God isn't going to let the investment He has in you go to waste."

"I think I'll spend the afternoon in the hospital. I want to spend some time visiting with people who have real problems. I don't want to think about Howard Dexter or Annual Meetings or Vestries or By-laws or Bishops. I just want to visit the sick. And maybe...." His eyes glistened, "just maybe someone will have had a new baby and they'll let me hold it." He stood up and started walking toward the shower. "Yes, that's just what the doctor ordered. I need to focus on being a pastor and priest."

He had just started making his rounds at the hospital when his beeper started vibrating. He did not recognize the number right away. He went to the chaplain's office to use the phone. Chief Sparks answered.

Steele listened in disbelief. Then he heard the Chief ask him, "Where are you?"

"I'm at the hospital," he replied.

"Wait for me out front. I'll pick you up in three minutes."

Steele stood near the fountain in the middle of the circular driveway at the hospital entrance. He didn't have to wait long. An unmarked patrol car pulled up and the back door swung open. He got in the back seat next to the Chief. A male officer was in the driver's seat. A female-uniformed officer was sitting next to him. They rode in silence. When they pulled into the circular drive in front of Chadsworth's house, Steele could not help but notice the large white columns on either side of the front door. They had an eerie quality about them. It was as though the shadows from the trees in the front yard had been designated as the solemn sentries to witness this scene.

The two officers got out first. They opened the doors for the Chief and Steele. "Are you all right?" The Chief asked. "You have done this before?"

Steele nodded, "Yes, but you never get used to it. I still get sick to my stomach. I guess, I never thought I would be doing it at this house."

The Chief agreed, "Me too."

The two officers led them up to the front door. One of them rang the doorbell. Steele took his station up front. He would be the first one that she would see when she opened the door. It would be his job to break the news. The Chief took his position on Steele's right, but just a step behind him. The two uniformed officers flanked the door. The doorbell rang a second time. They could hear Almeda's high heels clicking on the hardwood floor as she walked toward the door. She opened the door the width of the safety chain. It was just enough to see Steele standing there. "Mistuh Austin, did we have an appointment? I fear that you have caught me at a bad time."

"Almeda, I need to talk to you." He tried to keep his voice calm and steady.

She lifted the safety chain off the door latch and opened the door for him to come in. It was then that she saw Chief Sparks and the two officers standing with Steele on the front porch. The color drained from her face, "Chief Sparks—Mistuh Austin…is it Chadsworth? Did something happen to Chadsworth?"

Steele nodded, "Almeda, I have some really bad news." He started to walk toward her, but she stepped back and held her hand up for him to stop. She sat down in the chair next to the hall table. Steele could tell that she was trying to maintain her composure. "Almeda, I am so sorry." Almeda looked up at him. The tears started flowing down her cheeks.

Steele called a couple of her lady friends on the Altar Guild to come over. With the dispassionate order that is inbred in every woman raised in the South, the ladies took charge. Soon the place was swarming with women from the church bringing food, setting out a guest registry for visitors to sign, and making sure that the proper folks were notified. A schedule of who was to do what was posted in the kitchen. In a matter of a couple of hours, it was determined that Almeda's every need would be taken care of through the afternoon of the funeral. The ladies of the church would see to that.

"Did you know?" The Chief chewed on his unlit cigar. He looked directly at Steele. They were once again in the back seat of the patrol car. "Did you know that he was living a double life?"

Steele was embarrassed to have the Chief ask him that question. He did not want to lie to one of his strongest supporters, but he was not about to betray the trust that Chadsworth had placed in him. The Chief studied Steele's reaction and then looked away, "You knew. I thought you probably did." The Chief reached over and patted him on the arm. "Don't worry about it, Parson. You don't have to betray anyone. Let me tell you what I know."

Steele listened carefully. I know that he was arrested for soliciting an undercover officer at the health club a few months ago. I know that a member of the clergy bailed him out. My guess is that it was you."

The Chief turned to look at Steele's reaction again, "Yes, I thought so. It was you. That also explains all the stink that Howard Dexter has been raising about you laundering a large sum of money through your Discretionary Fund."

The Chief sat silent chewing on his cigar before he continued, "Then, there were some leaks about an underling over at the newspaper killing the police report."

"But why did he do it?" Steele needed some answers of his own from this answer man. "Why on earth would he kill himself?"

"Seems that just before he committed suicide he made a telephone call to 911." The Chief took the cigar out of his mouth and rolled it in his fingers. "According to the Atlanta police, their 911 Operator received a call from Room 1215 at the Ritz Carlton next to Phipps Plaza. The caller was a male. He said that he was calling to report that there was a suicide in room 1215. They would find the victim in the shower. Then, he told them to use extreme caution. The victim had AIDS."

Steele tried to absorb what the Chief had just told him, "Is that where they found him?"

"Yes Sir, they found him in the shower. He had taken a 45, put it in his mouth and pulled the trigger."

"Did he leave a note?" Steele was still struggling to absorb it all.

Again, the Chief turned in the car to look directly at Steele. "He did leave a note. It was in a sealed envelope addressed to you."

"To me? Why me?" Steele couldn't make any sense out of that information at all.

"The Atlanta Police are forwarding it to us. Of course, they opened it and have read it. Doesn't seem to have much in it. Just some final instructions on how he wants his ashes buried and the inscription he wants on his tombstone. There is also some information on an endowment he set up for outreach ministry at First Church." The Chief studied Steele's face, "Do you know a man by the name of Earl Lafitte?"

"Lafitte? Sounds French?" Steele shrugged his shoulders.

"More like Cajun. The only thing the police can find out is that he is at the Sisters of Mercy Care Center in Atlanta. He's dying of AIDS." The Chief frowned. "One and one equals two, or maybe in this case one."

"Why did you ask me if I knew him?" Steele was still confused.

"I just wanted to know if Chadsworth had ever mentioned him to you." The Chief kept studying Steele's face for an answer, but he did not get one. "I suppose it will all make sense to you when you get the letter in a couple of days."

They rode back to the hospital in silence. Steele was dropped off at his car in the parking lot. When he got out of the squad car, the Chief leaned toward the open door, "Father, I don't think anyone else in Falls City knows Chadsworth's secret but you, me, and that newspaper reporter."

Steele leaned back into the car. "Do you see any reason for that to change?"

The Chief put the cigar back in his mouth and started chewing on it; "I think we should let the dead take their secrets to their graves with them."

Steele extended his hand to the Chief. The Chief took it and they shook, "Thanks Chief, thanks for being my priest." The Chief smiled, saluted him with his cigar, and instructed the driver to take him back downtown.

CHAPTER 29

The people started arriving a full hour before the scheduled time for the funeral. Chadsworth was a third generation citizen of Falls City. He was a part of the fabric of the place. But beyond that, word on the street was that there would be many state dignitaries in attendance. The Governor and his wife, both of the United States Senators, the area Congressman, and several members of the Legislature were all to be present. Both the grieving and the curious wanted to secure seats inside the church.

Stone Clemons had told Steele that Bishop Petersen had called Almeda and volunteered to drive down and do the service. Stone was laughing, "She told the old egotist that he was welcome to attend, but that her Rector would be conducting the service. There would be nothing for him to do." Steele couldn't help but think that while that was probably gratifying for Almeda, it would not help his relationship with the Bishop.

As Steele came up the steps from the Sacristy behind the crucifer, he was overwhelmed by the number of people in attendance. Every pew was filled to capacity. People were seated in the choir. Chairs had been set up in every available space. People stood against the walls, out onto the steps, and into the very churchyard. These had no hope of hearing any of the service, but they would be able to see and be seen.

The procession remained in the back of the church until such time as the Governor's party, the Senators, and the members of state and local government could be seated in places of honor in the reserved front pews opposite the family. The head usher then led Almeda, her two sons, and a few distant relatives into the front two pews on the pulpit side. As was the custom, their black housekeeper, maid, and cook were all seated with the family.

Almeda created a stir in the congregation when she entered. She wore a large black hat. She had on a white dress spotted with a few black polka dots. Her makeup was immaculate. She walked erect with her head held high. She did not make eye contact with anyone in the congregation or even acknowledge that there was a congregation. She was a perfect example of poise and self-control.

At the sight of Almeda, the more emotional in the congregation reached immediately for their handkerchiefs and began dabbing their eyes. The curious strained their necks to get a better look at her. A whisper could be heard over the pipe organ as the nagging question continued to be asked: "Why did he do it? Do you have any idea why he killed himself? Poor Almeda, such a shock."

Of course, the rumor mill had been running the gamut. It was as though no one in Falls City had anything else to talk about but Chadsworth's suicide. The speculation moved from the sublime to the ridiculous. "He had major financial problems. You know, he has left poor Almeda with a tremendous debt, but no funds." Others speculated, "I heard he got a young girl pregnant over in Macon. She'd been blackmailing him, so he decided to end it.'" The only rumor that even came close was that he was diagnosed with an inoperable brain tumor."

Steele was always disappointed in gossip. He often wondered why the very same people who could be so creative with untruth couldn't use that same creativity for good. Each time someone had approached him with one of the rumors, he would ask that they not repeat that which they did not know to be fact. In spite of his appeals to them there were a few who insisted that their story was fact. They had it on the most reliable of sources.

As Steele started down the aisle behind the processional cross he asked the congregation to stand. He read from the Prayer Book, "I am the resurrection and the life, says the Lord..." As he passed Almeda, he could see out of the corner of his eye that she was looking at him. He turned to meet her gaze. She gave him a gentle smile and reached out and touched him on the hand. There was kindness and gratitude in her expression that he never dreamed would come from Almeda to him. It was at that instant that Steele made the decision that he was going to put an end to all of the rumors. The greatest gift he could give Almeda and Chadsworth would be to shut the mouths of all the gossips.

The Burial Office in the Episcopal Church is done with grace and dignity. The Prayer Book is very specific about the order and the rubric. It's said that whether one is a king or a pauper, all receive the same burial service. This, however, was the next thing to a State Funeral. The First Church Choir was present to sing the anthems. The Vestry was all seated together as honorary pallbearers. The lessons were being read by prominent members of the community. Chadsworth had left instructions that the hymns at the funeral were all to communicate God's love and mercy. Steele consulted with Almeda and chose three hymns to be sung. "O God Our Help in Ages Past," "The King of Love My Shepherd Is," and "Love Divine All Loves Excelling." The congregation and choir sang each with great gusto. He was pleased to see that not only Almeda joined in the singing of the hymns, but her two sons joined in singing them as well.

After the reading of the Gospel, Steele stood on the steps in front of the congregation. He asked them to be seated. "It is not our usual custom in the Episcopal Church for the priest to preach a eulogy on the life of the departed." He paused, "but because of the way that Chadsworth chose to leave this world I feel led to make a few remarks. We are all in this place today because Chadworth's life has touched each one of us profoundly. We gather to give thanks to God for the love, the laughter, the sharing, the friendship, and the companionship that the Almighty brought to each of us through His child Chadsworth."

Steele swallowed, took a deep breath, and took a slow gaze at the congregation. "Just as Chadsworth's life has touched each one of us, so has his death." Again he paused, "I cannot tell you why Chadsworth did what he did, but neither can any of you. There is no one who can tell us why Chadsworth chose to exit this life in the way that he did." He paused again and took another look around the congregation, "Do you hear me? No one—absolutely no one can speak for Chadsworth."

Steele looked over at Almeda. She was still smiling at him. Her every look encouraged him to continue. "While I cannot tell you why Chadsworth did what he did, I can tell you this. I can tell you that pain is pain. I can imagine physical pain being so excruciating that a person would prefer death to suffering. By the same token, I can imagine emotional hurt so great that it becomes unbearable."

He struggled to verbalize his next thought. "Just as none of us would choose physical pain, so none of us would choose emotional pain. Often physical pain is forced upon us by accident or disease. By the same token, emotional pain comes into each of our lives. None of us chooses to suffer. Sometimes it is the consequence of our own actions. On other occasions, we may truly be its' victims. The challenge for each of us is to guard against having our own words or deeds create emotional pain for our brothers and sisters. If our minds are closed to people who differ from us, if our hearts are filled with prejudice, if we use our Bibles as weapons, then we create emotional pain for others. If we prefer rumor to not knowing, if we prefer to gossip the bad news instead of proclaiming the good news, then we create a world in which there is emotional pain for others."

Steele could tell that he had the congregation's attention. "There is no part of me that believes that Chadsworth chose the emotional pain that led him to take his own life. If he did not choose it, then I have to ask whether or not I did anything to cause it. We each must ask ourselves that question. As long as we perpetuate a world in which our words and deeds cause pain and suffering for others, there will be those who choose death over living in such a world."

Steele paused in order to let the impact of that statement sink in. "Can you imagine a world in which understanding transcends judgment? What would our world look like if compassion overcame revenge, love conquered hate, forgiveness healed hurt, and acceptance replaced prejudice? Such is the world that God wants to give us. Such is the world that you and I are called to create. In such a world, men and women will not be left to suffer alone the pain they did not choose. In such a world, they will not be left without comfort. In such a world, they will not have to choose death, because you and I and people just like us will be opening their arms to them in love. In such a world they can choose life."

Steele paused again and looked at the congregation. He felt that just maybe he had penetrated the veil. He looked at Almeda. She was smiling. He lifted his arms and his voice, "Into Paradise may the angels lead you, Chadsworth. At your arrival may the saints and martyrs greet you and lead you into the heavenly city, Jerusalem."

Steele followed the crucifer and torches down the sanctuary steps and into the center aisle leading to the front door of the church. When he came to Almeda's pew he stopped, "Do you want to go out the front exit and go immediately to your car or do you want to walk with me to the rear of the church?" She did not answer; she simply reached out and took his arm. She lifted her head high and put a gentle smile on her face. She walked the length of the aisle holding onto Steele's arm.

There were many pats on the back after the service from the worshipers. Even Howard Dexter shook Steele's hand, "Well done, Mistuh Austin. Today, you were a true pastor to this congregation." One of the Governor's security officers led Steele over to the Governor's limousine, "The Governor wants to speak to you, Father Austin." He opened the back door of the limousine and Steele got in next to the Governor. "Steele, I wish I had a place for you on my staff. You are just what this congregation has needed. You are just the kind of minister we need here in Georgia. Don't give up, Steele. I know you may want to, but don't. Just let me know how I can help you."

"I appreciate your kind words, Governor. I fear that I do have my hands full. I know that there are a lot people who support me. For now, I'm going to take it one day at a time."

The Governor shook Steele's hand again. "Just remember that we're here for you."

Steele smiled and waved as the limousine drove away.

The service and all the events of the last few weeks had really taken their toll on Steele. He was exhausted. His body hurt. His chest was heavy. He had to force himself to go back over to the office to pick up his telephone messages. He really just wanted to go home and go to bed.

Most of the office staff had left by the time he got back over to the parish house. Steele glanced at his watch. It was well past 5:00 p.m. Daylight savings time would start on Sunday, but now it was already beginning to get dark. His secretary was waiting for him in his office. "Father Austin, Crazy Vera is down in the chapel. She wants to see you."

Steele collapsed into his chair. Vera Lake was one of the more unique characters in Falls City and First Church. Well into her eighties, she dressed in some of the most outlandish clothing. She drove an old beat up Dodge Dart ninety to nothing. She slowed for red lights, but not much else. She wore enough makeup to cause a clown to be green with envy. She self-dyed her hair and the colors varied from week to week. She was, to say the least, unpredictable. She would say whatever was on her mind whenever she wanted and to whomever she wanted to say it.

"Isn't there anyone else in the building that can take care of her?" Steele felt every bit of energy he had left drain out of him.

"She insists on seeing you." His secretary sympathized, but knew only Steele would be able to help her. "Father Austin, there is something else I need to tell you."

"Oh God, what else could there be?" Steele rubbed his eyes.

"Father Austin," His secretary's voice dropped to a whisper and her eyes widened, "She has a dead cat with her!"

"A what?" He could not believe what she had said.

"A cat, she has a dead cat with her." With that she gave Steele a sympathetic look and walked away. "She's in the chapel. She wanted to wait for you in the chapel."

Steele walked down to the chapel. It was completely dark except for the night-light above the altar. Crazy Vera had lit the candles on the reredos. Steele could see that she had placed the cat on the altar. She was standing there stroking it. She was crying. He walked up behind her and put his arm around her shoulders. "Vera, what's going on?"

"It's George. He's dead." She broke down. Through her gasps she continued, "He was run over by a car."

"I'm really sorry, Vera. I know how hard it is to lose someone we love. Pets are no different." He waited for her to calm down.

She looked at Steele, "Father Austin, I brought him here because I want you to do a funeral for him."

That one surprised Steele. "That's a really unusual request, Vera. We don't normally do funerals for pets."

Vera looked at him with determination. "Father Austin, I'm an unusual woman. I know that. I also know what people say about me." She continued with a smile, "In fact, I rather enjoy it. I just want George to have a proper burial."

Steele's heart went out to her. "When? Where? I mean, when do you want to do this and where?"

"Can't we do it now?" She had the most innocent look on her face. "I brought him over here so we could do it now. I own a grave in the churchyard. Let's bury him where I'm going to be buried."

"Oh, I don't know, Vera." Steele stammered, "The churchyard is just for human burials. It's not a pet cemetery. Perhaps we could bury him in your back yard, or we could find a pet cemetery."

With that she started to wail. "No, no, no...I want to bury him here in the churchyard with me. Please, Father, please."

She was now hanging onto his suit coat. Her tears were washing down his clerical shirt. Steele tried to comfort her. She continued to sob. After a few minutes, Steele relented. "All right, all right, Vera, I'll do it, but you have to promise me one thing."

"Anything, Father, anything."

He lifted her chin so that he could look directly into her eyes. "Vera, you can tell no one about this. Do you understand? No one must ever know that I buried a cat in the churchyard. Vera, you could get me in a lot of trouble if anyone ever finds out."

"I understand," she whimpered. "No one will ever know."

"You wait right here, while I go to the janitor's closet and get a shovel." Steele noticed that it was now dark outside. He was thankful for that. He found the shovel and returned to the chapel. Vera was standing before the altar holding the cat in her arms.

"Do you have something we can bury him in?"

"You mean, like a shoe box?" Steele's mind raced for an answer to her question.

"No, I don't want to bury him in a box. Don't you have a piece of cloth? We could wrap him in a piece of cloth." Vera looked at her dead cat. "Yes, I would like to wrap him in a piece of white cloth like they wrapped Jesus in."

Steele took the keys out of his pocket and opened the door to the Altar Guild Sacristy. "There ought to be something we can use in here." He began opening the drawers. All of the corporals, towels, and purificators were neatly lined up, clean, and well ironed. He continued to pull drawers. In the next to the bottom drawer he took out a wood box. In it were some old altar cloths. They looked moth eaten, frayed, and had started to turn yellow. He thought about just how slow the church is to throw things away. "These should have been burned years ago." He took out one of the corporals. It was just the right size to wrap the cat in. "This will do nicely." Vera agreed.

In the darkness they went out into the churchyard. Vera pointed out her grave. The headstone was already in place. She would be buried next to her husband who had died years earlier.

"Dig the hole here, near the headstone. Put him between my husband and me." Vera marked the spot with her foot.

Steele dug the hole. Vera wrapped George in the cloth. She gently laid him in the grave and Steele covered it over. He put the grass plug back in place and stomped it down.

"Thank you, Father Austin," Vera hugged him.

"Vera?" Steele started to speak.

"I know. I know." She put her hand over her mouth. "No one will ever know."

CHAPTER 30

A full month had passed since Chadsworth's funeral. The parish had been unusually quiet. Howard Dexter had pulled in his horns. When he saw Steele on Sundays he was filled with compliments and words of encouragement. By the same token, he had not heard any more from Bishop Petersen. His Chancellor had taken all of the records on Steele's Discretionary Fund to the Diocesan House, but returned them a couple of days later. There was a note signed by the Bishop and the Chancellor stating that they had reviewed the funds. The note stated that Steele needed to keep more accurate records. They also suggested that he could use better judgment, but that they could find no wrongdoing.

Chadsworth had left five million dollars to First Church to be used for outreach ministries. The terms of the trust were revealing. The interest was to be used at the total and complete discretion of the Rector. The Vestry was directly prohibited from interfering with the expenditure of the funds. Annually, the expenditures were to be audited by an independent auditing firm from Atlanta. Their only report would be to the Vestry stating that all of the funds were used to help people in need. The specifics were not to be revealed.

Steele announced at the last Vestry meeting that he was going to use the first year's income from the endowment as seed money to purchase a safe house in Falls City for homeless men living with AIDS. This announcement was met with the usual murmurings. Howard Dexter started to argue with Steele about his decision. Steele simply looked Howard in the eye and reminded him that the Vestry did not have the authority to interfere with the Rector's decision on how to use these funds. Howard relented, but encouraged Steele to keep the Vestry apprised of the details.

The morning paper carried a picture of Almeda Alexander and Howard Dexter standing in front of Howard's little bank. They both had big smiles on their faces. The accompanying article reported that she had just been elected chair of his bank board without term. Steele knew that Chadsworth's hand was in all this. The primary topic of conversation in Falls City the past few weeks had been the turnover of shares in Howard's bank that had been engineered by Stone Clemons. It was generally agreed that before his death Chadsworth had started the process and now Almeda was reaping the benefits of his good business sense.

Howard Dexter was now pretending to be Steele's lead supporter. The Bishop had backed off. The parish was at peace. And, if Almeda along with Stone Clemons were now the majority stockholders in Howard's bank, then she quite literally had Howard Dexter exactly where Chadsworth wanted him. Steele smiled to himself, "Congratulations, Chadsworth, you clever rascal. You pulled it off."

The intercom rang, "Father Austin, there is a messenger here with a box. He says that you have to personally sign for it."

"I've been expecting it. Send him in." Steele stood and greeted the messenger. He took the cardboard box. It was a cube six inches on each side. He knew what was in it. When the messenger left, he shut his door. He pulled the shipping label out of the plastic envelope. The shipping label verified his expectations. The box contained the cremains of Earl Lafitte.

Steele walked to the cabinet behind his desk. He opened the cabinet to reveal a small safe. He opened the door of the safe and took out a large brass urn. In it were Chadsworth's cremains. He sat it on his desk next to the cardboard box. He opened his top desk drawer and removed the letter that Chadsworth had written to him on that fateful day. After reading the letter again, he picked up the telephone and called the Hollingsworth Monument Company.

"This is Steele Austin over at First Church. Can you tell me if Chadsworth Alexander's marker is ready?" He waited for an answer. "Can we do it at 4:00 p.m. today?" He hung up the phone and called Almeda. "The monument company would like to put Chadsworth's stone in place this afternoon at 4:00 p.m. Do you want to be here?"

Just before 4:00 p.m., Steele spread a newspaper over the top of his desk. He then opened the urn containing Chadsworth's cremains. Next he opened the box containing the cremains of Earl Lafitte. As per Chadsworth's letter of instruction, he poured Earl's ashes into

Chadsworth's urn. He put the lid back on the brass urn and carried it outside to the churchyard and waited.

Almeda arrived first. "Are those his ashes?"

"Yes," Steele nodded.

"I just don't understand why he wanted to be cremated. It is just not our way." She shook her head. Then she really surprised Steele. "You know my Chadsworth's secret, don't you?"

The look of surprise on his face must have given him away. "I don't know what you mean, Almeda. What secret?"

"Mistuh Austin, you know and I know that you know, but we don't have to discuss it. I just want you to know that I am glad that Chadsworth had you to confide in."

Steele was moved to reach over and hug her. He did, but she did not return the gesture. She stood straight and poised with her arms hanging rigidly at her sides. He released his embrace. "I'm sorry. I guess I made a mistake or misunderstood. I was hoping that we could be friends."

The Almeda that he first met so many months ago returned. She looked at him with the haughtiness of royalty addressing a commoner. "Mistuh Austin, let's be straight with each other. We will never be friends. I really don't like you. I think you are the wrong man for First Church. I would prefer that our Rector be a man of breeding and letters. Having said that let me assure you that you will have my support as long as you are our Rector."

Steele started to interrupt. She held her hand up, "Please, let me continue. Because you were my husband's pastor and because you have been a pastor to me, I will see that no harm comes to you. That's Chadsworth's desire. He has left me instructions on this matter from the grave. But let me make myself clear, Mistuh Austin, I will protect you only so long as you behave yourself. If you choose to continue exercising your unusual style of ministry in Falls City, I will be the first to help move you along."

Steele's heart sank. He really didn't know how to respond to her. Just then the truck pulled into the drive of the churchyard. He and Almeda followed it to the Alexander family plot. The driver and an assistant got out. The driver looked at the urn Steele was holding, "You want to bury that urn underneath the headstone, right?"

"No," Steele took the lid off the urn. "My instructions are to pour the ashes directly into the earth and then have you cover them with the headstone."

"You're the boss." The assistant took a posthole digger and dug a hole about two feet deep. Steele then turned the urn upside down into the hole. He poured all the cremains into the hole. He offered the prayer of commitment from the Prayer Book and personally filled in the hole with dirt. He then stood back as the two men brought the monument over to the grave to set it in place. Once they had positioned the monument they stepped back. It was then that Steele was able to read the inscription for the first time:

Chadsworth Purcell Alexander III
"In his Sixtieth year on earth
He was finally set free"

EPILOGUE

Easter came and went with great flair at First Church. The pews were filled to overflowing. The choir and instrumentalists were magnificent. The dogwoods and azaleas were in full bloom for the Easter celebration. There was promise of new life and new opportunity. Steele Austin was beginning to settle into a routine. He and Randi had started talking about having another baby. The Vestry had become much more cooperative. The Altar Guild meetings had even become pleasant. Steel had developed a genuine affection for the ladies on the Altar Guild. He particularly admired their devotion and faithfulness to duty. He was struggling to respect their dedication to tradition and detail. He was beginning to believe that their "altar work" as they called it was a genuine expression of their love for God. Steel surprised himself one day in the sacristy by hugging Mrs. Gordon Smythe. He was even more surprised when she hugged him back. Even Mrs. Howard Dexter managed to give him an Ipana smile when she saw him.

Bishop Petersen, however, was the one who was really confusing Steele. He was full of compliments and deference. It was all so surreal. It was as though he had gone through a terrible hurricane and now was destined to live out the rest of his ministry in its eye.

Then one day, just as Steele was beginning to bask in the rural calm of South Georgia, his secretary came into his office. "The Altar Guild is meeting in the parlor." Her voice was shaking. "They are furious, Father Austin!"

Steele was perplexed. "Why, what have I done now?"

"It seems that the Centennial Corporal is missing."

"What on earth is the Centennial Corporal?" Now he was really confused.

"It is the Altar Corporal that they have had here for over one hundred and fifty years. They only use it on real special occasions. They say that General Robert E. Lee had his communion blessed on that corporal. They kept it in a wood box in the chapel sacristy."

With that Steele felt his legs go out from under him. The sick feeling that had been his cruel companion for so many months returned. He collapsed into his chair. He put his head down on his desk and began to pound the desk with his clenched fists. Then, a calm came over him. He lifted his head and a large smile blossomed on his face. He stood up. He was in complete control of his anxiety. An inner strength that he had discovered through all his ordeals at First Church rose up within him. He squared his shoulders and held his head high. He walked to the door of his office with the dignity of royalty.

And then, he combined his newly found royal air with the pride of a wrongfully convicted man who was about to be executed. With this newfound strength, The Reverend Steele Austin walked with determination out of his office. He moved gracefully down the hallway toward the parlor. He was now fully prepared to meet with the First Church Altar Guild. This time however, it would be on his terms...

SOON TO BE RELEASED
<u>When the Magnolia Blooms</u>
By
Dennis R. Maynard

Steele Austin finds himself in the middle of a murder investigation. He is the only person that believes the accused is innocent. This puts him at odds with his good friend Chief Sparks.

Almeda Alexander discovers love, but...but...oh, my!

Bishop Petersen tries yet another method to rid his Diocese of the recalcitrant priest he finds so unacceptable.

And through it all, the work of the Church goes on. Miracles of work and mercy do occur. You won't want to miss the second installment of life in Falls City, Georgia.

ABOUT THE AUTHOR

The Reverend Doctor Dennis R. Maynard is the author of four other books. Dr. Maynard's inspirational writings frequently appear in church periodicals throughout the Anglican Communion. His writing style has been described as "to the point with a liberal use of humor and inspirational stories."

His book, Those Episkopols, is one of the most widely used resources in the Anglican Communion for membership classes. Close to one thousand parishes in the American Church have used it in their new member ministry.

His most recent book, Forgive and Get Your Life Back, is a guide on the forgiveness process. Several hundred clergy have used it to do forgiveness training in their parishes.

He is also frequently requested to speak and lead retreats in the American and Canadian Church.

His books can be ordered through his website www.Episkopols.com or Amazon.com.

He lives in Rancho Mirage, California with his wife Nancy and their "daughter's cat", Lila.

Made in the USA